1973 1st EDITION

Japan Sinks

SAKYO KOMATSU

Japan
Sinks

Translated from the Japanese
by Michael Gallagher

HARPER & ROW, PUBLISHERS
New York, Hagerstown,
San Francisco, London

This work was first published in Japan under the title *Nippon Chinbotsu.* Copyright © 1973 by Sakyo Komatsu. English translation rights arranged through Japan UNI Agency, Inc.

FIRST EDITION

Designed by C. Linda Dingler

Library of Congress Cataloging in Publication Data

Komatsu, Sakyo.
  Japan sinks.
  Translation of Nippon chimbotsu.
  I. Title.
PZ4.K817Jap   [PL855.0414]   895.6′3′5   74–15876
ISBN 0–06–012449–0

76 77 78 79 10 9 8 7 6 5 4 3 2 1

This translation is for Rosemary and Maureen

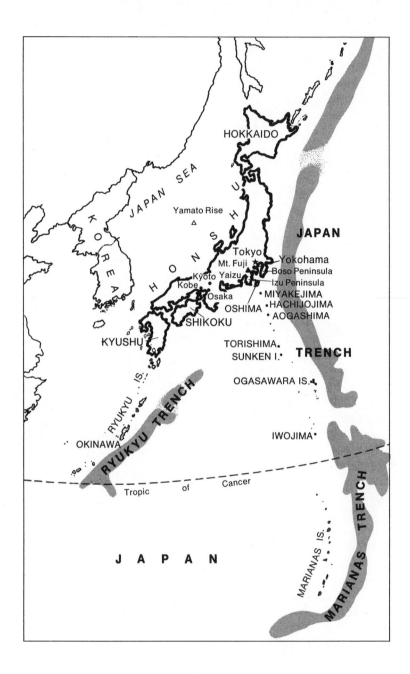

I

The Japan Trench

The area around the rear entrance of Tokyo Station was crowded as always. The air conditioning hardly seemed to be making any headway at all against the clammy heat that radiated from the flesh of the milling crowd, most of whom were bound for the seashore and mountains or else returning to their native places for the approaching Festival of the Dead.

Toshio Onodera looked around with a grimace of distaste as he wiped the sweat from his chin with the back of his hand. The spring rainy season had been cold, and the Weather Service had been forecasting a cool summer, but once the rain was gone, a fierce heat wave had struck. It had taken its toll in both Osaka and Tokyo, killing many of its victims. And then there was the usual summer water shortage.

Onodera had some six or seven minutes until his train pulled in. Since he had no desire at all to go into one of the packed and steaming station restaurants, he walked restlessly about, elbowing his way through the sweaty crowd. Each of the bodies mottled with sweat that slipped by on either side seemed to radiate heat like a foot-warmer—a short, thickset office worker in short sleeves, wearing his best suit and down-at-the-heels shoes; a middle-aged woman from the country in denim pants cut off at the knee, staggering along under a heavy load of baggage, her face red from the heat, her too-full breasts wrapped in a cheap striped blouse; a girl in her late teens, a stiff straw hat wound with a gaudy ribbon on her head and sweat dripping from the tip of her flat nose . . .

As he made his way through this assortment of people, the

thought struck him that his own hot, sweat-drenched body was in no way different from theirs, that it, too, reeked. And perhaps the lingering odor of the gin that he had gulped down the night before mingled even now with that of his sweat. Onodera shivered with disgust.

Finding himself in front of a water fountain, he stooped to take a drink. But then, ignoring the trickle of cold water, he crouched, mouth half open, with his gaze riveted upon a spot just to the rear of the water fountain. A thin crack ran up the wall, zigzagging ever so little, so thin as to be almost imperceptible. The wall on one side of the crack seemed about an inch higher than on the other.

"Something wrong?"

He heard a somewhat irritated voice behind him. Unnerved, he took a quick gulp of water and moved back from the fountain.

"Excuse me. Go right ahead."

So saying, he attempted to give place to the tall man behind him, but the latter moved to block his way. Taken aback, Onodera looked up into the man's broad face.

"Hello!" the man said to Onodera, seizing his shoulder with a huge hand. White teeth flashed in his dark, sunburned face.

Onodera, at a total loss for a moment, suddenly grinned in return. "Goh! Not you?"

"A hangover, eh?" said Rokuro Goh, wrinkling up his nose. "Now I see. You looked like a carp there, gulping down that water."

Paying no attention to Onodera's denials, the towering Goh bent over and began to drink as though he intended to drain the cooler right then and there.

"Where are you headed?" Goh asked, wiping his wet mouth.

"Yaizu."

"Still at it, eh?" Goh bent back the fingers of his right hand and made a dipping motion.

"Right. Where're you going?"

"In the same direction. Hamamatsu."

"What's in Hamamatsu? Work?" Onodera asked, as he sipped his beer in the train's air-conditioned snack bar.

"Yes, the usual thing—construction." Goh, already finishing

his second beer, made a grimace that pulled taut his sunburned skin.

"The Super Express?"

"Yes. There's been one problem after another. The work on the roadbed is stalled."

"What kind of problems?"

The train began to move. The view outside the window seemed to waver, catching Onodera's attention. Just for a brief instant, how beautiful seemed the confused, dusty scene at the platform, the row of heat-oppressed faces. . . .

"What kind of problems, you say?" said Goh. Gripping his glass of beer tightly, he stared moodily at the dissolving froth. "All kinds. But it wouldn't do to say anything about them yet. The newspapers might get on to it."

Onodera did not press him further. He poured himself a second glass of beer.

"I don't see how the survey could have been so far off," Goh muttered as though talking to himself. "We have to practically start from scratch. The work's in full swing, and then everything blows up in our faces."

"How do you mean?"

"Oh, it's nothing, I suppose. But take it from me, Onodera, Japan these days seems to be very, very shaky. Like a mass of jelly . . . Another beer? Or should we go back to our seats?" asked Goh, looking around the crowded dining car.

"What's going on in Yaizu, by the way? A sunken ship or something? Great work for hot weather."

"Not so great," answered Onodera with a wry grin. "A Security Agency ship is taking us south. It's a matter of doing some research using a deep-sea submarine—the *Wadatsumi.*"

"Where are you going?"

"Southeast of Torijima. There was an island there, and it seems that it disappeared."

"Disappeared? Was there an eruption?"

"No, there wasn't any eruption. It just sank—just like that."

2

The *Wadatsumi,* covered with canvas, was already loaded upon the rear deck of the Marine Security patrol boat *Hokuto* in the harbor at Yaizu when Onodera arrived.

Professor Yukinaga of M—— University caught sight of Onodera on the dock and waved to him: "Hello there. . . . I'm sorry about this. I hear you were on vacation."

Surprised at the stir aboard ship, Onodera glanced at his watch in surprise. "Is it sailing time already?" he asked as he came on board.

"Well, we have to sail as soon as we can," answered Yukinaga, looking down at the wharf. "Should the papers find out that the *Wadatsumi* is going out, you see, it would be awkward."

Onodera grinned. "The *A—— Journal* is especially eager, I hear. I understand they chartered a seaplane."

"They're making too much of it," said Yukinaga, shrugging. Though his field was marine geology and he spent much of his life aboard ship, his pale skin seemed untouched by the sun. "Anyway, I don't think there's any cause for alarm. They won't learn anything even if they do fly down there."

"Well, I suppose it's the slow season for news."

"There would be quite an uproar, though," said Yukinaga, dropping his voice and narrowing his eyes somewhat in the strong sunlight, "if something were to come out about the trouble they're running into with the new Super Express line."

"Oh?" Onodera was taken by surprise. "You know about that?"

"I've heard things," said the professor, his voice still low. "A colleague of mine was commissioned to make a confidential investigation. . . ."

Suddenly Yukinaga raised his hand. Down the concrete pier swarming with buzzing flies, a broad, plump figure was running toward them in a flurry of sweat. He banged the suitcase he was carrying against a capstan and almost went sprawling when he trampled upon one of the fish that lay scattered over the concrete, but, nevertheless, he finally reached the ship.

"Hurry up," said Yukinaga, laughing. "We're on our way."

"Without me?" the fat man shouted indignantly. "If you want to go, go. I'll come swimming after you."

"I know you would," said Yukinaga, reaching out for the man's suitcase as he came across the gangplank. "Onodera, this is Professor Tadokoro."

"Oh, yes, Professor . . . underwater volcanoes . . ." said Onodera, nodding eagerly. "I'm Onodera of Sea Floor Development."

"The truth is my field is geophysics," said Tadokoro, "but I stick my nose into everything." With that, he walked abruptly back to the stern, where the *Wadatsumi* lay beneath its tarpaulin.

He rapped his hand smartly against the steel plating under the canvas. "So this is it? You know, I asked that fellow Yamashiro at your place again and again. . . ."

"Well, there's been a constant demand for it," Onodera replied, smiling awkwardly. "The *Wadatsumi 2* will be finished soon, and then I think things will be better."

"It's the same design as the *Archimedes*. So it should be able to dive to thirty-five thousand. Right?" said Tadokoro, eying Onodera sharply. "How absurd to use something like this to study ocean currents and fishing grounds. Like using a laser beam to cut up a chicken."

"It's a tricky ship. The deeper you go, the less time you can stay under," said Onodera, stroking the side of the submarine.

"How many times has it gone down really deep?"

"Thirty thousand feet, four times. Beyond thirty-five thousand, twice. There was no particular danger, but . . ."

"How about the Vityaz Deep? Would it be safe to go all the way down there?"

"Well, if it were the new submarine . . ." said Onodera.

"Yukinaga!" said Tadokoro, moving away from the *Wadatsumi* with sudden resolution. "Let's talk for a bit." He threw his arm around Yukinaga's shoulders, and the two walked toward the cabin door, leaving Onodera to himself.

Now that everyone was accounted for, the *Hokuto*'s departure siren sounded. The crew cast off the hawsers, and white water boiled up at the stern as the sleek, shiny gray-blue patrol boat moved away from the dock. Though there were a few people on the dock to wave farewell, it was an austere leave-taking.

Shortly after they were under way, Onodera noticed a small man with an unlit corncob pipe in his mouth coming from the forward deck.

"Yuki!" he shouted. "I didn't expect to find you here."

"I'm just here to hand things over to you," said the little man, grinning nervously. "I've been a little concerned. Anyway, if I was back on shore, I'd only be suffering from the heat. I'll give you a hand with the repairs."

"I understand that the gondola was scraped," said Onodera, turning toward the submarine. A revolving gondola was attached to the bottom of the craft. Heavy and egg-shaped, it was made of steel bolstered with molybdenum.

"Where it scraped was on the side here. The window has a slight crack, but we have a spare one."

They began to discuss Onodera's mission. The request for the *Wadatsumi,* Yuki said, had probably come from scientists in the group already dispatched by the Weather Service to investigate the sinking of the island.

"Have you heard any news since then?" asked Onodera. "I thought that the meteorological people were concerned about volcanic activity in the Fuji area. And so to go to all this effort for the sake of one uninhabited island . . ."

"Not completely uninhabited," said Yuki, his face showing signs of fatigue. "Some Polynesian fishermen stopped there the night it sank."

"Really?" said Onodera, surprised. "Were they rescued?"

"Yes. A Japanese fishing boat happened to be anchored in the lee of the island."

3

While the *Hokuto* kept to its course to the south at high speed, Onodera and Yuki completed the repairs on the *Wadatsumi* and did the necessary maintenance work despite the fierce heat of the sun. Hachijojima appeared on the horizon and then fell away behind the ship's long white trailing wake. Now there was no trace of anything on the horizon—nothing to be seen but a vast, convex expanse of water.

With time hanging heavy, Onodera climbed to the crow's-nest and looked around him. From this vantage point, the *Hokuto* seemed no more than a tiny waterbug set down atop that vast globe of water of mind-numbing size. This was the area where the Pacific Tropics stretched far to the north, borne upon the ocean currents. Now the prow of this tiny, yet somehow brashly resolute ship was pointed toward the Torrid Zone and the islands below the Equator. Ever more to the south . . .

Down as far as Cape Horn, except for the small islands scattered like a handful of dust across that broad expanse, the face of the globe was covered with nothing but water, ever more water. The world's largest ocean, its mean depth was 14,155 feet, and at the Equator it stretched over nearly 180 degrees of latitude, nearly half the distance around the world—a vast sea that contained almost half of the water in the world, that covered one third of the surface of the world, that, even if all the continents were set within it, would still consist of over 14 million square miles of ocean.

"How about coming down?" Yukinaga called up to him, waving a can of beer. "It's cold. Let's have one."

Yukinaga was leaning against the ship's rail, beer can raised to his lips, when Onodera came down. When he pulled back the tab on the chill can Yukinaga gave him, the wind snatched at the clinging white froth that bubbled up and mingled it with the spray.

"I wonder if that's Aogashima," said Yukinaga, shading his eyes and looking toward the east where a cluster of clouds lay over the horizon. "I suppose it is. At this rate, we should be at Torishima before sunset."

"Look over there," said Onodera, pointing. "Do you think it's a ship?"

Straight ahead, almost directly to the south, there was a trace of black smoke upon the horizon. As it rose, the wind caught it and blew it in a trailing swirl to the northeast.

"That's no boat," answered Yukinaga, narrowing his eyes. "It's from a volcano. It's near the Bayonnaise Rocks."

"Is it Myojin Reef?"

"No. Myojin isn't active right now. But Smith Reef has shown signs of erupting, after more than fifty years. It stands to reason that there should be something in the Bayonnaise Rocks ready to erupt about now."

Onodera suddenly remembered something from his childhood—how he had read about the eruption of Myojin Reef. That had been in 1952. Could it have been that long ago? From the sea floor, covered by the glassy surface of the ocean, fire, smoke, and lava had suddenly come heaving upward. The fire had raged in the midst of the sea, the smoke boiling up right out of the water. How powerful an impression the news photo had made upon Onodera! A weather-survey ship, the *Kaiyo Maru,* had been destroyed, with the loss of thirty-one crewmen, when the cold, tranquil surface of the Pacific had dissolved in a cataclysmic surge of searing smoke and ashes. Even now the bizarre, disordered nature of the event caused Onodera's chest to tighten. A shiver ran through him.

"Torishima had its own catastrophe in 1886," Yukinaga said in a low voice, his cheeks a faint red from the wind. "A mountain right at the center of the island exploded. In an instant the whole population of the island, 125 people, was wiped out."

"There seems to be a lot of volcanic activity recently," said Onodera.

"Yes. Oshima, Miyakejima, Aoshima . . . and there's talk about Amagi now."

"Is there any connection?"

"There's not supposed to be—the way we've understood things up to now. But . . ."

"But what?"

"Well, the emergence of a volcanic region is linked with mountain-building activity, and so it seems that any change in the structure as a whole would have to have some general effect."

The two were silent for a time, looking at the sea.

The ship was now pursuing its southward course directly above the Fuji volcanic range running across the floor of the ocean. Beginning in Central Honshu with Mounts Shirauma, Hida, and Norikura, moving through Asama and Fuji, Hakone, Amagi, the Izu Islands, Aogashima, the Bayonnaise Rocks, Torishima, and farther down yet, to the Iwojima chain and almost to the Tropic of Capricorn, there stretched a long belt of fire covering 1,000 miles. Here and there along its length, volcanic peaks broke the surface of the sea, rising up from the ocean floor, some 13,000 feet below. These scattered islands, extending from the Equator north to the fire-spouting Kasai Archipelago, constituted the true western shore of the Pacific, a vast undersea mountain range over which the ship was now passing. They marked the great geological fold that began in Siberia and extended down through Hokkaido to Central Honshu. Thence it lay along the ocean floor beneath a thousand fathoms of water, its course marked by the Fuji Archipelago, the Ogasawara Archipelago, the Marianas, and the Palau Islands, curving at last to link up with the arc of Java and Sumatra. This ring of fire, this sunken shoreline, fell away on its Pacific side to trenches of awesome depth.

Suddenly there was a loud thump, as though something had struck the bottom of the boat.

"Did we hit something?" asked Onodera.

"I don't think there's any reef around here," said Yukinaga.

Just at that moment, though there was no sound, a wave of air struck their faces. Then came what sounded like the rumble of a far-off cannon.

A shout came from the bridge. Sailors were running across the deck and down the passageways.

"It's an eruption!" cried Yuki, coming out on deck.

The loud rumbling went on, and when they looked behind them, they saw gray-brown smoke pouring up from the Bayonnaise Rocks, orange flame glowing at the border between smoke and water.

"Dr. Tadokoro!" the captain called from the bridge. "What is the situation? Are we all right?"

"There's no need to worry about something no bigger than that," answered Tadokoro, who had appeared on deck and was holding a pair of binoculars to his eyes. "Warn the ships in the area, but we should hurry on to where we're going."

"Look, over by Myojin, too, there's vapor rising," said Yukinaga, looking through the binoculars he had taken from Tadokoro. "It doesn't seem too large a volcano."

"That shock before—was it a tidal wave?" asked Onodera.

"Yes. A small one, though," answered Tadokoro.

Onodera took the binoculars from Yukinaga. Tongues of orange flame rose up out of the ocean. The peak of the rock had been blown away. The surface of the sea about the island began to boil, and the brown smoke and the white steam seemed to be quenching the flames. The smoke climbed higher and higher into the sky, though a part spread out in a heavy layer over the water. Torrid projectiles and pumice stone peppered the surface of the sea like a sudden squall, whipping the water into a froth beneath the pall of smoke. And the surface of the sea shuddered as muffled explosions continued.

While they had been intent upon the volcano, the *Hokuto* had increased its speed. The waves at the bow rose so high that they broke over the foredeck, and the spray stung the men's faces. Tremors ran through the ship, and the groaning of the gas turbines took on the pitch of wind howling through a cave.

"I've moved up the rendezvous time," said the captain after coming down from the bridge. "After I get you to the survey ship, I have to go back to Torishima to pick up the Weather Service people."

"Torishima?" Yukinaga asked in surprise. "Are there indications of an eruption there, too?"

"I don't know. They say it's a precautionary measure. You're going to get wet here. I think it would be best to go inside." Then, as he was climbing the ladder to the bridge, the captain turned and said: "Oh, and by the way, that tidal wave seems to have had nothing to do with that underwater eruption. We just got a warning about an undersea earthquake in the eastern part of the Ogasawara Trench, and that's most likely what caused it."

For some reason, this news provoked a fierce frown on Tadokoro's face.

4

It was seven in the evening when the *Hokuto* arrived at its rendezvous point eighteen miles northeast of Torishima. At this latitude the setting sun had force enough to strike the sea with fierce intensity, but the water lay calm beneath the consuming rays, its surface slick and still except for a faint breeze from south-southeast.

The *Wadatsumi* was lowered into the water by a derrick and drawn by towlines to the Weather Service ship the *Daito Maru #3,* where it was lifted once more and secured to the rear deck.

When the work was completed at dusk, the *Hokuto* sounded its departure siren at once and sailed off at full speed, bound for Torishima.

Onodera, leaving to Yuki the overseeing of the *Wadatsumi*'s securing, left the afterdeck of the *Daito Maru* and went inside. As he was walking down a passageway, the door to the wardroom opened and Yukinaga put his head out.

"Onodera," he called. "Come in, we want you here, too."

When Onodera stepped through the door, he saw some ten or more men, scientists and research personnel, gathered around the wardroom table, which was spread with sea charts and other papers.

"The Polynesian fishermen who were on the island when it sunk—where are they?" Tadokoro asked in a loud voice. "Are they on board?"

"We've just sent for them," answered an elderly man who seemed every inch a university professor. "Tomorrow they'll be transferred to an American naval ship and taken home."

"It seems to me, gentlemen," said Tadokoro, sizing up the group around the table, "that this is a lot of fuss to be making over an insignificant little island. Here we have the Weather Service, the Fisheries Bureau, the Technological Bureau, all going to the trouble of outfitting and dispatching a ship of this size. What was this island like anyway?"

"Well, a weather-survey ship discovered it only five or six years ago," answered a man from the Weather Service. "It was very small—only one mile from north to south and eight hundred yards from east to west. The highest elevation was about two hundred feet."

The door opened and a man of about fifty entered. His shoulders were incredibly broad, and the sun had turned his complexion swarthy. His arms, bared by his T-shirt were thick and powerful, and his body reeked of fish and engine oil. Behind him three tall men came hesitantly into the room, their skins coal black, their eyes staring wildly. Two of them wore what looked like ragged aloha shirts bleached by the sun, and the third, a torn undershirt darkened to a muddy brown. Their lips were thick, and the hair that covered their long, narrow heads spread out softly like the crest of a crane. The one who seemed to be the oldest had hair sprinkled with silver, and his face, chest, and upper arms were covered with blue tattooing.

The squat man who had led them in took off his oil-stained work cap, gave a polite bow, and then stood there uncertain and ill at ease.

"This is Mr. Yamamoto, whose fishing boat, the *Suiten Maru 9,* rescued the Polynesian fishermen," the man from the Weather Service explained. "Since he can speak a bit of Polynesian, his captain was kind enough to send him to us with them.

These men, who were on the island when it went under, are fishermen from Uragasu Island, he says."

"Let's hear what you have to say," said Tadokoro, indicating that they were to sit down. "I'm sure you've told the others already, but we would appreciate hearing it once again."

"Well," said the fisherman, "the day before, our ship was somewhere north-northeast of Yamome Rock in the northeast part of the Ogasawara chain, and we were fishing. In the afternoon a weather report came warning about a tropical storm, and we got ready to clear out fast, but our engine started to act up. We could make headway, as far as that went, but it was slow going. The storm wasn't supposed to amount to much, but when you spun the wheel, it didn't respond right. And so we were in a situation in which something had to be done, and so we started thinking about what island we could shelter at. We decided to make for this island without a name rather than try for Torishima. We reached it just about sunset. We dropped anchor about seven hundred yards off the north side, and everybody but the engineers got some sleep. It was really a dark night, cloudy without a single star."

"What was the depth where you dropped anchor?" asked Yukinaga.

"I think it was about fifty feet. The radio report we heard said that the storm had just grazed us and moved off to the east. So everybody felt good about that, and then we really went to sleep. Then . . . well, let's see. It started to get light before three o'clock, I know. Up by the bow there was this sudden jerking like the ship was being pulled down. I was awake since I'd got up to go to the toilet, and it was just as I was coming back. I heard the captain yell from up above: 'What's the matter?' And then the watch yelled back: 'Everything's all right.' And so I went back to sleep, and when I woke up the next time, it was after four o'clock. I heard shouting up on deck, and so I went up to have a look. Everybody was yelling about the island being gone. The cloudiness had cleared up by now, and the surface of the ocean was fairly bright. And when you looked around, there wasn't a thing to be seen, not a trace of the island, when, the night before, there it was looming up solid as could be right in front of your nose. The ship was floating there all by itself on the open sea as far as you could look in any direction. We were just drifting, with our engine off. 'The anchor line's cut,' somebody said. But in fact the anchor was hanging there, not touching the bottom. Then suddenly the watch yelled: 'Somebody's in the water.' We looked and we saw some men swimming near the boat and yelling out something. We pulled them out right away, and it was this bunch here."

"I see," said Tadokoro, taking a quick breath. "These men, then—they were on the island that night."

"So they say. They had their sails torn in a gale, and so they stopped off there at noon the day before."

"I suppose you've been asked this any number of times," said Yukinaga, "but did you measure the water's depth at the rescue point?"

"Yes, sir. Right below the ship, it was two thousand feet. But, as we figured out later, we had been carried at least one and a half miles north from the spot where we had anchored. The captain said that it was the damnedest thing he'd ever heard of. And so, with the engine fixed, we got under way and headed south like a bat out of hell, taking depth soundings as we went. No more than fifteen minutes went by, before the mate yelled: 'Captain! The water's getting shallow all of a sudden. It's 160 feet here.' 'You don't often find anything so shallow in this area,' the captain answered. 'Come here,' the mate said. 'Take a look at the depth chart. You see?' Then the mate moved the compass bearing ten degrees to the west, and signaled for quarter-speed. Then he signaled for slow, and he kept a sharp watch as he moved the ship forward. The captain stood straight up in the prow—he had experience as a pilot, and with the sun finally out altogether, he kept his eyes fixed on the water in front of the ship, staring down into it. 'Was there an island here or not?' he muttered to himself. But then, all of a sudden, even I could see that there was a definite change in color coming over the water. 'Watch it, it's getting shallow,' the captain yelled. 'Captain, right now we're over the island,' the mate shouted. 'If we are, be careful,' the captain yelled back, 'it's getting shallow fast.' 'We're okay,' said the mate, 'we've already almost passed over the island. The deep part we went over just before must have been the inlet formed by the crater. One spot there was nearly three hundred feet deep. Right now we're passing over the peak on the southern edge of the island. But even so, the depth is thirty feet. . . .' "

Yamamoto closed his mouth, his story done. There was perfect silence in the wardroom.

Finally the elderly man spoke, his manner quite composed. Onodera had by now recognized him as an eminent authority on oceanography. "And, gentlemen, while this nameless little island was going under, Torishima itself sank three feet."

"Well, let's hear what these men have to say," said Tadokoro, turning toward the three Polynesians. "Can you interpret well enough?"

Yamamoto scratched his head and then set to work. Neither his Polynesian, however, nor the Japanese of the old man nor the English of the young one was of much help when it came to detailed questions. But rather the three natives, children of nature that they were, eloquently conveyed the circumstances of the sinking by skillful use of gestures and sounds.

After spending the day in repairing their damaged craft, the Polynesians had gone to sleep in a cave in the cliff face that looked down upon the inlet. In the middle of the night, they had been awakened by the sound of waves, and they had found the sea already at the mouth of their cave.

Had there been an earthquake? Had they heard any rumblings?

They answered that they had been aware of nothing of the sort. And when someone asked how fast the island had sunk, the youngest of the three, by way of answer, bent over to touch the floor with his hands and then raised them steadily until they were level with his chest.

"Like a submarine," someone said.

They had rushed up to the top of the cliff and thence to the island's peak, the encroaching sea hard on their heels. The peak had soon been reduced to a bit of rock on the black surface of the sea, beset by hungry white waves. Soon this, too, had been overwhelmed, and the three of them had been swept away, whirlpools of all sizes swirling all around them. Stricken with terror, they had felt themselves dead already, but a large piece of driftwood had happened to come their way, and they had taken turns clinging to it until daybreak.

"Well," said Tadokoro after they had finished, "there have been accounts enough of islands sinking—but an island so large . . . and for it to sink so fast . . . Well, gentlemen, that's not something you run into every day, now is it?"

"And there's more yet," said the gray-haired oceanographer coolly. "The fishing boat dropped a buoy to mark the island's highest point."

"You found it?"

"We found it all right. And we definitely established that we were over the island. But by then the peak was three hundred feet below the surface. What do you think of that, Tadokoro? The entire ocean floor in this area, in a mere two and a half days, has sunk more than five hundred feet."

5

At seven the next morning, after moving at a slow speed and taking repeated soundings, the *Daito Maru* stopped directly above the sunken island. The sea was peaceful. The tanker *Tatsumi Maru,* which belonged to Sea Floor Development, anchored some 300 meters from the *Daito Maru.* It functioned as a maintenance ship for the submarine, and now its decks were stirring with preparations. A derrick lifted the *Wadatsumi* from the deck and lowered it gently to the water. Onodera and Yuki went aboard, jumping onto the precariously rolling deck of the submarine. Onodera, going down through the passageway inside the conning tower, lowered himself into the gondola. Then, taking the directions that Yuki gave him through the open hatch, he guided the submarine over to the *Tatsumi Maru.*

The red no-smoking flag flew from the *Tatsumi Maru*'s deck, and the smell of gasoline filled the air. The *Wadatsumi,* its white hull set off in striking fashion by four stripes, two red and two orange, slowly settled to its proper draft. Three dives were planned, each in a different spot. The first was to last two and a half hours or longer if advisable.

The first passengers were Tadokoro and a young engineer from the Fisheries Bureau. After the two of them had preceded him down the hatch into the gondola, Onodera signaled with upraised thumb for the release of the mooring arm. Rattling loudly, the arm swung into action and pushed the *Wadatsumi* away from the side of the tanker. The submarine floated free upon the waves, its conning tower rocking from side to side.

Onodera bent his index finger, thrust it between his teeth, and whistled sharply, to ward off ill luck. From the work deck of the *Tatsumi Maru,* Yuki gave an answering whistle. Onodera made his way down the long, narrow hatchway, thirteen feet in height, and lowered himself into the gondola, closing the hatch cover behind him.

"Well, here we go," said Onodera to the two men sitting tense behind him as he gave the VLF radio a routine final check. After Onodera had dimmed the interior lighting, he put his hand to the control stick and released the air from the front and rear flotation tanks. The water churned noisily about the *Wadatsumi* and rushed upward past its observation windows. As Yuki watched from the deck of the *Tatsumi Maru,* the white-and-orange conning tower of the *Wadatsumi* slipped silently away, sinking down into the waves as it trailed bubbles from its prow and stern.

Onodera threw the power switch. The screw set in the stern at an upward slant began to turn over quietly.

"We are making a power dive down close to the island. The depth will be two hundred feet. Please hold on."

Onodera pushed the control stick forward sharply and then cut it to the right. The *Wadatsumi* began its dive, spiraling downward, its bow set at an angle of about fifteen degrees. Tadokoro and the engineer took turns peering at the TV screen and looking out the window.

"There it is," muttered Tadokoro, his voice like a growl. "There it is, all right."

It was nine o'clock by now, but down here in the depths there was as yet little light. The water was clear, however, and, on the screen of the free-ranging TV camera, one could dimly see, looming up from the dark depths, the massive and still darker bulk of the undersea island. Its peak alone was faintly touched with light. Its sloping side faded from sight as it trailed down through a thousand fathoms of black water.

"Point the nose right at it," said Tadokoro, throwing the switch to activate the videotape recorder.

Onodera cautiously, bit by bit, moved the control stick to straighten out the submarine's course and direct it at the island. Gently he shifted into reverse, and the vessel's forward motion stopped. He released a bit of the air used for stabilization, and after depressing the nose fifteen degrees, he gently edged the vessel into a dive. Like stage scenery rising into position, the crest of the nameless island loomed up from the bottom of the TV screen. The nose of the submarine was now about 300 yards distant from it. Professor Tadokoro pushed a button, and the compact videotape recorder began to spin with a faint whirring noise.

Onodera turned on the ultrasonic-wave fathometer.

"Turn it off whenever you think it's time," said Onodera, peering sharply at the trembling needle of the sonic depth-recorder and at the speed-of-descent needle. "We still have quite a distance remaining."

When the slope coming down from the crest was ten yards away, Onodera put the engine into fast reverse, and the *Wadatsumi,* its nose still tipped down at a fifteen-degree angle, darted backward like a killifish.

"Should we make a descent following the line of the slope, Professor?" Onodera asked.

"Hey, take it easy, will you!" Yuki's voice came in from the *Tatsumi Maru* on the VLF radio. "We thought you smashed into it for sure."

"Try circling the crest," said Tadokoro. "And then we'll go down the slope."

"Professor Tadokoro," said Onodera as he started to move the vessel forward, "even with the ocean floor sinking nearly six hundred feet in two days, there was no tidal wave or anything. Why not, do you suppose?"

"I don't know!" Tadokoro barked in answer. "Somehow equilibrium was maintained, I suppose, but I have no idea how. I just don't know!"

I just don't know—that's the same refrain I've heard ever since last evening, Onodera thought.

The *Wadatsumi* kept a distance of about 150 yards from the crest of the undersea island as it began to circle it at a speed of three knots. They were close enough to see clearly the creases that ran down the crater wall of the old volcano. As soon as he turned on the searchlight, even Onodera, layman though he was, was able to perceive the difference between water and wind erosion. The diameter of the crater at its mouth was some 200 to 300 yards. On its inside the sides of the crater fell away in a sheer, almost perpendicular drop. There was a deep V-shaped crevice in the crater wall. It seemed to have been caused not by the eruption, but by some earlier disturbance. The fathometer showed a depth of about 300 feet at the crater. Onodera felt a chill as the thought struck him that Tadokoro might say, "Let's go down into there for a look." There was no evidence of volcanic activity at the time of the island's sinking.

Just as though it had been there forever, the black bulk of the island lay in the cold gloom of the ocean depths, a pall of heavy silence shrouding it.

Onodera began his descent. Using the sonar to ensure the greatest safety, he fixed upon the slope line of the volcano, pointing the nose down at an angle of nearly thirty degrees.

"We're going down the slope, Yuki," he said into the microphone. "Keep a sharp watch."

"I've got you."

Onodera turned the rheostat lever. The sound of flowing water penetrated the thick metal of the gondola casing, and the vibrations of the engine shook it as the *Wadatsumi* began its descent at a speed of two knots. Professor Tadokoro and the young engineer tightened their seat belts, their eyes like saucers as they looked out the observation window and at the TV screen. The dull, twanging echo of the sonar reverberated through the gondola.

Schools of fish and huge shadows which might have been sharks crossed the screen. The side of the undersea crater loomed up outside the right window until at last the unmistakable traces of sea erosion came into view.

"Go back up to the water line," said Tadokoro.

Onodera raised the nose of the submarine until the erosion mark was opposite the window.

"Where's your level?" asked Tadokoro.

"In the drawer there."

Tadokoro laid the level on the ledge of the observation window and studied it with rapt attention. Finally he spoke abruptly: "If that's the sea-level mark as of three days ago, the whole island has tipped four to five degrees to the east."

"Should I continue down?" asked Onodera.

Tadokoro signaled his assent with a tap on the shoulder. The *Wadatsumi* resumed its descent. . . . 600 feet . . . 800 feet

. . . The sun was apparently high in the sky by now, for visibility remained fairly constant. The water outside the window, however, quickly took on a bluish cast. At 1,000 feet Onodera slowly brought up the nose of the submarine. The slope of the crater was gradually growing less steep as its skirts trailed down into the indigo-blue depths of the ocean floor. Onodera turned off both the television and the lights inside the gondola. A ghostly blue light poured in from the round observation windows. At 1,200 feet, the *Wadatsumi*, now almost level, continued to follow the gradual slope which trailed far off to the vanishing point in the darkness of the ocean floor. He jettisoned a small amount of ballast.

"We'll reach the bottom in just a bit," Onodera announced.

He turned on the searchlight. Beyond the cloudy wall of water ahead, the sea floor came dimly into view. The guide chain trailing from the bottom of the submarine struck with a thump, transmitting the shock to the gondola. Phosphorescent fish swam up to the window. The floor of the sea, beneath the powerful glare of the searchlight, seemed to loom up like some massive gray living thing. Onodera dropped their speed to a half-knot. The guide chain stirred up mud from the bottom as the *Wadatsumi* finally came to a gradual stop. There were only six feet between it and the ocean floor.

The bottom of the sea, as far as Onodera was concerned, showed nothing unusual. For the two men behind him, however, there was something that gave rise to great excitement.

"Ripple marks . . ." muttered the young engineer.

"Volcanic rock projectiles—right out in the open like that!" exclaimed Tadokoro excitedly.

"It's obvious, isn't it, that mud on the bottom shifted violently just a little while ago?" said the engineer. "Take a look—there!"

"Hmmmmm." Tadokoro nodded. "The sea floor here, keeping the same slope, seems to have shifted over a broad area, doesn't it?"

"Rather than shifted, wouldn't you say that there might have been something like a landslide?"

"Onodera," said Tadokoro, "what we have to do next is to see what we can see on the eastern part of the shelf."

Professor Yukinaga and a specialist in volcanoes from the expedition went aboard for the second dive. This time Onodera went down at full power and brought the submarine rapidly to a depth of 2,000 feet. And from there, following the slope of the shelf, they dove to the ocean floor, a depth of 6,050 feet. Again the two observers came across a wealth of exciting discoveries. Once even the ever-composed Yukinaga cried out shrilly. The sea was beginning to get rough when they surfaced again.

"We'll postpone the third dive until tomorrow," said Tadokoro. "The *Daito Maru* seems to have discovered something unusual about ninety miles east of here, in the Ogasawara Trench. This time we'll go down to the bottom of the trench to have a look. No difficulty in that?"

"No, sir," said Onodera.

6

Visibility was bad when the *Wadatsumi* slipped below the surface the next day, with Tadokoro and Yukinaga aboard. It plunged into the jaws of a vast black watery void, and at 3,000 feet darkness swallowed it up completely. The force of the water coming to bear upon a portion of metal no larger than the palm of a hand was more than 100 tons. The *Wadatsumi* continued its dive smoothly at a speed of three knots an hour into that freezing hell of crushing pressure, like a specimen sealed in blue glass. The interior of the gondola became cold. Moisture condensed in drops upon the inner walls.

"It would be good to put on your jackets," said Onodera.

The control board glowed with a green, firefly-like light. At 5,000 feet Onodera turned on the searchlight, and the water seemed to envelop the *Wadatsumi* like a gray-blue fog. From time to time, strange creatures of the deep floated up into the spotlight and then swam casually away without showing the least interest in the odd invader.

"Ten thousand feet," said Onodera, his eyes on the water-pressure gauge. "To the left there . . . the trench slope begins. The distance is eight miles. The slope angle is twenty-five degrees. According to the charts, it should be much steeper."

The temperature continued to drop. Yukinaga unobtrusively pulled his jacket collar tighter about him. The dehumidifier had begun to take effect. The drops of moisture on the walls and the pipes had disappeared. The inside of the gondola had the hush of a graveyard at dusk. The submarine seemed to Yukinaga like a metal coffin drawn ever deeper into the terrible pressure of the abyss.

Fifteen thousand feet. Professor Yukinaga felt his skin prickle at the thought of the water crowding against the outside of the metal wall a bare twenty inches from his shoulder. He heard a faint crackling noise, and he looked furtively about him.

"Everything's in good shape," said Onodera, noticing Yukinaga's concern. "The instruments contract and pull at their fittings when the temperature drops. Should I turn on the heater?"

"No . . ." said Tadokoro. "We'll soon be at the bottom?"

"We're at 17,200 feet," said Onodera, looking up at the pressure gauge. "The bottom should be . . ."

There was a loud ping as a downward sound wave gave back an immediate echo.

". . . 5,850 feet farther."

Only rarely now did any living thing pass through the searchlight beam. Sometimes a small jellyfish or shellfish, immune to the terrible pressure, would flash by. When Onodera turned off the searchlight, however, living creatures, like scattered stars, shone with blue-white phosphorescence in the pitch-black void. The water temperature fell to 1.8 degrees Centigrade. One hour and forty-two minutes had passed since they had left the surface behind.

"Twenty-two thousand feet . . ."

"That there!" exclaimed Yukinaga, a quaver to his voice. "Is it a ray?"

Outside the left window, a creature like a huge curtain was flapping its way slowly through the searchlight beam.

"Surely," said Tadokoro, his voice hoarse, "something that big couldn't be a living thing."

The creature, caught in the outer circle of light, took a good five or six seconds to pass by. It seemed to be more than 100 feet in length.

"Could we try to track it with the sonar?" asked Yukinaga.

"It's already way above us," answered Onodera. "We'll soon be at the bottom."

Suddenly there was a loud thump as the submarine took a shocking blow upon its side. The *Wadatsumi* shuddered, and its nose twisted sharply to the left more than twenty degrees, then thirty degrees back to the right.

"What is it?" Yukinaga asked, his voice harsh. "An accident?"

"No," answered Onodera calmly. "It seems like it was an undersea tidal current."

"At a spot this deep?" asked Tadokoro. "A current that strong? How's that?"

"I don't know," answered Onodera. "Sometimes we run into them. But I've never hit one that strong before."

"There's the bottom," said Yukinaga, his voice like a sigh.

Directly below them two mustard-colored circles seemed to loom dimly, the targets of the two powerful searchlights pointing straight down from the front and rear of the submarine. Gradually they got brighter, their outlines growing quite distinct. At several points doughnut-shaped clouds of mud whirled up, rising as they broadened, stirred by released ballast. The guide chain struck the sea floor, and the *Wadatsumi*, halting its descent, pursued a course barely five feet from the bottom.

The water was clear at this depth. Once the flowing clouds of ooze had thinned, there was almost nothing to catch the light cast by the searchlight. The melancholy brown desert of the sea floor stretched all around them. The distant portion was grayish with a tinge of indigo. Beyond that was blackness.

"Well . . ." said Onodera, breaking silence, his voice harsh, "this is the floor of the trench. The depth is 23,840 feet."

As though jarred by Onodera's voice, the two scientists began to exchange low, hurried whispers.

"Look there!" exclaimed Tadokoro, pointing his finger.

Yukinaga nodded. Running from west to east across the sea floor were any number of ripple marks.

"That over there," said Tadokoro, "what's that long thing like a rut?"

"I don't know," answered Yukinaga, shaking his head. He spoke to Onodera: "Could we turn in that direction?"

Onodera released a small amount of ballast. Once more a cloud of mud rose up outside the window. The *Wadatsumi* climbed a bit, and Onodera guided the nose of the submarine in the direction Yukinaga wanted by careful use of his jets rather than by the control stick, moving forward at extremely slow speed.

The long trench on the sea floor, some seven or eight feet wide, came into view through the cloud of muddy water. It looked as though some creature of fantastic size had dragged itself through the ooze.

"Over there, too," Yukinaga whispered. "Why, there are all kinds of them."

"What do you think they are?" asked Tadokoro.

"I don't know." Onodera shook his head. "I've gone down into a trench two or three times now, but this is the first time I've ever seen anything like this."

The sea floor was covered with these broad ruts. They ranged from fifteen feet in width to twenty or more. They extended east and west beyond the limits of the submarine's field of vision. Something had caused the sea floor to shift. Some force of unimaginable power.

"Could it be that there was some extraordinary gravitational variation in this area?" Yukinaga asked.

"No idea," answered Tadokoro. "Let's follow along and have a look."

Turning the wireless up to its full capacity, Onodera attempted contact with the *Tatsumi Maru*. At length Yuki's voice came through. The reception was terribly weak and marred by static.

"What is it?" came the faint response. "We lost all trace of you just now. We had been monitoring your sonar vibrations."

"We ran into some strange-looking ruts at the bottom of the trench," said Onodera. "So what we're going to do now is follow them, going east. Take a verification of my position."

"All right," answered Yuki. "In one minute give me a signal. And then let's have a sound wave every minute after that."

His eye on his stopwatch, Onodera let a minute elapse and then sent up a signal from the ultrasonic oscillator. When he had gotten a reply verifying his position, Onodera set the oscillator at one-minute intervals and started the submarine forward. He steered it into a shallow curve, and, passing over two ruts, he lined up the vessel's axis with the third and then moved forward at a speed of three knots. Apparently they had not yet reached the deepest part of the sea trench. In front of them there was a gentle grade of about twenty degrees, which fell off to the east. The vessel moved ahead, its guide chain maintaining a fixed distance from the sea floor. The water pressure began to climb slightly. After they had gone a mile and a half, the rut broadened, almost doubling in width, and it also grew shallower. Finally it disappeared into the ooze. All was silent save for the faint ping of the oscillator and the quiet vibration of the motor.

"We're down to 23,950," said Onodera. "The slope of the floor is getting steep all of a sudden."

"The water's gotten muddy," said Tadokoro.

Suddenly the nose of the vessel rose up with a thumping noise. It climbed some sixty feet above the sea floor before Onodera could check it.

"Are we all right?" asked Yukinaga, gripping his chair as the submarine pitched forward and back. The dim cabin light showed his forehead beaded with sweat.

Without answering, Onodera gripped the control stick and brought the vessel some ninety feet farther up. The pitching lessened at once. How incredible, thought Onodera, a current so violent that close to the floor of a trench! He leveled out on a course 180 feet from the bottom. The vibrations ceased almost entirely.

"Should we go down again?" Onodera asked.

"No . . ." muttered Tadokoro as though uncertain.

"How about a flare?"

"Give it a try."

Onodera opened the lid of a small control box to his right and depressed one of the six levers it contained. There was a faint shock. Then in the upper portion of the television screen a dazzling sphere of brilliance burst into view. Surrounded by a frenzied mass of bubbles, it slanted slowly downward.

The two scientists, clinging to the edge of the observation window, gasped with surprise. Onodera fixed his eyes on the television screen. What had come into view, lit by the blue-white glare of that underwater sun, was peak upon peak of gray-yellow clouds of mud, wavering in the current and stretching far into the distance like a vast sea of stratocumuli seen from an airplane.

"Can we go down?" muttered Tadokoro.

"We can try 150 feet," said Onodera.

"All right. Be careful . . ." said Tadokoro. "Make sure that we can go back up at any moment."

Onodera released a spurt of gasoline from the small tank used to trim the vessel, and the *Wadatsumi* began to sink rapidly. Startled, Onodera let go some ballast and lessened the rate of descent. They were already in the midst of the muddy clouds, however. Once more the vessel began to tremble violently. Gradually Onodera brought it up forty-five feet, climbing out of the clouds. Another blow struck the *Wadatsumi*, and it began to rock from side to side.

"Let's try another flare," said Tadokoro, absorbed in the instruments and oblivious to the new crisis.

As he fired the flare, however, Onodera, reacting to some instinct of danger, released a large quantity of ballast, and the whirlpool of brown cloud beneath them suddenly fell away. An instant later a fierce rush of water hit the *Wadatsumi* broadside, tipping it over and sweeping it far off course before Onodera could reassert control and start the engine. The submarine then began to rise steadily.

"Professor Tadokoro! Look there!" Yukinaga cried.

The flare that had been released before the current struck them was drifting in the distance, shedding its light upon the yellow-brown chaos below. At the extreme edge of the light, some huge thing was churning with terrible force—a mass of mud cloud tinged with green. Swelling as it came, it was pouring down the sloping side of the trench, down out of the darkness above.

"A turbulent mud current!" shouted Tadokoro, his voice uncharacteristically shrill. "We're the first ones to actually lay eyes on one."

"But . . . at this depth?" asked Yukinaga, trembling with excitement. "It looks as though it's pouring out of the side of the trench."

"I'm going to take us all the way up," said Onodera, regaining his voice. "There was a message from the ship. The surface is getting rough."

The *Wadatsumi* began its lonely ascent at a point some 240 feet above the rolling sea of mud which filled the trench. Like a balloon cut loose from its moorings, it soared upward with steadily increasing speed toward the silver sky that glinted nearly 24,000 feet above it. Onodera fired off the three remaining flares. They burst and hung suspended above the *Wadatsumi,* their burning blue-white glare creating a circle of light more than a mile in diameter.

For the first time Onodera was able to grasp something of the total environment that enclosed them—that vast, crushing environment of chill, clear water. Far off to the left, at the very edge of the light, loomed the dark face of the trench wall, merging into the blackness beyond. The twisting yellow-brown mud current was now far below them, but Onodera could make out the faint shadow of the *Wadatsumi* falling upon it, a tiny metal cylinder suspended in a void.

The Japan Trench. That deepest of trenches, whose broad expanse lay nearly 24,000 feet below the sunlit waves of the vast Pacific. Now in that immense watery void, something was stirring. That icy, monstrous serpent of blackness that lay within the trench, stretching from one end of it to another—it was beginning to writhe beneath the terrible weight of pressure piled upon it. It was beginning to edge its body forward.

II

Tokyo

1

After he had delivered his report to Yoshimura, his section chief, Onodera was turning to leave when Yoshimura, as though remembering something, called to him: "Onodera . . ." He turned back to see his boss, the report pushed to one side, tapping his lip with the end of a pencil and staring into space, lost in thought.

"What is it, sir?" asked Onodera.

"Ah, yes . . . I have it. Onodera, you going home now?"

"Well, ah, I suppose," he answered vaguely. "The day after tomorrow I was going to start that vacation I missed."

Yoshimura got to his feet. "I'm leaving," he said to his secretary. "When the report from construction is approved, send it around to the undersea section."

Onodera held the door open for him.

"What do you say to a glass of beer?" Yoshimura asked cheerfully. He pressed the elevator button. "Do you know a bar called the Miruto in the West Ginza?"

"Ah, I've heard the name," Onodera replied uneasily.

"There's a nice little girl there. Young, small . . . and she's got this unconventional way about her that's amusing."

I wonder what he has in mind, Onodera thought.

They hailed a cab, and, after a short ride through the stifling late-afternoon heat of a Tokyo summer, they arrived at the Miruto. The chief strode through the entrance under full sail across a luxuriant purple rug. He passed between a gently curving beige-colored wall and a narrow metallic pillar to sit down in a comfortable chair beside a potted palm. Onodera caught a glimpse of a small, blue-lit dance floor beyond a large, highly abstract sculpture of a harp. Quiet music flowed through the club.

"Well! You're early, aren't you?"

A slim girl in a white sharkskin minidress appeared beside the table.

"That's because it's so hot," answered Yoshimura brusquely, wiping his neck and chin with the wet towel brought by the waiter. "How's Tateshina? When did she go back home?"

"Well, she didn't go. She heard that there was a lot of trouble down there this year."

"Earthquakes? That was way south of Matsudai, wasn't it?"

"Yes, but there were tremors as far up as around Komoro. Some friends of hers had their car smashed by falling rocks. So she's splashing around at the beach at Hayama."

"Gin and tonic," Yoshimura said to the waiter.

"Give me a gin rickey," said Onodera.

"This is Onodera from our company . . . Yuri."

"I'm glad to meet you," said Yuri. "What sort of work do you do?"

"I'm involved in deep-sea dives."

"Oh! You're on a submarine?"

"Not an ordinary submarine," said Yoshimura. "He goes down more than thirty thousand feet."

"Oh, how wonderful!"

"Did Mako come yet?" asked the chief as he took hold of his gin and tonic.

"Just before. She's probably getting herself fixed up now."

"Call her. I want to hear about Nakagawa's golf match the other day."

"I hear it turned out very bad for him. He didn't say a word about it. If he won, it would have been terrible—he never would have stopped talking about it."

Onodera looked about him, ill at ease. His glass was covered with condensed moisture. He gripped it tightly and gulped down the light-green liquid.

"Another of the same, sir?" asked the waiter.

Onodera nodded. He was becoming bored with it all. The girl named Yuri left, and a hostess with a brown wig casually took her place. She, too, was beautiful, slim, expensively dressed. Yet both of them, though they were young girls of no more than twenty-three, had faces which bore the insidious marks of fatigue. There was no glow to their skin, and, graceful though their behavior was, there was something crass about them. They earned perhaps three or four times what Onodera did.

He raised his glass again. If he were a little drunk, maybe he might be able to bear up better, he thought. His eyes became heavy, and he began to feel more relaxed. He looked at Yoshimura.

"By the way, sir," he said, "weren't you going to talk to me about something?"

"Uhh?" said the chief, blinking as though taken unawares. "Oh, yes . . . that. Well, I thought we could go into it later, but . . ."

"Whatever you say, sir."

"Well . . . I was wondering, Onodera . . . Are you going to get married sometime or what?"

"Ohhh!" cried the hostess, on the verge of hysteria, it seemed. "What a marvelous topic! This fine-looking gentleman is single?"

"All right, now, why don't you just leave us alone for a bit?" said Yoshimura as though humoring a child.

"Let me hear afterward, okay?" the hostess said as she got up to go.

"Have you got a fiancee or a mistress?" Yoshimura persisted. "Does your family have any ideas for you?"

"No, nothing in particular," answered Onodera, shaking his head as he chewed some nuts. He was afraid that his facial expression might well be betraying his distaste for the topic.

"I suppose that you know about it, but, anyway, with the next stock issue there's going to be a big expansion. Now, this is something just between the two of us, but I think that there might be a very important position opening up for you. The recommendation would be coming from me. So, this being the case, I think it would be a good idea, about this time, for you to stabilize yourself in terms of both public and private reliability, you see?"

"It would be a desk job, wouldn't it?" asked Onodera, sensing as much from his boss's manner.

"Of course. You can't be taking that submarine down forever.

You have a good head on you, and I think it's meant for more important work."

Onodera said nothing. He felt himself getting drunker but no less discontented.

"How about a meeting so that you can see?" asked the chief, settling back in his seat, and speaking with deliberate cheerfulness.

"A meeting?"

"Yes, what I mean is a miai, with somebody who might be right for you."

"Oh, I see."

"If it's all right, we can make it tonight."

Onodera's hand, filled with cashew nuts, stopped halfway to his mouth.

"Tonight?" he said, meeting the chief's eyes. "Dressed like this?"

"It doesn't matter. Make it casual, she said. She's about twenty-six. Very beautiful, but she's a bit of a bitch. And so I think you might be just what's called for."

Onodera was acutely aware that there was nothing casual or haphazard about all this. He knew that the company expected a great deal from him and so took a keen interest in him.

"Who is this young lady?" Onodera asked.

"She comes from a good provincial family, the oldest daughter," said his boss, altogether nonchalant and still probing. "The family's rather wealthy, and even though it's a good provincial family, as I said, they're very unconventional. The father graduated from a European university, and this young lady, too, studied abroad for two or three years. So whatever you have to say to her, she'll have a comeback for you, you see?"

Yoshimura shook with loud laughter. And then he raised his hand to a hostess who was coming toward him.

"Hello, there," he called to her.

She waved in response, a tiny girl, slim and pretty.

"It's been a long time," she said to Yoshimura. And then as she sat down next to Onodera, she introduced herself: "I'm Mako. Hello." Her face was tanned, and when she sat down, she dropped her head abruptly, a mannerism that made Onodera think of a small bird.

"This is Onodera," said the chief.

"Ah!" she exclaimed, and, with that, she suddenly took hold of his arm, bared by his short-sleeved shirt, and, putting her pert nose to it, she sniffed vigorously. "The smell of the sea. I'll bet you have a yacht."

"It's a submarine," said Yoshimura.

"Ooh! It's you, then," said Mako, her eyes wide. "I've heard about you from Mr. Yoshimura, and I begged him to introduce me to you. How happy I am to meet you!"

"Thank you . . ." said Onodera, forcing a smile.

"A drink?" Yoshimura asked Mako. "How about cognac?"

"Too early. A whiskey sour or something."

The recorded music stopped. The club was somewhat darker now. The lights on the tables throughout the room glowed softly like scattered streetlamps. The spotlights focused on the dance floor grew brighter, and a small band began to play quietly.

"Order what you want," said the chief, getting up and leaving them.

Once they were alone, the hostess called Mako suddenly became like a little girl, tensing up and saying nothing. She seemed to be about twenty, perhaps more, perhaps less. She used almost no make-up, and the roundness about her chin made her look like a schoolgirl.

"Would you like to dance?" she asked with an embarrassed smile.

"No," said Onodera, smiling back. "I don't dance."

"Your submarine—is it big?" the girl asked.

"No. For its class it's big, but it's not anything like what you're thinking of. With four men in it, it's crowded. But it can dive as deep as thirty thousand feet."

"Thirty thousand feet . . ." Her eyes wide, the girl's expression took on a somewhat fearful look. "I have no idea how deep that is, but . . . down that far at the bottom of the ocean, what's it like?"

Onodera swallowed in surprise. He gazed at a pale-yellow table light for a moment. Then a vague smile formed on his lips, and he said abruptly: "It's a place where there's nothing at all."

Nothing but a ton of water pressure per square inch . . . and in the eerie glow of drifting flares, down there on the floor of the sea trench, a serpent some hundred feet long, its skin rippling convulsively . . .

"Aren't there any fish?"

"There are some. Deep as it is, icy as it is, terrible as the pressure is, a place with no light whatsoever—there are living things there. There are fish—there are vertebrates, too."

"Really? But if they live in such a deep, cold place, pitch dark and everything, what pleasure can they possibly get out of life?"

The tone of the girl's voice startled Onodera. He looked at her face. The girl's round eyes were brimming with tears.

"I don't know." He spoke gently as though trying to comfort a child. "But, at any rate, they really are alive." Yoshimura had been right about this girl, he thought—she *was* unconventional.

2

When Onodera awoke from the doze he had fallen into as soon as he had gotten into Yoshimura's car, his section chief was driving along a road next to a beach. Their destination, Yoshimura had said, was a villa on Sagami Bay. After they had passed through Zushi, he turned off onto a private road that climbed to a heavily wooded height, atop which stood an oddly built structure lit by floodlights, its curved roof thrust into the air like a huge plastic egg.

They got out of the car, and Yoshimura led the way into the house through French windows opening onto the garden. They passed an angular, powerfully built girl in the corridor. She was dressed in bell-bottoms, and she was holding a cigarette in the sinewy fingertips of the same hand that gripped her drink.

"Good to see you," she said. Her voice was somewhat slurred with alcohol. "They're all expecting you."

"Rei?" asked Yoshimura casually.

"She's here. She's a bit maudlin tonight."

They opened a white plastic door at the end of the corridor to enter what was apparently the main room. Its oval floor was spread with carpeting of a subdued, moss-like green, around which curved beige-colored walls. An ivory grand piano stood against the wall. Gathered around a glass palette-shaped table, four or five men and women were sitting in chairs of odd but evidently comfortable design. In another corner of the room there was a bar, behind which stood a girl whose pale face was half covered by her long hair. Holding a cocktail shaker in both hands, she turned to Yoshimura and Onodera as they entered.

"Hello," she said, her voice listless.

"Well, now," said Yoshimura, in full control of events, "let me do some introducing. This is Mr. Onodera of our undersea section."

"Please join us—here," said a pleasant, light-skinned young man, offering Onodera a chair. He wore an aloha shirt of subdued coloring. "What are you drinking?"

Onodera stood there awkwardly. These people, he was thinking, were sophisticated and refined men and women. He sensed that he would not readily fit in. The names he heard, one by one, as he was introduced were names he had somehow heard before, names that were always striking his eye whenever he glanced through a magazine or book. He began more and more to feel that he had without a doubt gotten himself into an awkward position.

Finally, Yoshimura brought him over to the girl standing by the bar. When he learned that she, Reiko Abe, was the owner of the villa and thus the one whom he was to meet in this informal miai, Onodera did not know quite where to look.

"Want to drink this?" asked Reiko, holding out the cocktail shaker and looking at Onodera with a weary, bored expression. "It's a martini. Here." She thrust it under his nose, the handle of a strainer sticking out of it.

Muttering his thanks, Onodera took the heavy cocktail shaker from the girl.

Reiko put her head back slightly and laughed a short, dry laugh. "Here you are a guest for the first time . . . Please forgive me," she said, her tongue somewhat twisted. "But, you see, we don't have a single cocktail glass left. I've smashed every one."

"It's quite all right," said Onodera, forcing a smile. "Thank you very much." So saying, he put the cocktail shaker to his lips, strainer and all, and drank the martini. Then, wiping his lips with the back of his hand, he handed it back.

"A fine drink." He turned abruptly and walked back to the table.

"Say, Mr. Onodera . . ." The young man in the aloha shirt, who had offered him a chair before, did so again, cordially bringing him into the conversation. "I've heard about you again and again from Mr. Yoshimura. Now, tell me, there'd be no problem about you being able to manage a submarine designed for sight-seeing, would there?"

"Well, it depends," said Onodera.

"What we have in mind is something truly unique—an under-sea amusement park," said another man, who was a well-known economist. "It's really nothing of consequence, of course, but what we want to incorporate in it are entirely new kinds of entertainment. From available tourism capital, funds should be forthcoming, you see."

"We'll even build an underwater concert hall," said the young man in the aloha shirt, casually spreading a sketch out on the table. He pointed to a young avant-garde composer by the piano. "He's now experimenting with an underwater symphony. It's quite interesting."

For some time, the sketch in their midst, they carried on an animated discussion of this novel project, and Onodera, despite himself, began to have a good time, helped, of course, by the liquor. At the same time, however, a suspicion began to take form in his mind. He noticed Yoshimura talking earnestly to Reiko, who might or might not have been listening to him as she held her cocktail glass in a limp hand and, from time to time, brushed back a troublesome lock of hair that kept falling over her face. Sometimes she giggled drunkenly and once she threw back her head and gave a loud, dry laugh. Was this cordial discussion about the amusement park part of Yoshimura's scheme? Onodera wondered. It would have been the shrewd sort of move to be expected from him.

Reiko left Yoshimura and came over to the table, her walk unsteady. She was tall, and though she was slender enough, there was ample evidence that she had the splendid figure of a mature woman.

"I'm going for a swim," she cried. She stripped off her dress briskly, and the sun-bronzed body so suddenly bared, save for a faded bikini, proved indeed to be surprisingly strong and well formed as she stood with her chest thrust out and her legs apart.

"Not again?" said the youth in the aloha shirt.

"Count me out," said the economist, stuffing his pipe.

"How about you?" asked Reiko, turning to Onodera. "A swim, Mr. Onoda?"

"I'll go." Onodera took off his shirt. "And by the way, my name is Onodera."

Reiko laughed, wholly unabashed, and led the way out of the room. Onodera followed her, his eyes on her splendid back, which shone as though rubbed with oil. Once out on the terrace, he got rid of his pants. Reiko led the way to a corner of the terrace, where there was a small elevator half hidden by pine branches. His body and Reiko's touched slightly during the ride down, though he drew back as much as he could. They left the glare from the house behind them, and all at once the night was filled with the sound of waves and of pine branches creaking in the wind. Onodera was acutely aware of Reiko breathing close beside him in the darkness, a sensation that stirred an odd embarrassment in him. There were no stars. The breeze was warm.

"In this elevator," said Reiko in a flat voice, breaking the silence at last as they were approaching the foot of the cliff, where a mercury lamp was burning, "how many men, do you think, have kissed me?"

"Well . . . ah . . ." Onodera hesitated.

"Just one."

A plank walkway led from the edge of the narrow concrete elevator platform to a large yellow rectangular cork float, wet from the waves gently rocking it.

Without a backward glance, Reiko headed straight for the float and plunged into the sea. Onodera went in feet first. The water was warm, and there were almost no waves. After taking two or three tentative strokes to attune his muscles, he began to swim vigorously, kicking up the dark surface of the sea as he looked for Reiko's head. She was swimming toward the open sea with an easy breast stroke. Concerned for her safety, Onodera pulled slightly ahead of her.

In the darkness there seemed to be a faint smile on Reiko's face.

"Don't you think it'd be wise to go back?" he said.

"Want to race?" she asked.

"We should stop."

"I've got a strong heart."

They swam on in silence. Reiko, instead of turning back toward the float, veered off in the direction of a small sandy beach some fifty yards to one side of the deck. When she reached it, she lay on her stomach with the lower half of her body still in the water. Onodera, still feeling somewhat awkward, stopped some little way from her and sat in the shallow water.

"Do you intend to marry me?" said Reiko abruptly, catching him by surprise. "You're not much interested?" she persisted when he did not answer.

"I don't know yet," he said, his voice subdued.

"Mr. Yoshimura wants to see me married," she muttered, burying her hand in the sand. "My father begged him with tears in his eyes . . . please, please get his daughter married. And so now he's come here with you."

"Look, tonight is the first I've heard of this."

"He's a shrewd one, you know. He knows just what kind of man I go for. . . . And, then, I wonder what's all involved."

"How do you mean?" he asked.

"I don't know, but . . . when he was trying so hard to convince me, I started to wonder."

Onodera said nothing for a moment as he collected his thoughts. "You're probably right," he said finally.

Reiko turned to him. "If there was something else involved, you'd say no?"

"No, not necessarily . . ." he answered awkwardly.

"But how do you feel about me? Do you like me or not?"

"I can't say. Unless we're together for a longer time . . ."

"I don't need a longer time. I like you." Reiko raised herself up on her elbows and spoke clearly. "But that doesn't mean that I want to marry you. You're set on marriage?"

"Uh-huh."

"Why? What advantage is there to it?"

"Children."

Onodera sensed that Reiko was gazing fixedly at him in the darkness. The waves lapped gently over their bodies, dissolving the sand beneath them, which tickled their stomachs and legs as it flowed back into the sea. She suddenly heaved a long sigh. Then, with a quick movement, she rolled over on her back, bringing herself near to Onodera. He heard a faint click, followed abruptly by the sound of music.

"What's that?" he asked, startled.

"A radio—it's in my bracelet. It's waterproof."

Her chest was heaving violently. She spoke in a hoarse voice: "What are you going to do? Hold me."

"Here?"

"Yes, here. Because we just met it's too soon? You don't have anything against sex, do you?"

Her passion was so intense that it choked her voice. In the darkness her broad breasts heaved. She stretched her arms up out of the water and wound them around his neck.

At the same moment a sudden flash, like a curtain of white brilliance, raced across the dark sky, silhouetting the mountains of the Izu Peninsula. But then the sound of music was directly in Onodera's ear, and Reiko's strong arms around his neck were pulling him down. Her lips were close to his in the darkness, and her breath smelled slightly of alcohol. She had loosened the top of her bikini, and her breasts, wonderfully soft, were crushed beneath his chest, the taut nipples caressing his skin. There was a taste of salt on Reiko's lips. Her arms were incredibly strong. He loosened the fasteners on either side of the bottom of her bikini, and as he pulled it free, Reiko spoke in a hoarse whisper: "Don't take your mouth away from mine . . . I always cry out."

After it was over, Reiko, as though her body had gone rigid, kept on clinging to his neck.

Suddenly something alerted him.

". . . the body . . ."

The voice was coming from Reiko's radio: ". . . was identified as that of Rokuro Goh, thirty-one, employed by Nagatsuka Construction Company and missing for a week. Mr. Goh is reported to have been distraught recently over his responsibilities in connection with the new Super Express line. His death seems to have been suicide."

"Look out!" Onodera tried to free himself from Reiko's grip.

"No!" said Reiko, clinging to him as tightly as before, her breath harsh in his ear. "Not yet . . ."

"Let me go," said Onodera.

It was at that moment that the shock hit them, rolling up from the depths of the earth, seeming to permeate their flesh. A sudden blast of wind struck their faces. Salt spray stung them. The beach upon which they lay trembled beneath them. Rocks came clattering down through the thick growth of grass covering the cliffside to strike close by them.

Onodera instinctively turned to look across the bay. Above the far-distant mountains of the Izu, black clouds had gathered, and slender streaks of lightning raced violently across the stretch of sky between cloud and peak.

"We've got to get up!"

Onodera shook himself free of Reiko. Then, with a swift movement, he reached down and pulled her to her feet.

"Put on your swim suit. Hurry up."

At first orange flames flared up to illuminate the mountain peaks across the bay. Then a red column of fire thrust itself high into the sky. It was then that the muggy atmosphere of the night itself seemed to tremble as a booming roar came rumbling out of the depths of the earth, followed by what seemed like distant thunderclaps rolling across the water together with a continuous roar as though massed cannon were firing volley upon volley.

"What is it?" said Reiko hoarsely. "What happened?"

"An eruption," he answered. It's probably Amagi, he thought. How could it have happened so suddenly?

"Quick!" he shouted at Reiko, trying to hurry her along. The trembling earth beneath them creaked and groaned incessantly, and stones, sand, rock fragments kept clattering down from the cliff above.

Realizing they had to get out from beneath, Onodera took Reiko's hand and rushed out into the water, but then a chilling thought took hold of him.

"Is there a path up the cliff to the villa?" he asked, turning to Reiko, his voice intense.

"On the other side of that rock there. But why?" said Reiko, her voice shaking. "It would be dangerous with all these rocks and stones. Let's go back along the shore."

Instead of answering her, he pointed down. A few moments before, the waves had been sweeping over their feet, but now the sand lay exposed several meters beyond them, and the dark sea was even then pulling back still farther, the tops of submerged rocks jutting up into view. Reiko's body stiffened. Onodera felt the girl gasp with terror. Somewhere out in the darkness, a tidal wave was mounting.

Across the water, the pillar of flame had tinged scarlet the volcanic smoke, and from the topmost peak a stream of lava had begun to flow like a thread of brilliance.

3

Sometime after midnight Onodera was at the wheel of a small hovercraft skimming over the surface of Sagami Bay. It belonged to the Abe family, and on board were all the guests who wished to get back to Tokyo at once.

Situated 150 feet above sea level, Reiko's villa had suffered little, but since the electricity had been knocked out and the road below blocked by a landslide, everyone had been in a state of high excitement.

On Sagami Bay, ashes were fluttering softly down from the sky, and the falling rain, lit by the probing beams of the hovercraft, seemed to merge with the surface of the sea. As the vessel skimmed over the water at a speed of forty miles an hour, Onodera's eyes strayed now and then from the bright radarscope to the distant view of Mount Amagi, where the night sky glowed red. A strange, indefinable foreboding rose up within Onodera like a dark, sinister tide. Somehow this foreboding seemed linked to what he had seen on the floor of the Japan Trench—down there, 24,000 feet below the surface of the sea, where the pressure squeezed the hull of his submarine at the rate of one ton per square inch—linked to what he had seen there, that massive, indescribable writhing.

"Onodera . . ." As they were rounding Aburatsubo, somebody called to him from the rear cabin. "It's a call for you from Tokyo. Person to person."

Though he heard, Onodera did not respond at once, still in the grip of the cold dread that was gnawing at him.

"Hello, hello . . ."

He knew he had heard that arrogant voice before.

"This is Onodera," he said.

"This is Tadokoro. I've been looking for you. What does Amagi look like?"

"The eruption is still going on," answered Onodera, glancing out the rain-streaked window. "Mihara, too. A lot of smoke is coming from it."

"I heard from your general manager that you have the records of the undersea survey you made in Sagami Bay two weeks ago."

"Yes. I was going over them at home before turning them over to the survey section."

"Is there anything in the records about any depth changes in the deepest section of the bay?"

Onodera caught his breath sharply.

"There is," he answered. "But since the previous surveys were not that accurate, all I could do was compare my previous impressions with what I saw and make an estimate. There seemed to be a lot of changes from a year and a half before. But that's based upon things as I remember them."

"Onodera, how soon can you get to Tokyo?" Tadokoro's tone was imperious as usual. "I know you must be tired, but I want those records of yours just as soon as possible. I'm at my laboratory, in Hongo. Where do you live?"

"In Aoyama, sir." He looked at his watch. It was 1:45 A.M. "At the earliest, I can probably be there by dawn. Where in Hongo?"

"Two Chome. When you get to the neighborhood, phone me."

"This data, sir, will bear on the earthquake?"

"The earthquake?" Tadokoro's voice became impatient. "There's something far more important at issue than the earthquake." There was a pause. "Or so it seems, at any rate. . . ."

Onodera seemed to lose Tadokoro's voice. "Hello, hello . . ." he said, fearing that they had been cut off.

"I'm still here. Onodera, I don't know exactly what we ought to do." Tadokoro's voice had abruptly changed, startlingly so. It had become a voice heavy with weary disappointment. "Maybe it's just a bad dream. But it's gotten hold of me, and I can't do anything about it. I'm obsessed. But, at any rate, please do what you can."

"I understand, sir," answered Onodera.

The emergency topic taken up at the regular meeting of the Cabinet on July 27 was the Izu Earthquake. The director general of the Prime Minister's Office gave a brief report on the damage done, which was expected to amount to hundreds of billions.

"The eruptions, the earthquake—in neither case was there any sort of forecast or warning, was there?" the Prime Minister quietly observed. He had just returned from abroad and looked as though he was still suffering from the rigors of travel. "For some time now we've been putting a good amount from the budget into earthquake forecasting, and so one would expect that some research is under way."

"Well," said the director of the Technological Agency, the youngest member of the Cabinet, "according to what the scientists tell me, leaving aside the matter of volcanoes, it will take five or even ten more years before we reach the stage where we can predict earthquakes. It seems that now we can't even say for sure why an earthquake occurs."

"I suppose the construction of the new Super Express line is going to be held up because of all this," said the Minister of Trade and Industry.

"The president of National Railways was raising a fuss even before," said the bent old man who was Minister of Transportation. "The matter of earthquakes be as it may, the area selected for the right-of-way has turned out, time after time, to be land that provides but treacherous footing. I understand the firms involved are clamoring about having to raise their estimates. Both the National Railways and the private lines are going to be very much in the red this year."

"Prescinding from the floods during the rainy season, because of these earthquakes, this is the third time this year that we've applied the Disaster Relief Act," said the Minister of Finance with a sour expression. "At this rate, we're going to have to have a supplementary budget."

"It looks as though from now on we're going to have to set aside a larger portion each year for damages from earthquakes and other natural catastrophes," said the Minister of Construction as he wiped off his glasses.

A silence came over the room. The words of the Minister of Construction stirred a vague sense of foreboding in the heart of each member of the Cabinet. Small as Japan was, she was laden with plan upon plan—construction plans, regional plans, municipal plans, plans for the reorganization of industrial areas. This year, however . . . Within the space of the first four months of the calendar year, the vague, somber shadow of something heretofore unknown had begun to fall across all of these plans. On the face of it, it seemed merely a matter of the perennial conflict with nature having become somewhat intensified, but once the data had been viewed in perspective, one sensed that something like a still faint mosaic was beginning to emerge, something sinister, its outline still no more than a pale shadow.

"The problem is the panic that could arise," the Prime Minister began and then stopped. He dropped his eyes to a teacup on the table. Sunlight from the window fell upon the now cold liquid within. Tiny circles of waves were forming, one after another, on its bright surface. "I'll be damned! How long are these earthquakes going to go on? Let's face it, gentlemen— we've had more earthquakes lately than ever before. Now are they going to keep on increasing? or what? If we knew, we could provide for them in the budget."

"Suppose we hear what the scientists have to say," said the Minister of Health and Welfare. "I, for one, would be interested in that."

"A good idea," said the Prime Minister, looking toward the director general of the Cabinet. "Let's find out how much these earthquake specialists know. But, as always, let's be circumspect about it. It wouldn't do at all for reporters to raise a howl. Let's get a few of them together and hear them out."

At that moment the room began to rock back and forth. Dust fell from the ceiling, flecks dancing in the sunlight. There was a brief pause, and then a much stronger tremor took hold. The floor shook violently. The earth itself began to groan, and the walls and uprights creaked and swayed. Tea spilled from the cups on the table.

"This is really a big one," someone murmured.

Then, just when the Cabinet members had risen from their chairs, their expressions tense, the vibrations stopped abruptly. The tea left in the cups was still trembling. The water in the flower vase still splashed back and forth with a noisy gurgle. Two or three acoustic tiles fell with a clatter from the ceiling.

"That was something!" said the Minister of Health and Welfare with a sigh.

There were wry smiles of relief as everyone began to talk a bit too loudly. Unnoticed in the uproar was a distant boom. A few moments afterward there was a knock at the door of the meeting room, and a secretary entered. He spoke into the ear of the director general, who nodded and turned to the others.

"Gentlemen, Mount Asama has just erupted."

When the earthquake struck, Onodera felt it through the ragged couch on which he lay on the second floor of Professor Tadokoro's private laboratory in Hongo. Such was his state of mind that he stared up at the swaying, soot-covered fluorescent light above his head as though he were dreaming. He vaguely heard the crack of a windowpane, the snap of something giving way inside the sofa. Finally he came to enough to wonder where he was. By the time he got up from the couch, the quake had stopped. He gave a wide yawn, and as he did so, he heard the clatter of footsteps on the stairs.

"Is there a fire?" he asked a young man running down the corridor.

"No. It looks like Asama's erupted."

Professor Tadokoro appeared in the corridor, wearing a wrinkled laboratory coat. When he came into the room, Onodera noticed that his eyes were bloodshot and he seemed completely worn out.

"Asama, uh?" said Tadokoro, his voice hoarse. "It's not worth bothering about."

"But, Professor," Onodera protested, "the whole world seems to be blowing up."

"Let it blow up," said Tadokoro, stifling a yawn.

"Well, sir," said Onodera, glancing at his watch, "I'm afraid I'll have to be going now. I took too long a nap."

"Onodera," said Tadokoro, hit by an onset of yawning, "could we talk just a bit downstairs?"

"Talk, Professor?" said Onodera, stopping in the doorway. "What do you want to talk about, sir?"

"Let's go downstairs," said Tadokoro. He shouted to his young assistants, who were still talking excitedly: "Hey, down there! Instead of doing all that chattering, get a report on the Asama eruption."

"Let me make a phone call, and I'll be right down," said Onodera.

When he had finished his call, Onodera went down to the basement.

The heart of Professor Tadokoro's private laboratory was a snug air-conditioned room with walls of double thickness. It housed a miniature LSI computer, and spread around it in disordered fashion were a desk, an open file, a locker, a drawing board, an old-fashioned dictaphone, and a variety of other instruments. The cool air of the silent room felt pleasant against Onodera's skin.

Professor Tadokoro was sitting in a chair in the corner, his chin propped up by his elbow, his mouth moving as though he was mumbling something. When Onodera walked over to him, he raised his bloodshot eyes and looked at him searchingly, as though he were seeing a stranger.

"Oh! It's you," said Tadokoro. "Now, let's see . . . Oh, yes. There was a call from Yukinaga just now."

"Professor Yukinaga?"

"His house is close by here. How about having lunch with us? I'll have something delivered." As he spoke, Tadokoro picked up the telephone.

"What was it you wanted to talk about, Professor?"

"Oh . . . yes." So saying, Tadokoro put down the telephone receiver and, once more lost in thought, said nothing for a few moments. "That submarine at your place—if you charter it for a long period, how much does it cost?"

"Well, it depends, I imagine," said Onodera, embarrassed. "Figuring out something like that would be beyond me, Professor."

"Something else, then," said Tadokoro, abruptly thrusting out a thick finger. "If I asked for it now, would I be able to get it right away?"

"I'm afraid that would be out of the question, Professor," said Onodera. "The *Wadatsumi* is being sent to Kyushu next, to do a survey for the Kanbu Tunnel project. After that there's an assignment from Indonesia waiting for it. And there's still more lined up after that. It would take several months before your turn came."

"This is for something of the utmost importance," said Tadokoro, thumping the table with the flat of his hand. "Isn't there some way that I can be given priority?"

"Well, sir, I can't promise anything, but . . . how long would you have to have it?"

"Half a year. Maybe longer," said Tadokoro, his stubborn expression showing he realized the extravagance of what he asked. "You know what I have in mind. The floor of the Japan Trench—I want to look over every inch of it."

"A half-year?" Onodera shook his head. "It's impossible, Professor."

"What kind of situation is this? In all Japan there's only one submarine in the thirty-thousand-feet class!" said Tadokoro, growing irritated at last. "Are we a sea-going nation or what? Incredible!"

"Well, once the *Wadatsumi 2* is ready, then things will open up a good deal, but that won't be until next year. Have you thought about chartering a foreign submarine? There's—"

"I know all about foreign submarines," said Tadokoro, interrupting. He thrust a paper under Onodera's nose. It was a list of all the deep-sea submarines in the world. "I want at all costs to use a Japanese submarine. This survey is intimately bound up with the national interest."

Behind him, Onodera heard footsteps coming down the stairs. Professor Yukinaga entered, tie neatly knotted, jacket on despite the heat, but there was not a drop of sweat on his decorous features.

"Well . . ." said Yukinaga, smiling at Onodera.

"So you're here. Will you have lunch with us?" asked Tadokoro. "Should we go out or have something brought in?"

"Either is all right," said Yukinaga.

"Wait a minute," said Tadokoro, jabbing the interphone button and bending his head. "No answer. They've all gone out upstairs. I'll go get something cold to drink." He went out the door and started up the stairs.

"The professor's a fine person, isn't he?" said Onodera with a smile as Tadokoro's footsteps faded.

"That fellow? He's a boor," said Yukinaga, not at all jocularly but rather with a sigh. "He's a rash, headstrong genius. So here in this country he's persona non grata with the scholars. It's abroad that he's gotten his reputation."

"It's certainly an excellent laboratory," said Onodera.

"It cost about four or five hundred million yen to build," said Yukinaga, looking around. "And then the operating expenses are incredible. Once he launches himself into a project, the sky's the limit."

"Well, where does he get the money?" asked Onodera.

"The Church of the Seven Seas," answered Yukinaga cryptically. "It's a new religion. Its headquarters is in Greece. Making the sea your god is an ingenious approach to religion. They've recruited men whose business is linked to the sea—everything from fisheries to shipping—and they've formed sister churches all over the world. It's quite rich."

All this came as quite a surprise to Onodera.

"Professor Tadokoro is a man unhampered by scruples, you see. If he has research to do, then he'll snatch money from the hand of the devil himself, confident that nothing will stop him from doing things his way."

Tadokoro appeared at the head of the stairs. From his right hand swung a kettle covered with beads of moisture, and in his left he was holding a tray with teacups on it.

"Professor Tadokoro," said Yukinaga, "I have some news. A classmate of mine, a very good friend, is a secretary in the Prime Minister's Office. He just called me."

"The Prime Minister's Office?" said Tadokoro, frowning. "Some bureaucrat?"

"Yes. He told me that the Cabinet members intend to have a confidential briefing on earthquakes from a number of scientists. He wanted me to suggest names."

"Bureaucrats!" said Tadokoro as though vomiting out the word. "The same old story. They say they want to consult a wide range of people, but the truth of the matter is that all they're interested in doing is setting up a serene consensus utterly devoid of anything resembling insight. Since their abiding desire is to avoid risk, they shrink from any venture that might entail it, and so they have no way of grasping the shape of things to come."

"I realize all that, Professor," said Yukinaga, nodding his head. "Would you be kind enough to participate?"

"Me?" demanded Tadokoro, his eyes straining at their sockets. "Me participate? You're out of your mind. Who'll be there? —as though I had to ask. Takamine from the Disaster Prevention Center, Nozue from the Weather Service, Kimijima from the Ministry of Education, Yamashiro from Tokyo University, Oizumi from Keio—a crowd of that sort, right?"

"That's right, Professor," said Yukinaga, intimidated.

"And suppose I join them in the bureaucrats' lair—what then? First of all, we'll be talking to people who don't know the first thing about science. And my colleagues, since they depend upon the bureaucrats for patronage, will be bending over backward so as not to disturb anybody. And then, finally, who are these scientists anyway? They're all splendid fellows. Each is tops in his field, but there's not one of them who knows much of significance outside of it. This damned compartmentalization! Nobody knows how to draw the big picture, and they gang up on anybody who dares to try."

"All the more reason, then, Professor, for you to do me the favor of joining in," said Yukinaga, cutting in quickly. "The research you're doing now—"

"The research I'm doing?" shouted Tadokoro, getting up out of his chair. "The research I'm doing now, you say? Suppose I were to talk about that—what would happen? They'd treat me as though I were insane—the mad scientist full of wild fantasies. Because as yet, you see, I haven't gotten my hands on any unmistakable proof. And if you're not careful about promoting me, it won't bode well for your future. Even your friends will attack you, and your reputation will be ruined. No, I'll not take part. Never!"

"What's this about my future and so forth?" Yukinaga asked, his voice very patient. "Professor, there's too much at stake for talk of that sort. It's hardly worthy of you. This is something that is vital for Japan, something that—"

"Japan? Japan, is it?" said Tadokoro, his face suddenly becoming contorted as though he was about to cry. "As for the likes of Japan, it can go whatever way it wants, as far as I'm concerned. Yukinaga, I have the world, this marvelous world full of inexhaustible mystery and richness. Japan—this threadlike line of islands—what's that to me?"

"But, Professor, you are a Japanese," said Yukinaga quietly. "You love the world, yes, but you love Japan, too. If not, why have you kept back some of your data from the headquarters of the Church of the Seven Seas?"

"What?" said Tadokoro, his voice suddenly sharp. "How do you know that I've concealed data from my sponsors?"

"It was just a guess. Forgive me, Professor. It was unkind of me to trap you." Yukinaga lowered his eyes and then raised them again. "And yet I have had occasion to wonder a good deal. I had paid almost no attention to the reports that you've been sending to the headquarters of the church. But, just recently it was, something in them happened to catch my eye here. It was very strange. The report dealt with our recent survey, and in it you went on at great length, tediously so, about various sea creatures and coral—something that's not very much in your line. But any nuance relative to what we saw— which, you intimated to me, might well be something that threatens us—was smoothly concealed." Yukinaga pressed the attack: "There's something pertaining to Japan that you didn't want foreigners to know. Isn't that correct? Something that you wanted to conceal from the headquarters of the Church of the Seven Seas . . ."

"All right, Yukinaga," said Tadokoro, his tone suddenly changing. "This conference or seminar or whatever it is of yours —I'll give it a try. That is, if they accept your recommendation."

"Splendid," said Yukinaga. His shoulders sagged as he sighed in relief. "As for lunch, I'd like a bowl of rice. And now let's have that cold drink."

4

The conference was held one evening ten days later in an office building in central Tokyo, a place chosen to throw an inquisitive press off the trail. After it was over and all the participants had left, an official in the Prime Minister's Office drove out of the garage beneath the building. When he reached the neighborhood of the Palace Outer Garden, he pulled over to the curb and placed a long-distance call on his car telephone. An old man's voice answered.

"It's finished, sir," said the official. "Nothing of significance came out. I'll summarize the main points." Then after he had read from his notes, he concluded by saying: "There was just one scientist there who came out with something unexpected. A man named Tadokoro. He said that it could happen that Japan would sink. The others thought he was out of his mind. . . . Yes, sir. Yusuke Tadokoro. . . . That's right, sir. You keep well abreast of things. . . . What, sir?" The official frowned slightly. "Yes, sir. If now is suitable, I'll come immediately."

After he hung up the receiver, he sighed heavily and looked at the dashboard clock. It was 10:35. "Something's on his mind," he muttered. "I wonder what."

Ten more days passed, and then a call from Yukinaga came to Tadokoro's laboratory.

"Who do you want me to meet?" demanded Tadokoro impatiently. He had been working through the night for some time, and his face was covered with a thick growth of stubble. "You know how busy I am. A hotel, eh? That means a necktie, I suppose."

"It won't take much of your time, Professor, No more than thirty minutes. I've taken the liberty of sending a car to pick you up," said Yukinaga, his tone frantically insistent. "This gentleman is a man who knew your father well."

"Well, who is he, then?"

The line went dead. And at the same instant the interphone buzzed: "Professor Tadokoro, the car sent by Professor Yukinaga is waiting at the front door."

Wearing a wrinkled, sweaty shirt and carrying his crumpled jacket, Tadokoro strode into the Palace Hotel to be met at once by a young woman in an exquisitely arranged kimono.

"You are Professor Tadokoro?" she asked. "Please, this way . . ."

They made their way through groups of foreigners, businessmen, elegantly dressed young women, and other guests to a lounge a level higher than the lobby, where a tall, husky young man dressed in a dark suit came forward to meet them. He bowed politely to Tadokoro.

"We have been waiting for you, Professor. Please . . ."

Looking in the direction indicated by the young man's outstretched hand, Tadokoro saw an old man crouched in a wheelchair. He was no more than skin and bones. Despite the heat, he clutched a blanket which lay over his knees.

"Where's Yukinaga?" asked Tadokoro, turning back to the tall young man. But he was no longer behind him.

"You're Professor Tadokoro."

The old man's voice was surprisingly strong. Beneath thick gray eyebrows, his sunken eyes were pale but bright, and they were focused upon Tadokoro's face with piercing force. The small, pinched face, flecked with the splotches of age, seemed somehow to be laughing.

"Well, well! There's certainly a resemblance. I knew your father. Hidenoshin Tadokoro. A stubborn young fellow, he was."

"And your name, sir?" asked Tadokoro, looking full at the old man, his irritability fading.

"Mmmm. Sit down there," said the old man, clearing his throat of phlegm. "What do names matter anyway? I tell you my name's Watari, and that means nothing to you, does it? I am, however, more than a hundred years old. Come October, I'll be a hundred and one. Medical science has made such progress that we old people aren't allowed to go to our rest any more. And we become more and more arrogant with each passing year. We've seen everything, and with the end drawing near, there's nothing left for us to be afraid of. Now today, having you come here like this—this, too, should be laid to an old man's arrogance. There is something that I want to ask you. Would you be kind enough to give me an answer?"

"What's the question, sir?" Tadokoro asked, wiping the sweat from his face. He had sat down in a chair beside the old man.

"There is just one thing that has caused me some concern," the old man said, his piercing eyes looking directly into Tadokoro's. "Perhaps you might think my question is childish. It has to do with swallows."

"Swallows?"

"Yes. Every year swallows come and build a nest in the eaves of my home. For more than twenty years now. Last year they came in May, as usual, built their nest, and then, for some reason or other, they left in July. They abandoned their eggs. And this year they didn't come at all. All around where I live, it was the same. What is the reason, I wonder?"

"Swallows, yes," said Tadokoro, nodding. "Yes, of course. In the past two or three years the number of migrant birds has fallen off at an incredible rate. Ornithologists say that perhaps it's because of a change in earth magnetism or in climate, but I feel that it's due to something far graver. And it's not just birds. There's been a great change, too, in the size of the runs of fish."

"Hmmm. My heavens," said the old man, "what does it all mean? Are these harbingers of something?"

"I can't answer in definite terms," said Tadokoro, shaking his head. "But I'm making every effort to find out what that something may be."

"I see," said the old man, coughing. "I have but one more question for you. For a scientist, what is the most precious thing?"

"Intuition," answered Tadokoro without hesitation.

"Mmm?" The old man cupped his hand to his ear. "What is it?"

"I said intuition, sir," said Tadokoro. "You may think it's strange, but for a scientist—especially for a natural scientist—far and away the most precious gift he can possess is that of keen intuition. Without it, he'll never make a notable break-through."

"I see. Very well," said the old man, nodding emphatically. "Well, then, I must say goodbye. . . ."

The tall young man suddenly reappeared. A polite bow to Tadokoro, and he began to push the wheelchair away with quiet efficiency. In a moment both were gone.

When Tadokoro recovered from his surprise and took another look around him, there was still no sign of Yukinaga. A bellboy, however, came by calling for Dr. Tadokoro. The message was from Yukinaga: "Please forgive me. I'll explain at some other time."

A middle-aged man with a sunburned face came to Tadokoro's laboratory one night a week later.

"I understand, Professor, that you're in the market for a submarine," he said without standing on ceremony. "How would the French submarine the *Kermadic* suit you?"

"How would it suit me? What do you mean by that?" said Tadokoro, frowning. "I'd like to use a Japanese submarine. However . . ."

"I'm not talking about chartering it. I'm talking about buying it and letting you use it. Furthermore, we'll supply the money for your research. Whatever amount is necessary—it doesn't matter. And you may select whomever you wish for colleagues. We ask only that you entrust to us the means for preserving the secrecy of your operation."

"Who are you? What connection do you have with Yukinaga?"

"We've requested Professor Yukinaga's cooperation, too, of course. As for me . . ." The man took a card from his wallet and presented it.

"The Cabinet . . . Department of Research . . ." Tadokoro mumbled, not at all happy.

At that moment there came the loud thumps of hurrying footsteps from the stairway outside the computer room, and a young technician burst into view.

"What is it?" asked the startled Tadokoro. "Can't you be quiet?"

"Professor!" His face showing his distress, the young man held out a note. "It happened again. In the Kansai. . . ."

For the first time in some years, Onodera was in Kyoto for the Daimonji Festival, watching from the veranda of an inn in Ponto-cho overlooking the Kamo River. The veranda was packed with people. And the bridges as well as the banks of the river were lined with a massive outpouring of spectators. So thick was the crowd that the auto traffic going from the west bank to Minamiya and the Keihan Railroad Station along brightly lit Yonjo Avenue was blocked entirely.

Etched in fire on the side of Mount Higashi, *Dai*, the Chinese character for "greatness," had been blazing brightly for some twenty minutes, together with the other traditional fires of the Bon Festival, all alike requiems offered for the souls of the departed.

Onodera listened with half an ear to his friends' conversation as he leaned against the railing watching the now subdued burning of the Daimonji fire. He had extended his vacation from two to three weeks and had not only attended Goh's funeral service but had gone to the trouble of traveling to Shikoku for the formal ceremony at his home place. The Daimonji fire flickered softly, Goh's requiem flame. In this country nothing was destroyed, nothing died, Onodera mused. Was it really so? Kyoto, for example. In it lived a thousand years of history. Today in this ceremony the past was alive, alive within the present. But what of the future? What of the next thousand years?

"Would you like a bit more?" A no-longer-young geisha was standing beside him. "Aren't you enjoying things? You seem a bit out of sorts. Let me fill your sake cup."

After the geisha had gone her way, someone began to play a samisen in the neighboring room. The breeze died abruptly, and the muggy heat became more oppressive.

"Is Mr. Onodera here?" From the main room of the inn, a waitress put her head through the doorway. "You have a phone call from Tokyo, sir."

Surprised, Onodera got up from where he had been sitting by the rail. He left the veranda and walked to the desk, where he picked up the receiver.

"Onodera? This is Yukinaga," said the voice on the other end. "I would like to get together with you as soon as possible. Are you coming back to Tokyo tomorrow?"

"Yes, sir. I intend to. If there's a great hurry, I can get a Super Express tomorrow morning. What is it about, sir?"

"I'll tell you tomorrow. I have the utmost need of your cooperation. And so . . ." Yukinaga faltered. "The truth is that it's work that pertains to Professor Tadokoro."

At that moment the line went dead.

"Hello, hello," Onodera shouted into the receiver. "Hello, hello."

As though he had suddenly become drunk, he felt his body begin to sway back and forth. A young geisha screamed shrilly. Sliding doors began to vibrate loudly, setting up a fearful racket. Before Onodera could even gasp with surprise, an awful, thundering roar seemed to roll up from the earth below, and at the same time the entire inn seemed to whirl about with terrible force. Wrenched from its frame, the crossbeam of a doorway came crashing down. Dust fell in thick clouds from the ceiling and walls. Together with the creaking of the building and the rumbling of the earth, cries of agony began to rise on every side. Onodera grabbed a doorpost to keep his feet. In the hall opposite the inn office a closet door came open, and what looked like a stoutly made desk bounced into the corridor. When he saw the desk, Onodera took hold of it. He tipped it on its side against the wall and then dived beneath it. A fraction of an instant later the inn was plunged into darkness, and something hit the top of the desk with a thunderous crash. Onodera glanced at his watch and noted the time. Since there had been almost nothing in the way of warning tremors, the center of the quake must be very near. How long would it go on? Onodera wondered. A thought struck him that chilled the back of his neck. Twisting his head, he took the risk of looking out from the shelter of the desk. A glimmer of light from the outside showed through a black jumble of door frames, walls, sliding doors, and other debris. Where the veranda had been, there was nothing at all.

The Great Kyoto Earthquake, coinciding as it did with a massive influx of people for the Daimonji Festival, claimed a large number of victims. Of the vast crowds gathered along the Kamo River, many were hurled in tangled masses from the bridges and from the houses lining the banks down into the riverbed, others were crushed beneath collapsing buildings, and still others were trampled to death beneath the feet of the terrified crowd. In one brief moment 4,000 people perished and 13,000 were severely injured. Whole sections of Kyoto were leveled. The effect upon the nation was profound. The plague of earthquakes had spread to long-tranquil Western Japan.

III

The Government

1

By April of the following year, Yukinaga was fully absorbed in a project that had been designated "Plan D," working day and night in an office building in the Harajuku district, one floor of which he and his colleagues had taken over. The heart and soul of Plan D was Tadokoro.

Yukinaga was filled with misgivings. Suppose all this turned out to be nothing more than a wild fantasy of Tadokoro's? He had taken a leave of absence from the university at a time that was especially critical for him. His superiors were just beginning to recognize his achievements, and if he behaved himself, he had a good chance of advancing to a full professorship the following year. But now he had let himself become entangled in a bizarre affair that defied rational analysis. How was he going to explain things to his academic patrons?

Kazunari Nakata, a friend from college days and one of the world's foremost authorities on informational science, frowned with concentration as he studied the reports. "No matter how you look at it, it's an absurd kind of game—like trying to grab hold of a cloud," he said with a groan. "The qualifiers are extremely complex. Why, even a PERT might not be able to handle them. What we have to do is think in terms of some sort of new softwear. The problem is that the government is going to give us money only on a stage-by-stage basis and not once during the intermediate stages are we going to come up with unequivocal evidence that this is actually going to take place. Can we persuade the government, then, despite this intrinsic uncertainty, to commit itself fully at some point, realizing full well that this will entail the expenditure of a fantastic amount of money? And then there's the whole business about secrecy!"

"It might even happen that new legislation is necessary," said Kunieda, a young man from the Prime Minister's Office. "In that case, secrecy would be out of the question."

Yukinaga, naïve as he was in such matters, had at first favored the open implementation of Plan D, but Kunieda and Nakata had persuaded him otherwise. According to Tadokoro's rough calculations, the earliest possible date was two years off; the most remote, fifty years. The phenomena in question were still extremely vague and impossible to interpret clearly. Should the evidence, however, begin to point toward an actual occurrence and that, if not in two years, at least in the next few years, then the formulation of a government program to deal with it would have to be done in secret in order to avoid public turmoil. Nor would secrecy be any less necessary in the area of foreign relations should the dreadful crisis come to pass. The news would have to leak out eventually, of course, and it would therefore be a question of how much the government would be able to accomplish before then.

Nakata's responsibility lay in coordinating the workings of Plan D. The group as yet numbered no more than five, and they were young, ranging from the late thirties to forty years of age. Besides Yukinaga, Nakata, and Kunieda, there was Yamazaki, of the Intelligence Section of the Cabinet, and Yasugawa, the youngest of the group, who had been taken from an architect's office to handle the accounts.

"About the money aspect," said Yasugawa, "it seems to me that we've already gone beyond the budget given us. And soon we'll need still more people and an incredible amount of equipment."

"Let's just leave worries of that nature to the Prime Minister and his friends," said Nakata. "No matter how much we thrash it around, we're not going to get anywhere with that problem. So let's get down to work with whatever means we have available and get some results. The rest is out of our hands."

The meeting broke up, and Kunieda and Yukinaga were left to themselves as the others went downstairs for coffee. Yukinaga envied Nakata his cheerful confidence. He stared moodily at the magnetized map of Japan on the wall. Large red arrows had been attached to the southeastern section of the Archipelago, which was mottled with a variety of colors, and to the Japan Trench. The start of Tadokoro's plan.

Suddenly Yukinaga realized that the board was shaking gently from side to side. "Another tremor," he muttered.

"The old gentleman, Watari, has let go a part of his art collection, I hear," said Kunieda absently as he puffed on a cigarette.

"And that's how we got part of our money?"

"I think so. They say that some of his pieces are classified as National Treasures."

That shriveled-up old man in the wheelchair—what was his game anyway? Yukinaga wondered. Kunieda came from the same village as he, and it was most likely the old man's influence that had put Kunieda into the Prime Minister's Office. A city boy himself, Yukinaga could not fathom the nature of that village solidarity whose deep roots remained firm even to the present. At any rate, Kunieda seemed to have maintained contact with the old man at all times, and it had been through Kunieda, to whom Yukinaga had confided the nature of Tadokoro's "concern," that Watari had come into the affair. Yukinaga had known nothing of this relationship, nor had he even heard of the old man, though after Kunieda had explained things to him, he had a vague recollection that he had seen the name somewhere years before.

Immediately after the earthquake meeting, he had been invited to come to see the old man with Kunieda. He had been astounded at the fierce spiritual strength that lay hidden behind Watari's withered appearance and at the keenness of the mind that posed such laconic, concise questions. Watari's manner was never anything but gentle, the very image of the good old man, but Yukinaga had gone away that day thoroughly awed. With his own eyes he had seen Watari summon the Prime Minister to his residence in Chigasaki and with a few words persuade him that Plan D should become a reality. And then there were the mysterious individuals and the hard-eyed young men, the latter obviously bodyguards, who surrounded the old man. There was also a beautiful young woman, mysterious enough in her own way. This was the stuff of legends, Yukinaga thought, a world whose depths he could not fathom, and he could not help feeling that something sinister lurked in the background.

"The old fellow—aside from this project, I wonder what goes on inside his mind," said Kunieda, snuffing out his cigarette.

"I was going to ask *you* that," said Yukinaga.

"I don't know much about him either. We're from the same town, it's true, but if you tried to follow up any lead about him as a native son, you'd quickly come to a dead end. But it's quite certain that his forte has been to work behind the scenes in two major worlds: politics and finance. He spans the Meiji, Taisho, and Showa eras, and he has a knowledge of their dark side that he carries with him into the present. Certainly, according to our way of thinking, he's done some evil deeds, I suppose. But at times it seems that unless some villain with immense power comes along, nothing at all can be accomplished."

"If you had lived for a century, what the devil would you think of things, I wonder?" said Yukinaga. "And more than just living, if you had exercised authority all that time, what would be going on in your mind? What would you want to do?"

"I have no idea," said Kunieda, getting up. "I'm sure only that it's because of his power that Plan D has actually gotten under way."

Kunieda went downstairs, leaving Yukinaga to his thoughts.

2

"Well, they're really getting down to it, aren't they?" said Nakata, laughing as he read a transcript of the secretary general's press conference at the end of September, in which he urged the nation to look outward.

"Is that your doing, too, sir?" asked the young Yasugawa.

"No, no. It's the brainchild of some politicians and bureaucrats acquainted with the situation. They seem, however, to have made use of some suggestions of mine—bringing up that slogan from the old days: 'A Bold Leap into the World.'"

"But they'd better be careful," said Kunieda, pointing to a section of the paper. "There might be somebody out there who can put two and two together."

He had indicated a humorous item enclosed in a box. It was a parody of an old song popular at the beginning of the Showa Era, when immigration to Manchuria was at its peak:

If you go, I go too.
Who wants to stay behind
In shaky old Japan?

Nakata laughed when he read it: "So you think there might be some people keen enough to tie this up with the earthquakes, eh? The Japanese people, it's true, are great for intuition."

The door opened with a frightful bang, and Tadokoro surged into the room, his shoulders squared.

"What's the news on the *Kermadic?* Is it here yet or what?" he demanded fiercely, a question he had asked countless times before. "What's causing all this delay? Has it sunk on the way?"

"Everything's all right. It's already passed Okinawa, and tomorrow it's going to dock at Moji," answered Nakata.

"Moji?" Tadokoro's face turned scarlet and his eyes bulged. "What's the idea, sending it there? What we want to investigate is the Japan Trench. We'll lose two days in extra sailing time."

"The idea is to keep it out of the public eye, Professor," said Nakata with great care. "If it was a matter of Yokohama or Kobe, the reporters would be on our necks. When it clears the port, they'll load it on a naval vessel there, the *Takatsuki,* which will then sail directly for Ise Bay. The diving tests will be in Toba Bay and the Kumano Sea."

"I'm going to Ise, then," said Tadokoro. "The main thing is that we've got to move. Look at this. One section of the Rikuchu coast is now sinking at the rate of .5 centimeters a day. At the bottom of the sea off Sanriku, shallow earthquakes of small to medium intensity are occurring at the rate of several per day. When will the survey equipment arrive?"

"Part of it has already been sent to Moji and Toba. But by the time all of it is put in order and installed, it will be another week or ten days, no matter how much hurrying is done."

"Ten days!" Tadokoro groaned like an animal. "Dammit to hell! With speed so vital! And while we're standing here, down below in the Japan Archipelago, here, there, everywhere, changes are taking place from minute to minute. We've got to get a line on things at the earliest possible moment. What will happen if we're late, I ask you?"

"We share your fears," said Kunieda distractedly. "But about the time factor there's nothing we can do."

All eyes turned to the situation chart on the wall. It was a board lit by electronic luminescence on which light lines indicated the progress of every task that had been programmed into the LSI computer. The board was still filled with categories altogether unlit. In the date-designation portion, marked by vertical red lines, however, several had already reached the point indicating their starting date.

"Don't you people see?" demanded Tadokoro, striking the hand in which he held his papers with the back of the other. "In essence, our work is a fight against time."

A buzzer rang. Yasugawa went to the phone and picked it up. His voice indicated surprise.

"It's from the *Christina.*"

"We're using a foreign ship?" asked Tadokoro sourly.

"Dutch. It won't be noticed as much as a Japanese ship," answered Nakata as he took the phone. "It's Onodera," he told them. Then he spoke into the phone:

"I see. . . . Well, right now we're sending Kataoka from Defense Research to meet you at Moji. There's nothing to worry about. I don't think you know him at all. He's one of those who just joined our group, and when it comes to machinery, he's a genius."

Nakata hung up and turned to Yamazaki. "Call Kataoka. He's at the arsenal in Yokosuka. Arrange for him to fly to Moji. He's to wait for the *Takatsuki,* which we're sending to meet the sub. The *Christina* will arrive tomorrow morning at ten o'clock."

"Why is that fellow going?" asked Tadokoro, not at all happy.

"There's some sort of problem with the engines on the *Kermadic.* Onodera can't fix it, he says," Nakata answered. "But this Kataoka is a wizard."

"Professor Tadokoro . . ." Yukinaga stood up from the desk, holding a sheet of paper upon which he had just done some calculating. "The total quantity of energy in earthquakes and in the movement of the earth's crust this past year in the Japan Archipelago surpassed—though just by a little—the theoretical limit."

"Well, I wonder where the excess energy came from," said Tadokoro, taking the sheet and staring hard at it. "Where from, eh? What caused it, do you think?"

Yukinaga gazed down at the relief map of Japan on top of the desk. It was made of clear plastic of varying tints, which showed the mantle beneath the surface.

"Well, this may be rash, but," he said at last, "it seems to me that the only way that we can track this thing down is to set up a simulation model involving the entire globe, focusing upon the crust and mantle of the East Asian land mass, especially the movement of the Japan Archipelago."

"What we lack is data," said Tadokoro, rapping the computer with his fingers. "That's of first importance." Suddenly he glanced at his watch. "Nakata, I'm going to Moji, too. Okay?"

"Well, Professor . . ." Nakata's eyes widened. "If you'd like to . . ."

"I'd like to check the situation again in the West," Tadokoro said, putting on his coat. He had all at once become like a boy. "I was thinking that maybe in the West . . . Well, I'm somewhat concerned about the Aso and the Kirishima volcanic belt."

"It's the only thing to do, I guess," said Nakata, clucking his tongue. "Yasugawa, call Yokosuka. Tell Kataoka that Professor Tadokoro will be going with him."

"Will it be a commercial flight?" asked Tadokoro.

"A navy courier plane. Needless to say, you'd like to fly over Aso for a look, wouldn't you?"

Tadokoro snorted, but a happy expression stole over his face.

3

As autumn advanced, the weather grew cooler, though, as happened every year, summer made torrid gestures of farewell even into October. Finally, these, too, came to an end, and as the blue of the sky deepened with each passing day and the lights each evening showed the ground more wet with dew, the memories of the turbulent and disastrous summer grew less vivid, and people began to regain their composure. Japan settled into the fall season in a manner scarcely different from that of other years. The streets, the people, the weather, nature itself . . . Yes, nature itself, or so it seemed.

Onodera had just finished a series of diving tests in the Kumano Sea and was about to return to Tokyo for a night before starting the actual exploration, which would be still more demanding. All its defects repaired now, the *Kermadic* was in satisfactory condition. Kataoka, the mechanical genius, had done a painstaking job of repairing and refitting it.

When Onodera had finally been able to drag himself from beneath a pile of tiles in Ponto-cho after the earthquake, he had made use of the quickly restored phone service to contact Tokyo, and, at Nakata's direction, he had taken off at once for Europe to negotiate the purchase of the *Kermadic* without even taking the time to stop at his parents' home. From Italy he had sent a cryptic cablegram announcing his resignation, which stunned his superiors at Sea Floor Development, who had been under the impression that he had died in the quake. Now, his work finished in the Kumano Sea area, he boarded a military seaplane and flew to Haneda Airport. The next day, together with Yukinaga and Nakata, he was to fly back to the *Takatsuki,* which was bound for a spot 310 miles east of Cape Inubo. Such was Onodera's frantic pace.

As soon as he stepped into the headquarters in Harajuku, he was taken in hand, especially by Nakata and Yukinaga, and swept up into an interminable discussion of the communication system and a variety of other aspects of the project. Onodera was astounded at the incredible tempo of Plan D. No sooner was one problem dealt with than still more loomed up. Can they expect, he wondered, to get through this fantastic amount of work with no more men than they have?

Finally, after a lengthy period of give and take, Nakata threw a sheaf of documents brusquely aside and yawned extravagantly.

"Well, no matter how long we stuck at it, we wouldn't finish," he said. "And the survey starts tomorrow. What do you say we get a good night's sleep tonight? Onodera, how about going out for a nightcap with us? After all, you won't be seeing Tokyo for a while, will you?"

"Thanks," said Onodera, glancing at his watch as he stood up. "An hour or two'll do no harm."

They went to a bar at the very top of a new building in Yoyogi which offered a panoramic view of the city. The lighting in the bar was so dim that it took time to make out the faces of the patrons, and though it was eleven o'clock when they arrived, it was rather crowded. At each table flickered a candle covered with a red or blue shade. Band music flowed quietly through the room, and well-dressed men and women talked as though in whispers. In the midst of a gloom like depths of indigo blue, the smooth faces of the women, their bare arms and shoulders, and the necklaces and pendants that hung at their breasts glowed pale, like the bellies of fish swimming over the dark ocean floor, while the tiny orange flames of cigarette lighters flashed from time to time.

The six of them sat at a table near the window, ordered a bottle of white wine, and then quietly touched their glasses together.

"Well," said Kunieda, "here's to the bold project that we start tomorrow."

"I don't know anything about bold projects," said Onodera with a half-smile, "but here's to the success of our research."

"And here's to the safe performance of the *Kermadic,*" said Yukinaga.

"And, finally," said Nakata, in a last toast, "here's to Japan and the road ahead for her."

The glasses clinked softly. The cold, mellow liquid flowed down their throats. After he had filled his glass a second time, Onodera leaned back in his chair as though to withdraw somewhat from the quiet conversation that had begun at the table, and gazed at the scene spread out below him, beyond the sheet of glass that extended from ceiling to floor—the city at night.

Tokyo by night was, as always, a flood of lights. The white beams of headlights and the red flash of taillights coalesced in swift-moving currents between the chilly glow cast by lines of mercury lights. Yellow sodium lights shone on the freeways winding about the city like huge snakes, and here and there skyscrapers towered up, giant black slabs studded with thousands of lights despite the lateness of the hour.

How could one possibly conceive of such a thing happening! Onodera stared out into the night beyond the dark sheet of glass.

Like a black, ominous bird, a huge passenger plane, flashing red and white lights on its approach to Haneda, seemed to graze the peak of Tokyo Tower, etched in the night sky with specks of brilliance.

Everything he looked at—should the thing that Professor Tadokoro feared come about, if it turned out to be real . . . this vast city, the teeming life that pulsated through it, what would become of it all? The 110 million people of this race that had come into being and flourished on this soil rich in history—what of the dreams cherished by each of them as they looked toward tomorrow? To build a home. To raise children. To go to college. To travel abroad. More than 100 million people, with their petty hopes—what in heaven's name was to become of all of them?

Go ahead and enjoy yourself, thought Onodera, as he looked out on the scene flooded with lights, his mood almost that of a man offering a prayer. Go ahead, for now at least, enjoy yourself to the full, all of you. Enjoy every moment like something never to come again. The memory of even paltry pleasures is better than none at all. So enjoy yourselves for now. As for tomorrow . . . maybe it will never come.

"I guess it's time," said Nakata, looking at his watch as he stood up. "Let's everybody get a good night's sleep tonight."

While they were standing by the cashier's counter, a short, slim girl, wearing the kind of beige suit touched with pale blue that was stylish that fall, glanced at Onodera and then cried out in a small voice: "My goodness! It's . . . ah . . . Mr. Ono . . ."

"Well," said Onodera, placing the girl. "Mako—right?"

"Yes! You're kind enough to remember me. Oh, how nice! Mr. Onoda—no, Mr. Onodera."

"That's right. Your place is the . . . let's see . . . the Miruto, isn't it?"

"You haven't been there at all since then, have you? Yuri's just heartbroken that you never taught her how to use an aqualung."

While she talked, Mako clung to Onodera's arm as though she were intent on abandoning the stout, distinguished-looking gentleman she was with. "Please come back. Oh, yes—Mr. Yoshimura has been in, but he said that you left the company. Is that so?"

Frowning slightly, Onodera nodded.

"Well, anyway," said the girl, "please come again. And give me a call, please. Don't forget."

"A cute little girl," said Kunieda ironically. "Is she a hostess?"

"Yes. It's awkward to run into her like this," muttered Onodera as he watched the girl disappear into the bar, chattering to her companion like a sparrow. "Should I tell her to keep her mouth shut?"

"No, there's no need. With a girl like that, there couldn't be cause for concern," said Nakata. "Besides, tomorrow you'll be at sea—or, rather, at the bottom of it."

4

Kataoka was frantically at work at Yokosuka supervising the refitting of factory ship *Yoshino* to serve as the command vessel for D-1, and in the meantime the *Takatsuki* was doing duty as mother ship for the *Kermadic*. The *Takatsuki* was an old ship, a former American corvette which had served as an anti-submarine vessel during the Second World War. Just the previous year the Sea Defense Force had refitted it as a specialty ship. In place of its depth-charge racks, a platform had been installed on its broad afterdeck, which was used to secure the *Kermadic* on the way from one diving site to another while the *Takatsuki* kept to a grueling schedule calling for some twenty dives within two weeks over a wide area of the Pacific above the slope of the Japan Trench. Often the submarine, caught in the flux of converging currents, was buffeted like a leaf, and there were many days when the sea was so clouded to the very floor of the ocean that any visual estimates were impossible.

The grind told upon Onodera. His skin became pallid. His eyes were bloodshot, and his cheeks hollow. A growth of beard covered his face, and his joints ached from lack of sleep. Time and time again he guided the submarine down through turbulent seas to the ocean floor in dives of more than 20,000 feet, taking it where the shouting Tadokoro directed, turning on lights, releasing flares, taking pictures, and operating the television camera. Often it was necessary twice in one day to do the work of placing the automatic measuring devices on the trench floor and on its sides. The consequent strain on mind and body had a cumulative intensity. With the temperature of the ocean floor at two or three degrees Centigrade, the instruments in the gondola were as cold as ice, and the moisture inside was so heavy that the dehumidifying compound had to be replaced after every dive. Then, too, since the refitting of the submarine had been carried out very quickly, the various instruments to be installed had been crammed helter-skelter into the narrow confines of the gondola, leaving almost no space in which to move about during the dives of some hours' duration.

On the seventeenth day the *Kermadic* developed mechanical trouble as a result of the hard use it had been put to, and further dives had to be put off for a while. Tadokoro shut himself up in the wardroom with a vast amount of research data, and Onodera, fighting the weariness that had taken hold of him, threw himself into the repair of the submarine, working in grim silence beside the *Takatsuki*'s engineers.

Two days later the *Yoshino* finally arrived at the rendezvous point. Its three radar masts roused a cheer when they appeared over the horizon. Two large derricks were mounted on the low afterdeck, which was also equipped with a launching slide. It would be a simple matter for the two interlocked cranes to lift the submarine out of the water and place it on the deck, and the use of the launching slide would make refloating it a speedy operation. Things would go much smoother from then on.

Kataoka was on board the *Yoshino*, a short, bright-eyed young man whose plump brown face was like that of a young boy.

"It took more time than I thought. I'm sorry," said Kataoka, grinning as he spoke through the loudspeaker on the bridge. "We'll load the sub onto the *Yoshino* right away. Professor Nakata and Mr. Kunieda are on board, too. Mr. Yamazaki will be coming soon on the courier plane. We can have a conference on board here, if that's all right."

When Tadokoro and the others were ready to leave the *Takatsuki*, they went to the captain's cabin to take their leave. The captain handed Tadokoro a message he had just received.

"It says that Hakone shows signs of erupting," the captain said. "And it seems that there's the sound of rumbling at Miyakejima. The timing's good, anyway. We're to proceed at full speed to Miyakejima to aid in the evacuation."

The *Kermadic* was already in the water, its yellow hull bobbing in the troughs of the waves as it was drawn slowly to the fantail of the *Yoshino*. As soon as the submarine was secured, the *Takatsuki* steamed off at once on a southerly course, its prow cleaving the waves as it rapidly grew smaller in the distance.

"Well, as you see," said Nakata, "we don't have a welcoming banquet prepared for you. What do you say? Should we start talking right away?"

"Of course," said Tadokoro without hesitation. "As soon as we pay our respects to the captain. Where can we have a private conference?"

"Well, first let's get your luggage to your cabin," said Kunieda. "Then I'll show you to our Plan D command room."

Twenty minutes later they gathered in the command room on the top deck at the front of the ship. The walls were banked with flashing computer lights, and at one end of the room hung the luminescent progress chart and the magnetic plastic board on which was drawn the Japan Archipelago. In almost the center of the room was a huge rectangular block of clear plastic. The block seemed to contain nothing at all, but when Kataoka pressed a switch at its base, the Japan Archipelago came into view in the form of a vividly clear three-dimensional image in full color. Everyone responded with a gasp of admiration.

"Rather nice, isn't it?" said Kataoka, flashing his white teeth. "It's a hologram projector screen developed by Defense Research. The plastic block seems to be empty, but actually it's filled with very small metallic particles."

Kataoka pressed other switches, and smaller-scale images appeared one after another in the plastic block. One of these showed the topography of the ocean floor.

Moreover, as Kataoka moved his fingers over the board, a wide variety of symbols such as spots of light, arrows, lines, and the like appeared. Heat currents, gravitational abnormalities, vertical and horizontal movement of the earth crust, volcanic activity—these and almost every other sort of data could be projected into the hologram.

"There's a direct link-up with the computers, and so the data, as soon as it comes in, can be shown as is. It takes in everything," said Nakata.

Tadokoro, in the meantime, had sat down in a corner of the room in a chair facing the wall. His head was bent forward, and he seemed lost in thought. His face was gray and covered with sweat, and Yukinaga was taken aback to see how painfully contorted his expression was.

"Professor Tadokoro," said Yukinaga, as he went up to him and put a hand on his shoulder. "Aren't you feeling well?"

At Yukinaga's touch, Tadokoro started as though he had received an electric shock. He jumped up from his chair. "Oh," he said, expelling his breath harshly. "Oh, yes . . . of course."

Tadokoro then walked with dragging footsteps toward the desk around which the others were gathered. He looked vacantly at the computers along the walls, the control board, and then he stared at the three-dimensional image of the Japan Archipelago that glimmered in the huge block of plastic, as though noticing it for the first time. As he stared, the light gradually came back to his hollow eyes.

"An interesting device," said Tadokoro, his eyes now boring into the plastic projection screen. "Can you show more—not just the Japan Archipelago but the whole area, taking in the Western Pacific to Southeast Asia?"

"Right now this is the widest area we can show," said Kataoka, pressing a switch to project a view that, with Japan at its center, took in the Ogasawara Islands, Okinawa, Taiwan, the Philippines, together with the Korean Peninsula and a section of the Chinese coast.

"Good enough. Leave that on, please."

With that, Tadokoro walked away from the screen and stood beneath the plastic board on which was drawn the map of the Japan Archipelago.

"Sit down, gentlemen," said Tadokoro, his voice low and hoarse. "I'll tell you what has to be said."

The group took seats around the desk. Tadokoro stood for a few moments with his eyes cast down as though considering something. As Yukinaga gazed at Tadokoro standing thus, he suddenly felt his chest painfully constricted. This man, Yukinaga thought—how much he's aged in just two or three months! It's as though he's ten years older. His hair has gotten whiter, there's no vitality in his expression, his wrinkles have grown deeper. . . . His eyes are heavy and bloodshot, and his whole expression is that of a man who's burned out.

"This Plan D of ours," began Tadokoro, his voice lifeless, "took its origin from a possibility that had arisen in my mind as a result of the varied research I had been doing for the past ten years, research that had begun with marine volcanoes and then had gradually spread to mountain ranges, geology, and, finally to the basic structure of the earth beneath the ocean floor. The possibility is that there might take place a vast alteration of the earth crust of the Japan Archipelago."

As Tadokoro paused, a chill seemed to sweep over the group around the desk.

"The plan is presently divided into D-1 and D-2. D-1 is our concern—further investigation. The burden of D-2 is to formulate an evacuation program, should worse come to worst." Tadokoro paused for a moment, his hand to his head as though marshaling his thoughts. Then he placed both his hands on top of the plastic-block screen. "Let me take things in order. The thing that first led me to suspect that something was wrong was the manner in which marine gravitational irregularities were distributed in the areas adjacent to the Japan Archipelago. There was an incredible change from what had been recorded in a survey made a mere decade before. Furthermore, there was the same sort of radical change with regard to earth magnetism and electrical and heat currents, especially the heat currents on the Japan Sea coast. And then in the Ogasawara group, as you know, an island with an elevation of some two hundred feet sank in a single night—an event of extraordinary significance."

Tadokoro glanced down at Onodera.

"As it happened, in the course of investigating that, something further came to my attention, something that our most recent explorations have confirmed: it seems to me that the pattern of mantle convection far beneath the Japan Trench is changing radically."

"Professor," said Kunieda, "would you be kind enough to explain what a mantle convection is?"

"Very good," said Tadokoro, some color returning to his lifeless skin. "Our specialties vary, so some basic explanations are in order. First, a convection: for the present, think of it as the transfer of heat through fluid motion, especially motion upward. Now let's take the structure of the earth." He drew a circle on a blackboard and then a much smaller one within it. "At the center of the earth, like the yolk of an egg, is the core.

Surrounding it, like the white of the egg, is the mantle. Finally, the thinnest and outermost layer, the crust. Judging from the way that earthquake waves are transmitted from deep within the earth, we believe that the mantle is solid, the outer core liquid, and the inner core solid. The mantle is some two thousand miles thick, approximately half the radius of the earth. The crust, on the other hand, is a mere twenty miles thick beneath the continents and still thinner beneath the ocean floor—apparently no more than three miles. We like to think of the ground beneath our feet as solid, but the truth is that the thickness of the crust upon which we and all our history and civilization rest is, relative to the size of the earth, like the stretched rubber of an inflated balloon. And within the mantle itself, solid though it seems, the evidence indicates that, over vast stretches of time, convections take form here just as they do in liquids. The mantle, in fact, flows beneath the crust at the rather rapid rate of two inches per year in its deep portion and at the rate of six inches per year in the portion near the crust, which, in turn, provokes great movement on the surface of the crust, especially beneath the ocean. This seems to be the motive force that moves the continents. . . . Kataoka, let's have a topographical map of the world."

Kataoka pressed a switch, and a brilliantly colored map appeared on the projection screen on the desk. Tadokoro took up his explanation, tapping the map with his pen.

"Note the respective concave and convex portions of the European and African coasts and the North and South American coasts, so aligned that it seems as though they would fit neatly together. It is this configuration that gave Wegener the hint that they had in fact once been joined and so led him to his famous theory of Continental Drift."

Tadokoro next ran his pen down the middle of the Atlantic Ocean, indicating the massive Mid-Atlantic Ridge, which reached a height of 9,000 feet and was 600 miles wide, stretching in an S shape from the Arctic Circle all the way down to the southern polar region.

"In the midst of this ridge, the source of almost all the quakes in the Atlantic," Tadokoro continued, "there runs a deep crevice containing an extraordinary amount of heat. This heat is being conveyed upward from deep within the mantle by means of convection, and this Mid-Atlantic Ridge itself is nothing else but the upward thrust of this mantle convection. Here we have the motive force that long ago, in accordance with Wegener's theory, opened up a great chasm in the continental mass and set what is now the American continents moving in a westward direction. Furthermore, this same kind of protuberance, resulting from the upward thrust of the mantle convection and constituting the same kind of break in the crust, runs along the sea floor of all the oceans of the world." Professor Tadokoro stopped for a moment. He looked around at everyone before going on, his voice somewhat lower. "Now with regard to these mantle convections, using a method that I've developed myself, I have not only been able to make a detailed diagram of them and formulate a comprehensive explanation, but I am certain that I can predict the emergence of phenomena that will be completely new."

Yukinaga felt his pulse quicken. What a sensation Tadokoro's theory would provoke if he could make it known! But that, of course, was out of the question. And then, too, even granting that the history of man's scientific scrutiny of the earth was a short one, the thrust of Tadokoro's argument seemed fantastic. . . .

"All right," said Tadokoro as he turned a dial and brought a relief map of the Pacific into focus, "now let's take a look at the Pacific." He picked up a pointer and indicated the undersea ridge off the coast of Chile. "You see how the ridge line of the Atlantic continues into the Southeast Pacific. Now look here." He now pointed to an undersea mountain range that extended up through the Indian Ocean. "If one credits Wilson's theory, it was the upward thrust of the mantle, represented by this range, that pushed the Indian subcontinent, formerly separate from Asia, to the north, thrusting it finally against the continent. And in the process the coastal impact area was pushed upward to form the great Himalayan fold. And even now this seems to be the explanation for the continual increase in the height of the Himalayas." The pointer moved back to the Southeast Pacific. "It seems evident that the general flow of the Eastern Pacific mantle is from southeast to northwest, something corroborated by the fact that the Christmas, Hawaii, and Tuamotu groups run in that direction. Furthermore, this flow collides eventually, we believe, with the mantle flow coming from the Asian continent, as a result of which a part of it takes a downward turn, something that would account for the long trenches that characterize the eastern side of the island arcs of the Western Pacific. But now let's consider how all this pertains to our immediate concern."

There was dead silence in the room as Tadokoro flipped a switch to change the picture. The area now spread across the screen was the Northwest Pacific, taking in Japan and a portion of the mainland. "The Japan Archipelago was once joined to the continent, and some time in the distant past the continental mantle current I referred to thrust it out into the Pacific in a southeast direction. According to my theory, it is still doing so to this day at a speed of from one to three inches a year. In the first stages of this process, say twenty-five million years ago, the Archipelago lay much farther to the north and it lay straight rather than curving away from the continent. The constant pressure, however, bent it into its present arc shape and opened the fossa magna that divides Central Honshu. Furthermore, at this break line we have the Fuji volcanic zone. But now let's consider the mantle current coming from the opposite direction, from the Southeast Pacific. What happens when these come together?" Tadokoro paused for a moment and then suddenly looked at Yukinaga, a gleam in his eye. "Yukinaga, what discipline concerns itself with the behavior of masses of fluids of varying temperatures on the earth's surface?" he asked.

"Meteorology, Professor," answered Yukinaga, his voice hoarse.

"Good. But you want perhaps to protest that vapors, liquids, and solids are quite different things, isn't that right? But would it be too absurd to think that, given a sufficiently long period to overreach the difference in nature, meteorological analogies might be used to explain the behavior of the mantle? For it not only forms convections, but in the upper mantle there is a distribution of masses of varying temperatures. Would it be out of the question to think of these as behaving like vapor masses, given enough time?"

They stared at Tadokoro's unshaven face in amazement. Could there really be any similarity between atmospheric currents, ever moving and never knowing rest, and those heavy,

solid masses of rock moving deep with the earth at high temperatures?

"To put it in simple terms," said Tadokoro, "let's take a look
at the kind of pattern that occurs when a cold front meets a
mass of warm air."

Tadokoro drew a horizontal line on the blackboard. Above
this he drew a line cutting down into it which formed half an
oval, its long axis parallel. Within the curved line he drew an
arrow pointing from right to left. "This is a vertical section
diagram of a cold front. The straight line below is the earth's
surface. On the right is a mass of cold air. The cold air mass
plunges beneath the warm atmosphere on the left. The warm
air is pushed upward and is chilled. And along the line of discon-
tinuity, clouds take form and rain begins to fall. In the case of
a warm front, the reverse happens. The warm front climbs over
the cold mass." Tadokoro turned away from the blackboard and
singled out Onodera this time. "Onodera, do you see where I'm
going?"

"I think so, Professor," answered Onodera. "In terms of your
analogy, the cold front moving from right to left is the mantle
flow coming up from the Southeast Pacific, and the warm atmosphere on the left is the mantle flow coming from beneath the
continent."

"Exactly. The continental mantle flow is much warmer because of the radioactive elements it contains, because the crust
of the continent is some six times thicker than the crust of the
ocean floor, and for other reasons I needn't go into now. Thus,
it climbs up the advancing mantle. And this is the force that
moved the Japan Archipelago away from the mainland, forming the Japan Sea in the process, and eventually bent the Archipelago into its present arc shape. Now bear this in mind: the
Archipelago is still bending and moving, and the Japan Trench,
formed by the descent of the Pacific mantle, is still growing
deeper."

His intent listeners swallowed hard as they heard Tadokoro's
explanation. The Archipelago on which they lived was like a
line of clouds that had taken form along the leading edge of a
moving mass of warm air. Outside, the wind seemed to have
risen and the sea grown rougher. The *Yoshino* began to pitch
and roll, though gently at first. Since Tadokoro had paused once

more, they could clearly hear the echo of creaking throughout the ship, the moaning of the wind, and the breaking of the waves. A gloomy mood took hold of them.

Kataoka broke the silence: "But, Professor, hasn't all this been going on for millions of years?"

"Yes, it has. And you're thinking that it will go on for still more millions in just this way?"

"Well, yes."

"If so, we of course have nothing to worry about. But my research, my intuition also, if you will, leads me to think that we are on the verge of a sudden, a violent alteration of that pattern. I readily grant that a change of this nature would be something unheard of, but please remember this: since man as we know him now appeared on the earth, some hundreds of thousands of years have passed—no more. What incredible events may have happened before he appeared we have no idea. And even after he appeared, even in historical times, much has occurred that we know next to nothing about simply because our scientific scrutiny of the earth has barely gotten under way. For example, the fact that the earth's axis has moved, the fact that terrestrial magnetism is lessening and will be gone in another two thousand years, the fact that creatures upon the earth will be subject to cosmic rays—these and many other things we've learned in just this past decade, and we've no more than scratched the surface. So we must be very slow to say that such-and-such a thing cannot happen."

The cabin lurched to one side. There came the noise of doors crashing shut.

"There's always a reason, though. There has to be a reason." Tadokoro turned to Yukinaga. "Yukinaga, do you remember how, when Runcorn resurrected Wegener's Continental Drift theory, he explained how the process began—the break-up of the single land mass and the westward movement of the Americas?"

"I remember," answered Yukinaga, feeling his throat dry. "He proposed Chandrasekhar's calculations, the great Indian astrophysicist working in America."

Tadokoro nodded and then pointed to the diagram of the earth that he had drawn earlier.

"Take another look at this cross-section, gentlemen. At present the diameter of the core is more than half that of the earth, having a diameter of about four thousand miles. It seems, however, that in the beginning the core was smaller. The earth as a whole has been contracting, by force of its own gravity, while the core, its heat and pressure growing more intense, has been expanding. And this has had its effect upon the mantle surrounding it. In the beginning the mantle convection pattern was like a single whirlpool, but as the core expanded, it altered. Nor was this alteration a gradual process. Rather, once the core reached a certain size, the whirlpool suddenly was torn asunder and a multitude of small whirlpools took form, a theory verified by Chandrasekhar's calculations. And so, after having remained a single mass for so many millions of years, the continents suddenly began the movement that would give them their present form. But you see what I'm driving at, Yukinaga?"

"I think so. The still-expanding core has brought about another sudden alteration of the mantle convection pattern," Yukinaga answered. "Still smaller whirlpools are taking form. And somewhere near the Japan Archipelago, the mantle mass has developed a fine split or is on the verge of so doing."

"Basically, that's it. Why things should be moving so fast, I don't know. But, in any case, the mantle mass on the Pacific side of the Japan Archipelago is rapidly shrinking." He tapped the block screen on which was projected a three-dimensional map of Japan. "This may be the harbinger of a crust change of unprecedented kind extending over the whole earth. Or perhaps it will affect only this area."

Tadokoro's tone was much softer than it had been, his voice lower. The room was hushed. There was not a murmur. Holding their breath, the group sat with their eyes fixed upon Tadokoro. Behind his back the computer lights flashed on and off incessantly. Outside, the whine of the wind and the crash of the waves seemed to be growing louder.

Onodera noticed that his hands, clenched into fists, had become sweaty. He wiped his brow instinctively, to find it, too, slippery with sweat.

"And what would its effect be, Professor?" Onodera found himself asking.

"If the present speed and direction are maintained, there's reason enough to believe that once the shift in matter reaches a certain point, the present dynamic balance existing between the mantle and the crust structure will collapse at a stroke. Up to now, you see, the pressure from the Pacific side has held the Archipelago relatively firm against the pressure coming from the continental side. And so, should the convection pattern on the Pacific side suddenly change, the result would be a crushing blow to Japan."

A single image took hold of Onodera's mind: the bar holding the Japan Archipelago in place suddenly falling away. . . .

"If the worst were to happen," Tadokoro went on, swallowing noisily, "the usual way of thinking of greater or lesser quake damage would have no place. For if the worst were to happen, the greater part of the Japan Archipelago would sink beneath the sea. We have to think in terms of annihilation."

A chill silence fell over the room. No one dared release his breath. The whine of the wind, the creaking of the ship, the sound of waves beginning to break over the decks—all these seemed but to intensify the silence that held them in its grip.

Out of the corner of his eye, Onodera noticed that the red lights of the computers and the communication gear had begun to flash steadily. Because no one was taking the messages, the equipment was starting to do its own recording. The telex was chattering. The facsimile machine began to crackle. But still no one moved.

All at once there was the sound of hurrying feet in the corridor. When they reached the cabin door, there was a loud knock. Someone in the room answered, but Onodera had no idea who. The door opened and a sunburned young officer came in. He made a polite bow. His face was tense, and the paper he held in his hand shook slightly.

"Just now a message came from Fleet Command in Yokosuka," said the officer, looking at the paper, his voice unsteady. "A large-scale quake has occurred in the Kanto Region. The epicenter is twenty miles out to sea off Tokyo Bay. Its magnitude is 8.5. Tidal waves have struck the entire shoreline of Tokyo Bay and Sagami Bay. In Tokyo the force of from 6 to 7, together with the suddenness with which it hit, appears to have caused extensive damage. This vessel, on orders from the Sea Defense Force Headquarters, is changing its course and is proceeding to Tokyo Bay for rescue operations. . . ."

IV

The Home Islands

At a little before five, Yamazaki was about to leave Plan D headquarters, on the sixth floor of a building next to Harajuku Station. At six o'clock a high-speed helicopter of the Sea Self-Defense Force was to land at Harumi Pier to pick him up and fly him to the *Yoshino,* then approaching the Sea of Enshu.

"Well, I think I'll be going. Tonight I'll be on the waves."

"Sorry to hear it, answered Yasugawa breezily as he punched the keys of a computer. "I've got a full night's work ahead of me."

"Don't overdo it," said Yamazaki, putting on his hat. "It wouldn't do to ruin your health while you're still young." As he spoke, Yamazaki moved over to the window to see how bad was the rush-hour traffic in the streets below.

Just as he came to the window a mass of dark specks, like a billowing cloud of pepper, rose up into the sky in the direction of Yoyogi Grove. Pigeons, sparrow, crows—birds of every kind were taking to flight as though seized with a sudden frenzy.

A cry formed on the lips of the startled Yamazaki, though no sound came from his throat. At the same instant, bolts of lightning, one after another, flashed down from the lead-colored clouds gathered in the already darkened eastern sky and darted over the ground. The staccato flashes covered the horizon with glaring sheets of light.

"Yasugawa!" Yamazaki, whose eyes had been fixed on the scene outside, turned and shouted to his friend in a shrill voice. "Come here! Look! Something's happening."

There was no way of fixing their points of origin, but beginning somewhere in the east and extending into the city itself, pillars of light were boiling up from the earth as though to tear it asunder and climbing toward the clouds. The columns—two, three of them—keeping a fixed distance from one another, shimmered brilliantly. A crimson-tinged ball of light spurted up from one of them and, describing a flashing arc, fell back to earth.

"What is it?" asked Yasugawa, rising from his desk.

But at that instant a thunderous shock struck, and the floor seemed to billow up beneath them. Before they had time even to register alarm, the floor rose again, as if a giant hammer were striking from below, blow upon blow, as though to pound everything to rubble. While the two men struggled to keep their feet, ink bottles, water glasses, and the like bounced up into the air with each shock. A box of thumbtacks turned over in mid-flight, the tacks spilling out over the floor.

"An earthquake!" said Yamazaki. "It looks like it's going to be a big one."

When the violent shocks rocking the building lessened, Yamazaki quickly took stock of the situation. Was it best to use this breathing space to dash downstairs?

But they were given no time to flee. There was a rumbling like a distant volley of massed artillery, and then the whole building groaned as it began to sway from side to side. Yamazaki clutched at the wall to keep his feet, but the counter-sway sent him sprawling onto the floor. Two or three of the spilled tacks bit into his palms. Fear gripping him, he struggled to his knees, but, far from being able to stand, he could not even manage to get on all fours. The floor shook from side to side at frenzied speed, and Yamazaki was flattened again.

"Mr. Yamazaki!" Young Yasugawa's high voice sounded.

"Under a desk," shouted Yamazaki. "Get under a desk!"

There was a loud crash. A heavy bookcase had fallen over. Cracks raced across the walls and ceiling. Pieces of cement began to rain down amid clouds of grimy dust. Clutching his head, Yamazaki looked out from beneath the desk under which he had finally been able to crawl. In shocked amazement he watched as the glass of the adjacent window, ripped from the strong sash that held it, broke apart in the air with a shattering crash. The lights went out. Outside, glowing curtains of sparks seemed to swirl about one another in the gray sky.

For a moment the rocking slackened off, but then it started up again with renewed fury. A desk computer went sailing through the air, trailing its cord, and smashed into the wall close to Yamazaki. The tremors this time were fiercer yet. The building swayed crazily, its whole frame groaning with terrible force, and chunks of cement crashed down from the ceiling. Yamazaki felt the floor lurch sharply upward.

Would the building go over? With relative calm, he considered the situation. They were on the sixth floor of a seven-floor building. Were it to collapse, their chances of survival were almost nil. To be caught in the midst of that shattered mass of concrete falling to earth!

Now there was a staccato pounding. The window frame swayed again and then came free, and as Yamazaki watched, it sailed leisurely out into space. Was he about to die? In one part of his mind, he coolly weighed the question. Were he to die now, he thought, how void of meaning his life would be!

The rumbling gradually subsided. The floor was tilted several degrees. In the dim light Yamazaki could see that the room was filled with a cloud of dust. When he tried to crawl out from beneath the desk, he found something blocking his way. A section of fallen ceiling was draped over the desk. The aspect of the room, seen by the faint light that came in through the windows, was one of frightful disorder. Through the dust that choked the room, Yamazaki saw cracks in the walls, holes torn in the ceiling. The floor was covered with shattered concrete. Bookcases and lockers were overturned, desks were crushed. All order had been obliterated, leaving nothing but a shambles. The thing that ever lurked behind the geometric patterns of rational order had shown its terrible visage.

The raw dust from the broken concrete struck Yamazaki's nostrils with pungent force.

"Yasugawa!" Yamazaki called in a hoarse voice. "Are you all right?"

"Yes," came the weak reply. "Something hit me on the head, but I'm all right."

Again there was creaking as the room started to rock once more. A tipped bookcase fell over with a crash.

"What should we do?" Yasugawa asked, his voice shaking like a child's.

Outside the noise of explosions sounded rapidly, one after

another. At each report a red glow filled the windows. And now, abruptly, the sound of people shouting and crying out began to reach them, as though coming from a long way off. Mixed with the smell of dust was a scorched, burning stench.

"The first thing we have to do is to get out of here," said Yamazaki. "There might be aftershocks."

"The elevator's no good, I guess. Would the stairs be all right?"

"The fire escape would probably be the best."

The door to the fire escape was at the end of a short corridor. Broken glass covered the floor and made a grinding noise beneath their shoes. Yamazaki felt a shudder run down his spine as through the gloom he saw the cracks that covered the walls and ceilings.

The steel door leading to the fire escape turned out to be jammed. Yamazaki resolutely threw his body against it, and it finally burst open. Smoke and searing hot air struck their nostrils. The frame building next door was in flames. The gloom of early evening was filled with the sound of running feet, shouts, and cries of pain. The quake had derailed a commuter train at Harajuku Station just below, and people were milling about along the twisted length of track. The scream of fire sirens came from every direction, and black smoke was starting to pour up.

"Come on!" Yamazaki shouted as he dashed out through the fire door. He felt the steel plates beneath his feet rattling ominously, and he could hear Yasugawa's footsteps behind him. Since the building was tilted, the slightest misstep on the fire escape would be disastrous. They climbed down past the fifth floor, then the fourth, turning one way, then another with agonized care. They had reached the third floor when heaven and earth began to groan once more.

"Careful!" Yasugawa shouted, his voice shrill. "Watch it, Mr. Yamazaki."

But Yamazaki had already lost his footing. He plunged downward, struck the steps heavily, buttocks first, and slid on his back until a landing checked his fall. He tried to get to his feet, but he could not. The steel fire escape shook violently, vibrating like a giant gong. The aftershocks seemed to turn heaven and earth alike into a massive, howling whirlpool. The burning building next door collapsed like a house of cards, and showers of sparks burst in all directions. Something whizzed by, grazing Yamaza-ki's cheek, whether a tile or a fragment of zinc roofing he could not tell. A deafening roar broke from the somber sky rumbling overhead, and the fire escape shook still more violently. The strain was such that the steel plates and rods that held it fast to the concrete face of the building began to burst free one after another, as though a rapid-fire cannon were going off in Yamazaki's ear.

When evening came, the sinister rumblings that followed the quake gradually quieted, but the destruction went on. For, since there was no means to check them, the fires that had broken out in well over a hundred places throughout the city gradually spread, and in the gathering darkness the red glow that lit the sky grew ever more vivid. Along the shoreline ravaged by tidal waves, flames burst like red lotus petals from ruptured storage tanks and warehouses, and smoke billowed skyward to form massive black columns.

No trains were running on either the National Railways or the private lines. Fires had broken out in some sections of the subway. Others were flooded. The streets were everywhere blocked by either fire, rubble, or burning vehicles. The elevated expressways were in still worse condition. Near Nishi Kanda and Shibaura the supporting girders had been twisted out of position, and, all along the expressway, sections of the cement pavement had fallen away, and burning cars, melting the guard-rails and turning the asphalt to flaming jelly, had come tumbling down like balls of fire. The seething mass of asphalt on the higher sections of the roadway was flowing down into the tunnels, which were belching fire and thick black smoke. Culverts throughout the city were filled with gas vapors, and periodic explosions sent manhole covers flying. Here and there, rushing water from broken mains clashed with the raging flames to give rise to clouds of steam.

When Yamazaki once more became aware of his surround-ings, he was in a grove of of trees on the grounds of the Meiji Shrine, dragging one leg as he walked. His left ankle seemed to be severely sprained, and with every step fierce pain shot through it. Up to this moment, however, he had taken no notice even of this. He looked around him, but Yasugawa was nowhere to be seen. Instead there were masses of men and women, sobbing, breathing harshly as they hurried along distractedly. To Yamazaki's rear, beyond the grove, the sky was red.

How had he survived? Yamazaki wondered dully as he dragged his leg along. He was sure that the building had collapsed. Hanging on to the landing of the fire escape, he had watched as though in a dream as, undermined by crevices, it had tipped more and more. Together with the fire escape, together with the building, he had been falling as though in slow motion toward the ground below, against which all alike would be pounded and shattered. And then he had been hurled free. Something had struck him painfully in the back, and his body had bounced about like a ball. Sparks had exploded in his face, and a bitter, pungent smell had struck his nostrils. Somebody had let out a piercing scream. He remembered nothing after that.

The strength was drained from his body, and every part of it ached. He felt something wet and slippery rolling down his face. The arm of his jacket was torn as though slashed with a razor, and his shirt and even his undershirt were ripped in the same way. Blood flowed down his bare arm. The left leg of his pants hung in shreds from the knee down. His shin was covered with abrasions. Oppressed by his weight of pain, he groaned instinctively. Then his heart began to beat at an alarming rate, growing gradually more intense until his ears were ringing.

Just as he was coming out of the grove, Yamazaki felt his legs giving way beneath him, and he fell to his knees. Sweat rolled down his body. His breathing became painful, and he felt a dizziness taking hold of him. Then the whining roar in his ears gradually subsided, and the cries of distraught men and women came to him from a distance like ripples striking his ear. He took two or three deep breaths, and his head cleared at last.

Here beneath the trees of the Outer Garden, thousands of people had already come together. Sometimes the glare of some blaze shone through the trees to light with a dim glow the chaos of this terrible night.

"All of downtown is gone!" somebody shouted. "Akasaka and Shibuya, too. Aoyama is going to be next."

"Tokyo Bay is a sea of flames, I tell you." This last was said in low and hurried tones by somebody passing by. "From Tsukiji to Shinagawa . . . the whole area . . . and the Ginza, too—all wiped out."

Feeling the pain in his leg, Yamazaki got to his feet. Suddenly he began to worry about his family. His weary, grumbling wife . . . his pimply-faced oldest son, who had let his hair grow womanlike in keeping with the latest fad . . . and then his older daughter, who resembled neither of her parents and whose strikingly beautiful face gave him all the more cause for concern now that she was growing into adolescence, and his younger daughter, somewhat retarded because of a mild case of polio . . .

"Excuse me a minute, please," said Yamazaki to a passing stranger. "Have they got the trains going again?"

"The trains?" the stranger burst out, his voice harsh. "Why, the tracks are twisted like pretzels. And then there've been landslides and everything. Why, at Shibuya . . . when a train packed with people was leaving the station, and just as it was starting to move, it jumped the elevated tracks. There're bodies everywhere. I've just seen it with my own eyes."

"It's horrible on the expressways," somebody said in a high-pitched, tearful voice. "In Kasumigaseki it's horrible. In the tunnel there . . ."

"What are the police doing anyway?" asked somebody else. "Where are they? Any other time you'd see them all over the place."

Suddenly there was a loud, joyful shout at the edge of the crowd. Yamazaki heard the sound of truck engines, and from beneath the trees the glaring beams of headlights lit the faces of those around him. Three trucks pulled up and stopped, and helmeted soldiers in khaki uniforms began to jump down.

"Ladies and gentlemen, we're a relief squad of the Ground-Defense Force," a loudspeaker announced. "Are there any injured among you in need of immediate attention? We'll take charge of them at once. As for those of you who can walk, please proceed to the gymnasiums and indoor pool at Yoyogi. Emergency relief stations have been set up. Please remain calm and maintain your normal behavior. The earthquake is over with. As for the fire, due measures are being taken. It's too early to say how soon rail service can be restored, but engineer battalions of the Ground Defense Force are laboring right now to open the lines leading from Tokyo to each outlying area."

"Can you take us home?" somebody yelled. "My family's in Mitaka. They're worrying."

"Any time now transportation units should be arriving over by Yoyogi Sports Center. So please go to the Sports Center. Only, ladies and gentlemen, because there will be such a crush of people, please stay calm and don't get excited. At the Sports Center there should be news available about the damage sustained in each district and about the resumption of travel. As much food and drink as possible has been prepared there. So, calmly, orderly, proceed to the Sports Center, please. The troops will guide you there."

A searchlight went on, sending a stir through the crowd. They had yearned so much for light that now that they had it they were uncertain as to whether they could trust it. By the light spilling from the searchlight, Yamazaki studied the face of the officer talking to the crowd. His intrepid face was sunburned, and his cheeks were touched with an odd trace of childish innocence. From overhead came the whirring racket of a helicopter. A wind was beginning to rise. That helicopter will have a hard time of it, Yamazaki thought, as he glanced over his shoulder at the scarlet glow of the fiery destruction behind him.

Climbing black smoke covered the sky, lit by the baleful glare of the flames. Thunderous booms, probably exploding petroleum tanks, shook the sky again and again.

Suddenly Yamazaki found himself reliving an old memory. During the war . . . the night of the great raid on Tokyo . . . He had been in his late teens then. The night that his neighborhood in Shinagawa had been burned out, the night that his mother and his younger brother had died. The heavy, listless feeling he had felt then came back to him all at once, the mood that had gripped him that night when he had stood straight up, not going down into the shelter, watching the heavy rain of incendiaries and the fiery chaos around him—a sullen mood, a sense of helpless frustration . . . Since that long-ago night, Tokyo had expanded to a city of fabulous proportions. The destruction must be incredible, Yamazaki thought. If the oil floating on Tokyo Bay took fire, there would be a dreadful holocaust. And even after the destruction had been checked, civil paralysis, given the incredibly complex system of metropolitan government, might persist for a long period. Disorder could spread throughout the whole country.

What a situation, thought Yamazaki, dragging his leg painfully as he walked in the midst of the now-moving crowd. If the Cabinet should fall in the near future . . .

Black specks and white specks fluttered in the air, lit by the beam of the searchlight. Yamazaki looked up. In the lead-colored sky a seemingly infinite number of black spots danced in the wind, blown along across the sky like a million flickering bat wings.

"Ashes are falling," muttered an old man next to Yamazaki. "We'll get soaked. It always happens. There'll be rain. After a big fire there's always rain. Isn't that right? That's the way it was during the big raids."

Yamazaki felt a drop strike his cheek from the shower that was indeed beginning. In a corner of his overburdened mind, he gloomily considered the future of Plan D. If the Cabinet should fall, what in the world would they be able to do then?

2

At eleven that same night, the *Yoshino* passed through the Uraga Channel. Those on board had already seen from afar the fiery destruction raging along the Sagami Bay shoreline while the *Yoshino* was approaching the Miura Peninsula, but when the ship entered the channel, the salt breeze carried a peculiar, undefined stench. When they were passing Cap Kannon, the rain, which had been intermittent till then, suddenly began to fall in sheets, and little could be made out. Yet Onodera could see from the bridge the flames rising from underground storage tanks, glowing with a deep scarlet intensity like the fires of hell.

"Tokyo is burning," muttered Kataoka, who was standing beside Onodera at the end of the bridge. "Kawasaki, too, and Chiba . . ."

"I guess the tidal waves hit about three hours ago," said Onodera, pulling the hood of his raincoat tighter about his head. "The damage must be terrible."

The *Yoshino* was proceeding at a reduced speed of seven to eight knots. A steam whistle echoed in the midst of the rain.

Flames shot suddenly upward at a point either in Kawasaki or Yokohama, probably from exploding tanks, and the noise was like the rumbling of the bowels of the earth.

"What an awful stench," said Nakata, frowning and wrinkling up his nose, wet from the rain. "I imagine we'll put in at Yokosuka. The city is probably in chaos, but they say that it would be dangerous to go too far north. Because of poisonous gas, heavy oil fires, and wreckage from the tidal waves."

Peering down at the dark surface of the sea, Onodera realized that for some time they had been surrounded by all sorts of floating objects. Crates, tatami mats, oil drums, planks of wood, shattered fragments of every kind, and what looked like corpses.

"Off the port bow—something adrift!" shouted the watch at the bow.

A searchlight flashed on. There was a groaning roar set up by the front screw, and the *Yoshino* suddenly veered to one side. A derelict of some thousands of tons passed closely on the port side, nearly submerged, its capsized hull just above the surface.

From out of the rain and darkness came a faint cry.

"On the starboard bow—man in the water!" Again the watch's voice sounded through the rain.

"Reverse engines!" the captain ordered, speaking into the intercom in a low voice. "Lower a starboard lifeboat. Pick the fellow up."

While the boat was being lowered with a clattering noise, the glaring beam of the searchlight turned to the right and probed the water, but there was nothing to be seen on the surface of the sea lashed by the rain.

"Up ahead there's a lot of derelict ships," said the navigator, studying the radar screen. "Probably fishing boats and lighters smashed by the tidal waves."

"The lifeboat is coming back," called a sailor from the end of the bridge.

"How'd you do? Did you find him?" somebody shouted over the rail.

"We got him," a sailor answered. "The only thing is he's out of his head."

"Professor Tadokoro," said Onodera, turning around to where Tadokoro stood behind him, wearing not even a raincoat. "The whole coastline around the bay seems to have been badly hit. It looks like the Tokyo waterfront has been wiped out."

"That's jumping to conclusions," muttered Tadokoro as the rain beat against his unshaven face. "To say that now would be jumping to conclusions."

"How are they at home, I wonder?" said Kataoka absently. "I live in Tamachi."

That night of fire and destruction and tidal waves, of inky black rain came to an end with clear skies at dawn, but the fearful aftermath of a city in ruins remained. Fires still burned along the shore. Black smoke, spreading out like a gigantic sea monster, hung low over the bay.

Onodera left Yokosuka in a helicopter, accompanying Tadokoro and Yukinaga, who had been summoned by the Prime Minister. He looked out the window, his eyes fixed upon the frightful scene below. In Yokohama, Kawasaki, and in Tokyo itself, thin smoke still rose here and there. Beneath a blue autumn sky in which floated high, fleecy tufts of cloud, an eerie quiet lay over that vast population center, the home of more than twenty percent of the Japanese. Aside from the fires still burning along the shoreline, the scene at first glance seemed little out of the ordinary. But when Onodera looked down more intently, the whole panorama of ruin slipped into view, the terrible aftermath of that swift rush of fiery disaster. The packed-together houses lay half in ruins, and burned-out sections, like frightful black blotches, spread out in every direction. In the center of the city, however, the large buildings had come through surprisingly well, despite being cracked and tilted.

"Chiyoda Ward seems to be in pretty good shape," said Onodera. "Look! There's a train running on the Yokohama Line."

Beneath a clear autumn sky, Tokyo had begun to come alive once more. A fleet of bulldozers was already at work beginning to clear away the shattered ruins. Large trucks, probably loaded with relief materials, were streaming into Tokyo. And in the opposite direction moved military trucks and buses loaded with commuters who had finally been given the means of returning home. The Japanese, it seems, are on intimate terms with disaster, Onodera said to himself, feeling tears come to his eyes. Such was the surprised observation recorded by a German visitor to Japan in the middle of the nineteenth century, who had seen the great fires that ravaged Edo and then heard the ring of hammers as the people who had lost their homes to the flames cheerfully started to rebuild without sparing a sigh of distress, even while the fires still smoldered.

This time, however, the scale of destruction was overwhelming. Even allowing for the "traditional" reaction, once the full extent of the disaster became known, and once it became necessary to confront the major problems that would stem from it, what, finally, would be the outcome? Still more—suppose *on top of all this . . .*

"The government has come out with an interim report," said Yukinaga, his ear to the radio. "The dead—estimated at more than two million. The total amount of damage is expected to surpass one billion yen."

"What's that?" muttered Onodera, who had noticed from time to time something shiny falling from the windows of tall buildings.

"Even after the earthquake is over, the glass will come loose and fall out like that, given some tremor or other," answered Tadokoro, looking straight ahead. "The same thing happened at the time of the Peru earthquake. People would have their heads slashed by glass like that and die long after the quake was over."

3

When Nakata, Yukinaga, Onodera, and Yamazaki entered the Executive Building, which housed the Prime Minister's Office, everything was in disorder, with all sorts of people hurrying up and down the corridors.

Nakata turned to Yamazaki and asked: "Have you been in contact with our patron?"

"Yes . . . finally," answered Yamazaki in a weary voice. His tie was crumpled and his collar dirty. He had aged greatly in a short time. His unshaven cheeks were hollow, and there were wrinkles around his eyes. Besides having suffered the ordeal of the earthquake, he held himself responsible for the severe injuries suffered by young Yasukawa, who had been found in a temporary hospital. "Mr. Watari's in Hakone. Kunieda is with him."

"Good. Professor Tadokoro should go to see him. He's wasting his time trying to corner the Prime Minister in the midst of all this disorder."

"In any case, it looks like we'll have to close up shop for a while, doesn't it?" Yamazaki asked as he opened the door of the small room that had been set aside for Plan D.

"You think so?" Nakata said dryly.

"Well, with everything up in the air the way it is, we couldn't expect to accomplish anything for the time being, could we? And then, besides, even if it happens, it wouldn't be for some time, would it? Say for four or five years or even longer?"

"It's hard to say," Nakata said quietly. "According to a very rough calculation, it could happen that D would equal two."

"Equal two?" asked Yamazaki, his jaw dropping. "Two years? Are you sure?"

"Yes. If worse comes to worst."

Yamazaki looked at the three of them, his face haggard. He shook his head. "That's hard to believe. . . . Well, at any rate, make yourself at home. I can't offer you tea because of this chaos. How about a glass of water?"

"Never mind," said Nakata with a laugh. "The thing I'm concerned about is for you to think about getting in touch somehow with the old Mr. Watari in Hakone."

"We don't have a car, and anyway gasoline rationing is really stiff," Yamazaki answered as he threw himself into a chair in front of the desk. "Somehow, I just can't believe it," he went on as he looked out the window. "Could something like that really take place? This thing . . . couldn't it be nothing more than the delusion of a senile old man and a scientist a little touched in the head?"

"I suppose we've all wondered that," said Nakata. He paused for a moment. "I'm afraid it's really going to happen."

"Well, if so . . . what then? There are a hundred million Japanese, you know."

"Most of them might die," said Nakata. "And why? Precisely because nobody is going to believe that such a thing could happen. We ourselves are of two minds, and we're up to our neck in it. And in the midst of the will-it-or-will-it-not, maybe-so-maybe-no debate, time is slipping away. And the longer the delay, the greater the number of those who will die."

"You don't seem to have any hope," said Yamazaki in a low voice.

"Oh, I can hope as well as the next man. I hope that there's some equilibrium process at work unknown to us, something that will prevent this from happening, or something, at least, that will greatly lessen its impact. But in the meantime we've got to act as though it is going to happen, so that we can save as many as possible." Nakata smiled ruefully. "I have no desire to be vindicated as a prophet. If this thing happens, it will be pure hell, and there's no point in putting on prophetic airs in hell."

Yamazaki crushed out his cigarette. "I've got a wife and children," he said in a hoarse voice. "I wonder what you people think . . . about your families, I mean. If only somebody would take the initiative . . ."

When they arrived at Hakone, it was already the middle of the night. The roads were damaged so severely and the traffic jams had been so fearful that they had been able to average no more than six miles an hour.

A small, almost hidden private road wound through the cryptomeria forest at a point midway between Ubako and Gojiri Pass. As the car was climbing the steep, winding road, a one-story house came into view. A brushwood fence surrounded it, and an air of stillness hung over it. The car stopped beside a gate crowned with a crossbeam. And after someone had gotten out and announced their presence into an interphone, it swung open by remote control. The Oribe votive lanterns in the garden lay overturned. Their stone caps had left gouges in the mossy ground.

The old man was sitting by himself in a rather small room ten mats in size, his legs covered by a quilt concealing a foot-warmer. A cushion seat covered with purple figured silk supported his back. He wore a sleeveless padded robe of dark brown over a fine kimono of Yuki pongee. Around his neck a wide scarf of white linen was loosely wrapped. His solitary figure with its bent back looked small and shriveled. His eyes, sheltered by the white brows above, were closed, and he seemed to be dozing.

Their party of five, including Tadokoro, knelt by the doorway, but Watari gave no sign that he had noticed, merely nodding as though in his sleep.

"Well, Hakone is cold, as usual," said Tadokoro in a loud, heedless voice, very much in character, as he got to his feet and strode boldly into the room. His greasy socks were baggy at the toes, and they made a floppy sound upon the tatami floor.

A faultlessly groomed girl, dressed in a short Chichibu Meisen kimono too sober for her age, invited them to take places around a huge quilt-covered foot-warmer. Her hair, so thick as to be unruly, was gathered in back. The eyes, set in a face showing no trace of cosmetics, were large. She was tall, and her firm mouth gave her a formidable air. When she happened to laugh, however, one caught a glimpse of dimples and a single crooked tooth which seemed altogether becoming, and her expression became one of artless innocence.

"You've taken a little punishment, I see," said Tadokoro, stretching his neck as he looked at the alcove behind the old man. Up where the ancient alcove posts of cryptomeria from the northern mountains joined the ceiling, raw cracks ran along the wall, and sand had spilled down upon the alcove step of black persimmon.

Yukinaga, noticing the Southern Sung painting that hung in the alcove, spoke abruptly. "I believe that's a Tanomura Chokunyu, is it not?"

"Very perceptive," said Watari, his voice hoarse as he laughed. "But it happens to be an imitation. Well done, isn't it? Do you like the Southern School? What about Tessai?"

"No, I don't care much for him."

"I see. Well, I'm not too fond of him myself. At my age, that sort of style becomes tedious, you see."

The young girl came in with tea, pointing her white tabi-shod feet gracefully as she walked. How like a Noh actor, thought Yukinaga as he watched her.

In the teacups that she distributed, instead of ordinary tea there was a beverage in which lay a single brownish leaf of some sort of plant.

It's an orchid, thought Onodera as he took a sip. Through the steam that rose from the cup, he gazed absently at the scarlet color of the maple leaves in the Mosochiku vase that stood in the alcove.

"Well, then," said the old man, coughing faintly, "how do things stand, Professor Tadokoro?"

"That's why we're here, sir," said Tadokoro, leaning forward.

"As far as the Tokyo disaster goes, I'm well informed."

"I expected that," answered Tadokoro, gulping down the rest of his orchid tea. "The way I see things now is exactly in line with what I told you before. We must by all means mount an investigation of still larger scope in order to get the facts more certainly in hand. The question is how are we going to accomplish that. And how, furthermore, are we going to broach our desire to the government?"

The old man, his wrinkled hand like a withered branch, gave the Rakuyake teacup a slight shake. The surface of the orchid tea trembled. His eyes were hidden, sunk deep within their sockets, and there was no way of knowing which way they were looking. He seemed to be staring with a child's detachment at the trembling liquid. Was he lost in thought, oblivious to everything? A silence came over the room, and Onodera became aware of a rustling from the dark forest outside. And farther off, the mountains themselves seemed to give off a faint, indistinct noise that was like a moan.

"From now on . . ." Nakata, urged by some impulse, suddenly spoke out, his voice little more than a whisper. "If we go on as we are, it's hopeless. If you say go on with the number of men we have now, using the means we have now, we'll go on . . . but it won't do much good. As the day approaches, of course, more and more people will become aware, but by then it will be too late."

The old man was still jiggling his teacup. A faint cough echoed from the throat covered with wrinkled folds. Everyone stared fixedly at the teacup.

"Professor Tadokoro," said the old man, raising his eyes and moving his head slightly to one side, "have you seen the flower in that vase there?"

Tadokoro raised his eyes. From one of the posts at the rear of the alcove hung a gourd vase. Within it was a small flower of vivid red, picked in full bloom and set off by two or three branches of dark green leaves.

"A Chinese camellia, isn't it?" muttered Tadokoro.

"That's right. Every bush is blooming with wild profusion. It seems to me, Professor, that nature is running wild in all sorts of ways in Japan this fall. A scientist looks at this, and perhaps it strikes him as not too significant. But as for me, I have lived with nature for one hundred years, and I can't escape the feeling that nature in Japan—plants and trees and birds and insects and fishes—all alike have grown fearful and have lost their composure."

The sound of quiet footsteps came down the corridor and stopped outside the door.

"Did you call, sir?" came a voice.

"Hanae," said the old man, "open the door, and then open the outside ones, too. All the way."

The inner door slid open. "But, sir," said the girl, her eyes wide, "it's really gotten rather cold."

"It doesn't matter. Open them."

The girl slid open the glass outer doors with a slight scraping noise. The chill of the autumn night in Hakone rushed into the room, which had no warmth of its own save that from the foot-warmers. There was a ghostly murmur of insects. Branches rustled in the pitch-black darkness of the grove of cryptomeria trees.

One could look beyond the garden and through the tree trunks down to where Lake Ashi lay. The moon of the seventeenth day of the month hung in the sky. The awesome, chill brilliance of its beams shattered itself upon the rippled surface of the water. The ring of peaks surrounding Hakone loomed up, linked together like a huge black screen touched by the light of the moon.

"Professor Tadokoro," said the old man in a voice of surprising strength, sounding behind them as they gazed out transfixed by the beauty of the scene. "Do you see? Take a good look. Take a good look at the mountains and lakes of Japan. As you know, Japan is large. From southwest to northeast it extends nearly 1,700 miles. It has islands large and small. It has ranges of mountains with peaks over 9,000 feet. The extent of its land is 142,000 square miles. And here live 110 million people whose gross national product ranks third in the world. This Japan, this massive group of islands—do you still think, really, even now, that it will sink? Do you really believe, even now, that such a thing could occur in the very near future—the swift submersion of all this?"

"I . . ." Tadokoro spoke as though heaving a deep sigh. "Yes

. . . I do believe it. And our next survey will deepen that belief still more."

Onodera felt his chest tremble as he gazed at the mountains bathed in the light of a moon just short of being full, and at the dark, brimming surface of the lake, over which that same brilliance was scattered in a thousand silver waves. The sensation was uncanny.

"Very well," said the old man's voice. "That's what I wanted to hear. Hanae, that's enough. Shut the doors."

Looking up at the moon, whose brightness in that cloudless sky was almost painful, Onodera suddenly frowned. For the ring of brilliance that surrounded the moon sailing through a clear sky suddenly wavered as though a wave of heat had covered it. And then he realized that the chirping of insects had stopped. Even the rustle of the wind in the trees had grown quiet, as though every breeze had died.

Suddenly there came the shrill cry of night birds from the midst of the dark forest, a distressed chorus that sounded on every side. Nearer at hand, on the shore of the lake, dogs began to howl and roosters to crow.

"It's coming, you see," whispered Tadokoro.

Before he pronounced his last word, the mountains and forests spread before them began to rumble. Tiles trembled. The posts and lintels began to creak and moan, till finally the whole house began to vibrate loudly and the lights went out. The furniture rattled, sand fell from the wall with a dry rustling noise, and there was the light sound of something spilling over the tatami. The girl gave a frightened cry.

"Don't worry. It's just an aftershock. Hakone and Tanazawa, after sinking a bit, are now coming up somewhat to restore the balance. It's nothing of significance." Tadokoro's composed voice spoke in the darkness. "This isn't what we have to worry about."

Before they realized it, the quake was over. The whole group sat in silence within the darkened room, looking out upon the night scene of the bright moon shining down upon the shimmering, tranquil surface of Lake Ashi as though nothing had happened. The moon was rising higher and higher, and its pale brilliance covered an ever larger portion of the tatami floor.

"Nakata . . . that was the name, wasn't it? The young fellow

who said something a moment ago," came the old man's voice
from the darkness behind them.

"Yes, sir," Nakata answered.

"Do you have a fair idea of what has to be done with regard
to this next stage?"

"I have a plan in mind, sir," said Nakata, altogether composed. "It's not yet complete in all respects, but I have the
general scheme laid out."

"Good. Get it in final order as quickly as possible. Tomorrow
I'm going to phone the Prime Minister. I want to meet with
him. And furthermore, tomorrow I want somebody to go to
Kyoto. Two of you go. In Kyoto there's a scholar named
Fukuhara. He's still very young, but I know from reading his
writings that he's genuine, a true scholar. Take him a letter
from me. I'll explain the circumstances and ask for his cooperation. Tomorrow I'll tell you what to say. It's essential that we get
the benefit of his thinking on this matter. The scholars of Tokyo,
if you'll pardon me, have from long past shown a propensity for
fads and an incapacity to think their way through complex
problems."

"Fukuhara . . ." said Yukinaga in a low voice. "He's in compar-
ative civilization, isn't he? Have you known him for some time,
sir?"

"I've never met him," said the old man, coughing slightly.
"But we've exchanged one or two letters. I'm sure he'll be
receptive to us."

A light shone from the crack in the doorway at the rear of the
room. The door slid open, and the girl came in holding an
old-fashioned lamp.

"Oh, my!" she said frowning. "The camellia . . ."

In the pale yellow circle of light cast by the old lamp, the tiny
flower, fallen from the alcove post, lay like a spot of vivid color
on the tatami, red as blood.

The next morning Onodera left for Kyoto with Kunieda, carrying Watari's letter. The Super Express was in operation west
of Shizuoka, but because of the precautions that had to be observed, it took more than three hours to get from there to the
express terminal in Osaka.

As he stood swaying back and forth in the jammed aisle, a

sensation hard to define suddenly took hold of Onodera when he noticed that the train was crossing the Tenryu River. It was just a year ago that he had run into Goh at that water fountain near the rear entrance of Tokyo Station.

Now, as he thought back, he realized that that was when everything had started. He had not had the least idea at that moment what the future held in store for Japan or that he himself would become caught up in this kind of mission. A sense of secrecy and peril weighed upon him with oppressive force.

Osaka had almost entirely recovered from the effects of the great earthquake of the year before, but in Kyoto there was no way of missing the devastation evident in Gion, Ponto-cho, and the other districts making up the old Gay Quarters, which were the heart of the city, and in the close-packed downtown areas wracked by quake and fire.

When they arrived at the professor's house in the northern part of the city, they learned that he had become somewhat ill the day before and had not gone out since. When he appeared in the parlor, wearing a pongee haori jacket, he seemed so youthful, with his boyish face and with no trace of gray in his hair, that Onodera, who knew that he was over fifty, would have had a difficult time guessing his age.

Professor Fukuhara read the old man's letter again and again, his head tipped to one side, and Onodera and Kunieda, in turn, explained the situation to him. All the while he pursed his lips and finally uttered but a single phrase: "My, what an awful thing . . ."

And with that he got up at once and walked out of the parlor. Thirty minutes passed, then an hour, and still there was no sign of the professor. Their legs aching from being bent so long beneath them on the tatami floor, Onodera and Kunieda called the maid to find out what happened.

"The master is lying down upstairs," was the answer she gave them.

"What the devil! This is what you call a Kyoto scholar? Making fools of us like this?" said the furious Kunieda. "We come all the way from Tokyo to tell him this, and all he can do is say 'My, what an awful thing!' and go up to take a nap."

V

The Sinking Country

1

In a room in the Prime Minister's residence, which still showed the effects of the earthquake, three men sat around a table with somber expressions: the Prime Minister, his face worn and haggard; the secretary general of the Cabinet; and its director general. On the table lay a single sheet of paper upon which was written:

$$\min$$
$$D \doteq 2$$

"It's altogether ridiculous," said the director general, rubbing his face vigorously with a thick hand. "If it were true, it would be terrible, of course. But it's an absurd mistake, a fantasy of that eccentric scientist Tadokoro."

The secretary general eyed the Prime Minister shrewdly. He was like a foster son to him, and, a graduate of the same high school, he had come a long way with him down the road of politics. From the first, the secretary general had been bedeviled in this affair by the dread that this man who held the chief responsibility in the nation might, by some mental lapse, have become entangled in a great hoax and be on the way to a misstep from which there could be no recovery. Up to this point it had been possible to keep things concealed, and if the affair had taken a suspicious turn, it could easily have been hushed up. But from now on . . . should things advance to the next stage, then in terms of budget, in terms of organization, the affair would begin to take on a scale that would attract public notice. And then should something go wrong, the question of political responsibility might well be raised. The least blunder might prove fatal, not only to the Prime Minister but also to the party.

"The investigations haven't yet enabled us to come up with an unqualified answer," said the Prime Minister, unfolding his arms and raising his head. "So let us go on with them. The budget, the personnel needs are going to increase considerably, of course. And what are we going to do then?"

The Prime Minister's words by themselves indicated nothing more than a prudent continuation along roughly the same lines, but the secretary general caught his breath. Oh-oh—he's finally made up his mind, he thought. He intends to move ahead, no matter what. He'll even risk political suicide.

"I don't think there'll be too much of a problem," answered the director general, his big body rocking as he nodded. "The secretariat meeting is tomorrow."

"Good enough." The Prime Minister stood up. He took a bottle and three glasses from a shelf. "I'm a little tired," he said, pouring out some cognac for the others and himself. "Should we take this up again tomorrow?"

"Fine," said the director general, nodding as he took up his glass. "It would be good to get a little rest. What I have to say can wait till tomorrow."

The three men raised their glasses in silence. The director general, whose huge frame was like that of a professional wrestler, downed his at a gulp. He got to his feet, bowed to the Prime Minister, and turned toward the door. The secretary general was right behind him a moment later, and the Prime Minister, too, rose to follow. As they walked down the corridor, with the director general a few paces ahead, the secretary general turned and whispered to the Prime Minister: "A change in the Cabinet?"

Caught somewhat off guard, the Prime Minister studied the face of his keenly perceptive confidant.

"Once the turmoil dies down," the Prime Minister whispered, his face rigid. "In some respects, the earthquake is a good opportunity, I think."

After the two Cabinet members had left, the Prime Minister returned to the parlor and poured himself another cognac. After the earthquake he had sent his family to Shinshu, and now in the huge house there was no one besides himself but a middle-aged maid, a steward to attend to his personal needs, and his bodyguards. Since even from this group no one was ever much in evidence, the interior of the residence was as quiet as though he were there by himself.

Things have come to a strange pass, he thought. As he felt the effect of the brandy lessening his fatigue, the Prime Minister raised his forefinger and rubbed his right eye. Then he closed his eyes, and a sense of weariness suddenly bore down on him from behind. He felt as though he were being dragged down into the depths.

The physical obliteration of a nation great in size, in economic power, and in historical tradition . . . Had an event so incredible ever occurred before? Had any politician ever been faced with a problem of such vast proportions?

The Prime Minister gazed absently into space as he gently jiggled his brandy glass. Had he the strength to steer a way through this peril? Should he perhaps give way to someone else? He downed his cognac abruptly. For the present there *was* no one else, he decided. When the situation grew more critical, perhaps a man might come to the fore and distinguish himself, someone more capable than he to deal with this crisis. But since that time had not yet come nor that man appeared, he had no choice but to carry on, to make the painful, frightening series of decisions. How odd, he thought. He had never detected any impulse toward the heroic in himself, neither before nor now. Furthermore, like all his colleagues, he held as an implicit article of faith that the politician's role was not to *do* but to *let become*. Political acts, after all, were but a portion of the great stream of fate.

Now, however, confronted with so perilous and complex a crisis, the Prime Minister found himself profoundly disturbed. He had always thought of courage as nothing more than a marginal necessity, but now it seemed an indispensable component of judgment.

To go somewhere for a day or two, even in the midst of his work, he thought, gazing at his brandy glass. To meditate in the Zen manner . . . so as to quiet the spirit and see beyond the darkness ahead . . . To consult with the old man . . .

2

Winter descended upon a Tokyo still bearing the raw claw marks of disaster. At the year's end, like another blow following upon that of the quake, a cold wave hit.

Onodera, the collar of his overcoat up, was walking from Tameike toward Toranomon as a powdery snow fluttered down from a frozen sky. He intended to stop at the Prime Minister's Office and then go to the Maritime Safety Agency, but he ran into a milling crowd by the Diet Building, the first large-scale demonstration since the disaster. In one place a clash had already broken out between students and riot police. To avoid the crowd, he decided to cut in front of the patent office and take a detour by way of Kasumigaseki.

The universities had been relatively undamaged, and the greater number of them had reopened. They still were being used to some degree, however, to house refugees, and since many of the faculty had been killed or injured in the earthquake, many classes were canceled. A number of boardinghouses had been destroyed, and many students had returned to their homes after the quake. As a consequence, then, although the traditional paraphernalia was in evidence—helmets, masks, long poles—the students were few and their spirit was not robust. Nevertheless, workers and ordinary citizens were also involved, and since there were never lacking some willing to take on the police, two or three struggles had broken out. Though no one threw any Molotov cocktails, they hurled chunks of concrete and bricks from destroyed buildings. Finally the riot police charged and scattered the demonstrators.

More than the students, the dark, somber mood of the ordinary people who had silently joined in with them unsettled Onodera. "Give us houses!" "Throw open your buildings!" "Money enough for refugees to get through the winter!" The faces beneath these signs seemed dark and shrunken from the cold, and a strange anxiety seemed to hover over them.

Maybe, Onodera thought, these people sense something.

It was as though a kind of darkness floated above the heads of the demonstrators, colored by a desperate anxiety that the eye could not perceive. As though it spoke of a people once determined to do great things who had lost their will to act.

As the demonstrators lowered the placards with the violent slogans, their sullen faces conveyed an anxiety to Onodera, like a kind of ill omen. People, of course, never took at face value the daily headlines—"A Great Depression Coming?" "Black Market Price of Fresh Foods up 40%, Fear of Food Crisis Next Spring"—but now, more than ever, they were on their guard.

We're a sensitive people, thought Onodera as he passed the lines of demonstrators moving the other way. And he himself felt what they did, his skin prickling. All at once a painful sensation struck his chest. Suppose, he thought, suppose these people, who, on the one hand, have no definite information but who, on the other, are becoming ever more perceptive in the way they feel . . . suppose they learned of this thing, this thing which now stands a better than fifty-percent chance of occurring . . . what would happen? Would a great panic break out?

In a room at the Maritime Safety Agency, Onodera met Kataoka, who had arrived there just before him. The round, boyish, sunburned face of Kataoka had changed terribly in a very short time. He did not show his white teeth nor flash the bright smile that once had appeared so often. His eyes were without expression in a face that showed fatigue, its features somewhat blurred. He seemed to have aged ten years. Like all the members of the Plan D group, he was suffering from overwork, but more than that . . . the death of his entire family in Tamachi had crushed his high spirits, apparently forever.

"Did you run into the demonstration?" Kataoka asked in a listless voice.

Onodera nodded.

"It seems that lately the reporters are starting to get wind of things," said Kataoka almost in a whisper as he gazed at the snow piled on the window ledge outside. "Today one of them came to the Defense Agency. He's never talked to anybody of importance connected with Plan D, of course, but they say they had a hard time getting rid of him at the public-relations office."

"That looks bad," Onodera muttered. "What put him on to the Defense Agency, I wonder?"

"He probably saw Professor Yukinaga and Professor Tadokoro there. He knows who Professor Yukinaga is. And then with his suddenly leaving the university like that . . ."

"Kunieda told me something in confidence," Onodera said. "Tonight the secretary general is having a quiet meeting with a group of major newspaper publishers. And then there seems to be in the offing a highly secret conference between the Prime Minister and the leaders of the opposition."

"But how much is going to be held back?" asked Kataoka in a flat voice. "Weird rumors are cropping up everywhere. And with more people getting involved in Plan D every day, the greater the chance of leaks. By the way, how about that scholar from Kyoto they brought in? Fukuhara?"

"He's at the old man's place in Hakone."

"And what's he occupied with?"

"Well, I'm not sure, but—" Onodera smiled ruefully— "Kunieda was a bit perturbed. He told me that he did nothing but sleep all day."

The door opened, and the assistant director of the Hydrographic Bureau came in.

"Hello . . . sorry to keep you waiting," he said. He laid some papers on the table. "All the arrangements are made. At eighteen o'clock tomorrow, the *Seiryu Maru* will arrive at Yokosuka."

"Thanks," said Onodera, taking the papers. "Then, some time the day after, we can have our equipment and personnel on board."

"And as it turned out," the assistant director went on, "we were able to charter the sea lab and the submarine from a Japanese firm."

"A Japanese firm!" said Onodera. "What firm is it?"

"Sea Floor Development. The sub is the *Wadatsumi 2.*"

Just as Onodera and Kataoka were leaving the Maritime Safety Agency, a man struck Onodera a hard blow on the chest. Stopped in his tracks, the startled Onodera saw a short, dark man blocking his way, eyes blazing with anger. The next instant a fist struck his left cheek with a flat thump. And then a third blow landed solidly on the right side of his nose.

"What do you think you're doing!" shouted Kataoka, reaching for the man's arm.

"It's all right, Kataoka. Let him alone!" cried Onodera as still more punches struck home. "Take the papers and go ahead. It's all right, I tell you!"

Since there were people all about, Onodera retreated to a
place at the side of the building, taking punches all the while.
Out of the corner of his eye, he saw Kataoka glancing back over
his shoulder as he walked away. Punches struck his eye, the
bridge of his nose, his chest, his throat until finally Onodera
stumbled over something and went sprawling backward.

"Get up, damn you!"

The short man stood with his legs spread, his breath racing.

"Well, Yuki . . . it's nice to see you again," said the supine
Onodera as blood gushed from his nose. "How have you been?"

He felt the chill of the frozen ground penetrating his back.
He watched the dark snowflakes falling like motes of dust from
the gray sky. The shock of Yuki's blows seemed to be stirring a
long-absent sense of vigor.

"You bastard!" said Yuki, breathing fiercely as he looked
down on Onodera. "Quitting without a word to me . . . without
a word! Running off to another company!"

As Onodera got to his feet unsteadily, Yuki pulled a crumpled
handkerchief from his pants pocket and thrust it close to
Onodera's nose. Onodera, opening his swelling right eye, took
the dirty handkerchief with a smile.

"You bastard! All you had to do was say one lousy word! I
thought . . . I thought first that you were missing in the earthquake. I was upset. I went to Kyoto a few times. And then when
I heard that you deserted the company without any explanation, I tried to get in touch with you time after time. But you
wouldn't give me any answer at all, not a word. You clear out
and you don't think about your friend at all!"

"I'm sorry," said Onodera, laying his hands firmly on the
shoulders of Yuki, who was a head shorter than he. "It was
inexcusable. I did get your notes, but at that time the situation
was such that I couldn't get in touch with anybody."

"You're going to dive in the *Wadatsumi,* right?" said Yuki, his
eyes averted. "Somebody I know saw you hanging around here
lately, and then he said that the Defense Agency put in a rush
order for the *Wadatsumi.* And so I thought I'd come over for
a look." He hesitated for a moment. "You know what I'm going
to do? I'm going down in the *Wadatsumi* too. I made up my
mind to quit like you did."

"What?" said Onodera. "Have you submitted your resignation already?"

"Tomorrow. I made up my mind. Listen, without us two together, how are they going to get the most out of that sub? One of us has got to be manning that phone up on the ship."

"Thank you," said Onodera spontaneously. In that instant he, too, made up his mind. Himself, Yuki—they made a fine team. He could depend upon him.

"Well, great! It's settled, then," said Yuki with a sheepish look as he withdrew the hand that Onodera had grasped firmly a moment before. Then a broad, happy grin split his features. "The two of us are going to be together again." Suddenly he seemed to recall something: "Say, do you know some girl named Reiko, I think? She's been at the office looking for you."

3

Onodera heard the news of the Hachijojima eruption submerged at a depth of 6,000 feet at a spot in the ocean about thirty miles northwest of Torishima. The message came by phone from the *Yoshino* at the surface, and because of noise he had difficulty understanding it. He was able to hear that the eruption had already claimed many victims among the island's population of 12,000. And even as he received the message from the *Yoshino* 6,000 feet above, he felt a shock strike the *Kermadic*. The ascent that followed was a hazardous one, and when the derrick from the *Yoshino* had finally secured the *Kermadic*, Onodera saw that the surface of the sea was covered with pumice stone.

"Koshu blew, they say," said one of the deck crew. "Some fishing boats got damaged a little. Imagine something like that erupting!"

"It looks as though we ought to get out of here as quick as we can," said Onodera, wiping off his face with a towel. "Something's stirring down there."

"As soon as the recovery's finished, we're leaving," said the crewman.

Onodera was in the communication room drinking a cup of coffee when, the *Kermadic* secured, the *Yoshino* got under way, this time on a different course. Sailing northeast, it cut through the waves at full steam, leaving the dangerous sea area behind it.

"What's the Hachijo situation?" the technician who had been down with Onodera asked a radioman.

"They say that the Mount Nishi eruption killed two hundred people. And because they're afraid of a still bigger eruption, Defense Force and private ships both are being sent there to take the people off."

"The whole population?"

"Yes. It'll amount to twelve thousand in all. The whole island. They can't carry a thing with them. There are signs of eruptions on the other Izu Islands, too, and I understand that the people are being evacuated to Shizuoka."

"A Sea Defense Force anti-submarine patrol plane has landed in our area," said another operator. "It's going to take off right away. Then it's going to land beside us and pick up the data we've gathered, they say. They want us to guide them."

The communication officer sent a message to the bridge, and the captain instructed the radar room. The plane was soon picked up on the radar screen, and the communication room directed it to the *Yoshino*'s position.

"Mr. Onodera," said the operator in contact with the plane, "there's someone named Kataoka on the patrol plane. He says that he wants you to go back with them."

"Kataoka?" said Onodera, who was about to step out of the communication room.

Two or three crewmen ran past the door outside. Overhead the sound of motors was drawing closer. When Onodera stepped out upon the deck, the wind had grown stronger and the waves were covered with whitecaps. The four-motored flying boat began to make its descent extremely close to the ship.

Wearing a raincoat against the spray from the rough sea, Onodera got into a motor-driven rubber boat. It dipped so on the crossing that he had to cling to it to keep from being thrown out. He was covered with sweat by the time he climbed up into the plane. Once the documents had been transferred in a waterproof bag, the PS-1 began its takeoff run immediately. To Onodera it seemed as though it did no more than skip through two or three waves before the noise of the sea striking its hull was heard no more. Before he realized it, they were circling above the *Yoshino*.

On his way to the front of the plane along a rather narrow passageway packed with equipment, Onodera passed the radio room. There he saw Kataoka looking over the shoulder of a crewman. When he tapped him on the shoulder, Kataoka turned.

"Oh, hello," he said, nothing more, and then he went back to peering at the instruments the crewman was manning.

"That's what it is, all right," the crewman muttered. "A big sub. In the four-thousand-ton class . . . probably bigger."

"If it's four thousand tons, it has to be a nuclear submarine," said Kataoka, his voice dry and harsh. "It's following the *Yoshino*, I suppose. At 850 yards . . . very close."

"A submarine? Couldn't it be the *Uzushio?*" Onodera asked. "It's working with Plan D now, isn't it?"

"The *Uzushio?* It's by the Izu Peninsula now," said Kataoka. "Besides, it's too small. It's no more than 1,850 tons."

"I wonder what he's up to," said the crewman, twisting his head. "Is he spying on us?"

"He might be. It would be good to let the *Yoshino* know. Tell them it would be best to use only passive sonar and not tip their hand to the sub," said Kataoka.

"It looks as though there are a lot of countries interested in what we're doing," Onodera muttered.

"Off to port—volcanic smoke!" cried a voice over the speaker.

They rushed to the observation window. Blown by a strong west wind, clusters of white cloud seemed to dot the dark blue surface of the sea below. Farther ahead, like the genie of the lamp in the *Arabian Nights,* dark brown volcanic smoke poured up from a small spot in the sea and then swelled into a spreading cloud which climbed steadily higher into the sky until it had soared into a great column towering over even the cumulus clouds. The patrol plane was at 15,000 feet, and even here the air seemed to tremble slightly at each explosion that echoed from below. When Onodera peered intently downward, he could see red flame flickering in the midst of the smoke. Ash and pumice stone rained down, lashing the sea on the east side of the volcano, as though a curtain of gauze were hung there. And in the midst of the swelling column of swirling brown smoke darted flashes of lightning. Small tidal waves slowly spread outward in concentric circles.

"Is that Smith Reef?" asked Onodera.

"No. Aogashima," answered Kataoka. "Today's the second big eruption. And with that, almost the whole island went."

"Were there people on it?"

"About 270, I guess. Almost all of them died, they say. Some of them might have escaped in fishing boats, but it's not certain."

"What? They just let everybody die like that?"

"There were almost no ships in the area. According to the report of a passenger plane, the first eruption came just ten minutes after the island sent a message by wireless saying that there were signs of volcanic activity," Kataoka explained, not a trace of emotion in his voice. "Unlike Jogashima, Aogashima is very much out of the way."

How often was this to recur in time to come? Onodera wondered, feeling a chill gathering in his stomach. But on a scale thousands of times, millions of times as great as that of Aogashima.

"The entire Fuji volcanic belt is spouting fire," said Kataoka, frowning and indicating the sea below with his chin. "There've been chain eruptions there before now, but never to this degree. Oh-oh! Look—over there's the smoke from Hachijo."

The plane continued to climb, tipping its huge wings. Beyond the tip of the right one, more volcanic smoke was rising. And to the north of Jogashima there was still more.

"And over there?" asked Onodera, feeling his voice catch in his throat.

"Miyakejima. About two hours ago a series of eruptions began, running from Akabakyo to Oyama. The birds knew it. This year they didn't come back, apparently."

"I see," said Onodera softly, his tone as flat as Kataoka's now.

The PS-1 had reached an altitude of 25,000 feet and was still climbing. As they went farther north, the clouds began to thin out and the sea to glow with the clear beauty that it showed in winter in this latitude. The Izu Islands, stretching from north to south, lay scattered upon a dark blue ocean, filling Onodera's field of vision from the observation window from one end to another. From each of the five islands a plume of black smoke rose high up into the clear sky. Caught by the west wind, the murky columns trailed off to the east. It was as though a line of great battleships was steaming grandly toward the north.

But the smoke was not from gallant warships. The column of islands had been shattered by a terrible destructive force thrusting its way upward from beneath the sea. Thrashing about in its death throes, it was on the verge of going under.

Onodera instinctively shut his eyes. And when he opened them again, clouds had covered the ill-omened scene, and in front of him was Mount Fuji rising like a white phantom against the dark blue of the sky.

"Niigata—in the Tomiyama region—an earthquake," the speaker announced. "Medium intensity, its magnitude 7.0. Its epicenter forty miles north of Niigata. Depth thirty miles. A survey ship reported unusual elevation of the Yamato Rise."

"Now it's the Japan Sea coast, eh?" muttered Kataoka, glancing up at the speaker. "We're getting hit from both sides."

In the parlor of a villa belonging to a certain high government official, located in a suburb of Canberra called Red Hill, the Prime Minister of Australia had been sitting plunged in silence for nearly five minutes. His hairy hands, fingers linked, were thrust beneath his chin. The February heat was oppressive. And since the two other men present, the owner of the villa and a small, dark man, were also silent, the hum of a large air conditioner filled the room.

The Prime Minister began to tap his fingertips together, as though working to control something surging up within him. Then, like a huge tree being uprooted—he was more than six feet tall—he rose energetically from the low armchair in which he had been sitting. He linked his arms behind him and, keeping his eyes on the floor, walked slowly across the room. Then, hooking his thumbs behind the lapels of his coat, he turned toward his small-statured guest.

"Your story, Mr. Nozaki, is something to make the mind boggle. And the problem involved is a frightful one."

The Japanese was short and thin, and his hair was nearly white. The fine wrinkles in his face and at the corners of his eyes gave him a tranquil look. His eyes were extraordinarily bright. He had obtained a secret interview with the Prime Minister by going through the man who was their host. There were less than a handful of people in the entire Commonwealth who knew that the Prime Minister would never refuse a request from this particular official. The Prime Minister had no idea how Nozaki knew of this nor why this old man had been so anxious to see him.

"As I imagine you're well aware, the population of Australia has grown by nearly a million in the past ten years. It is now more than twelve million," said the Prime Minister, beginning to move across the carpet again.

"I realize that," said the old man, nodding, his bright eyes revealing nothing. "During the same period Japan experienced a population increase of some eight million. The total now stands at 110 million."

"Roughly ten times ours," said the Prime Minister, frowning.

"And in terms of population density, the rate is two hundred times that of your country."

"But you realize, of course, that more than seventy percent of that is barren desert."

The Prime Minister gathered his thoughts as he looked at the window. There was one topic that he now had no way of avoiding. A reddish moon had begun to rise in a dark blue sky, in which some trace of sunset lingered.

"Japan," the Prime Minister muttered as though to himself. "I have worked to make this continent a land open to the world, a land of promise. My father and my grandfather, however, were men who championed a 'White Australia,' " said the Prime Minister almost in a whisper as he took a cigar from his pocket and sniffed it. "At the beginning of this century, there was a gold rush in the North. Chinese laborers came pouring into the country. I don't think that my father and grandfather were outright racists by any means. Just consider the circumstances. Australia was a continent with nothing but kangaroos and aborigines, a continent to which criminals were banished. The whites shipped here raised sheep and cattle in the well-nigh unlimited open spaces, and bit by bit they developed areas in which a man could live decently. Now, these unruly and unsettled Chinese laborers were not the sort to fit into this kind of world. And this uneasy situation was aggravated still further by the Oriental-exclusion movement, which was then at its height throughout the world. Thus came about the immigration restrictions and a certain measure of tragedy."

The Prime Minister smiled wryly. He felt somewhat vexed toward this old man, Nozaki, who, almost without saying anything at all, had steered the conversation in this direction.

"So, then," said the Prime Minister, finally putting a match to his cigar, "what is the extent of what you wish?"

"The first stage, a million people," said the old man calmly. "For the future, should it be possible, we would like you to be kind enough to accept some five million."

The Prime Minister was silent for a long time. He inhaled to draw the match flame into the tip of his cigar. Five million people? That would be forty-five percent of the population of Australia. Australia would become more than one-third Oriental!

"A million—that's about nine percent of our population," said the Prime Minister, blowing out a huge cloud of smoke. "And that would be in . . . a two-year period?"

"Perhaps it might have to be quicker." For the first time a trace of something that might have been anxiety appeared on the old man's face. "If possible, we would like to begin bringing in the first contingent before the year is out—a hundred thousand, say. The idea would be a settlement in an undeveloped section of the interior."

"That could present some problems," said the official, breaking silence. "Without some adroit maneuvering, there'd be no getting Parliament to approve something like a settlement. Our country, you see, is very much attached to setting its own pace."

"Wait a moment—perhaps we can carry it out," said the Prime Minister, abruptly taking the cigar from his mouth as though something had occurred to him. "There's the North-South railroad."

"Ah, yes," said the official. "There are still no firm plans for the section from Tea Tree to Newcastle Waters, are there? It would be a matter of opening that up to international bidding, and then having Japan take it with far and away the most favorable bid."

"There remains the possibility that whatever we do will be too late," said the old man. "What would you say to this, gentlemen? Japan will provide credit backing at the most favorable terms possible, and Australia will see to the rapid implementation of the plan. We shall, of course, bring our own equipment.

We shall put our technical skill in railroad construction at your service without reserve. We only ask that you obtain without delay—say, within the next six months—the approval of your Parliament."

"But if we go at it too hastily, if you give us conditions that are too favorable, might not that stir some suspicion in this country?" said the official.

"Perhaps we can provide a reason. Because of the recent series of earthquakes, the Japanese government is carrying on a full-scale inspection of the Super Express network, and, consequently, work on the new Super Express line has been virtually halted. And so, in order to put to profitable use what had been set aside for that project, we offer it to Australia. And we shall, of course, pursue like negotiations with Africa, South America, and so forth."

It's something worth doing, thought the Prime Minister. There was no doubt that the enterprise would be a profitable one. There would come a vast influx of energetic, earnest, and well-educated workers with varied technical skills, of equipment of the most advanced kind, and of capital goods. And then it would happen that the country to which payment was to be made would be wiped from the face of the earth. . . . But the Prime Minister's mind was far from at ease. What sort of shadow would be cast upon the future of his country?

"Still and all, a hundred thousand people at one stroke might be too much of a strain," said the Prime Minister, shaking his head. "And then a settlement of a million . . . Well, what I mean, there are pertinent laws in the context of all humanity. What of the United Nations? Of course, I suppose you have already become active in that regard."

"We have had three confidential meetings with the Secretary General. We have begun to approach the various nations who are permanent members of the Council. However, the truth is that the United Nations simply does not wield power enough to cope with a matter of this sort. Right at the moment, we are conducting secret negotiations of our own with the American President, with South America, and with several countries in Africa. Beyond a doubt, our aspirations are self-centered, of course. What I must do—rather, what my country must do is to come to you, to come to all the nations of the world, to go down on our knees and make an earnest plea that you come to our aid. On the brink of disaster, the people of my country are pleading through me that, somehow, their lives may be spared."

The old man's tone had become fervent. It seemed as though at any instant his emotions might burst through the barrier he had set. Perhaps he might cry out, shed tears, actually fall to his knees, grasp the Prime Minister's legs, and beg in heart-rending fashion.

In fact, however, he sat on his chair, his knees neatly aligned, his hands resting upon them. There was even something like a smile upon his tranquil face. But those eyes of his were shining with a more earnest brightness than before, a fire kindled by the tragic intensity of his plea.

What incredible self-discipline, thought the Prime Minister. How few men there are today with control of this kind! The quality that characterized the whole peculiar race—at least, those of it whom the Prime Minister had had personal relations with—was this incredibly strong self-discipline which held all emotion in check behind the famous "inscrutable smile." And might not this be a drawback in international society, this unwillingness to cry out with an earnest plea? This eschewing of emotion?

"I understand, Mr. Nozaki," said the Prime Minister, laying his huge, hairy hand on the thin shoulder of the old man. "We will do everything within our power. I promise it. I will speak to the leaders of the other nations of the British Commonwealth also. As far as the Commonwealth nations go, I will undertake the responsibility of obtaining assistance for you. And, of course, as the largest of these and the closest to your nation, Australia, acting on its own, will not stint in our efforts to be of help."

"Thank you very much, sir," said the old man, bowing his head. Tears seemed to glisten in his eyes. "I shall be staying at our embassy for a time. I shall ever take comfort in the thought of Your Excellency's magnanimity and the love of humanity that you manifest to the world."

"Have you opened negotiations with the Soviet Union?" asked the minister. "Their country is vast and it includes a large portion of Asia."

"I believe that talks have already begun," said the old man, nodding, all trace of emotion now gone from his face. "To speak frankly, many things about that country are beyond our comprehension. However, in terms of its history, its record with regard to racial minorities gives grounds for hope."

"Except for the problem of the Jews, that is," said the minister quietly. "I suppose that you can't expect much from Mainland China, with its eight hundred million people. . . . Still, when one considers the historical ties that exist between the peoples of both countries and what the future may hold . . ."

"I have brought a gift for Your Excellency," said Nozaki, standing up. "Rather than from our Prime Minister, please think of it as coming from our country."

The old man went to a table in the corner of the room and brought back a wooden box over a foot and a half high. He quietly took off the cover.

"Why, this . . ." The Prime Minister, who had a fair knowledge of ancient Oriental art, was at loss for words. He took his glasses from his pocket. "This is extraordinary. It's about the thirteenth century, is it not?"

"This is correct, Your Excellency. The beginning of the Kamakura Era. As an image of Buddha, it ranks as a National Treasure. We can't specify its exact date," said the old man in a low voice. "It was purchased from a country temple. There are many objects of this sort scattered through every district of Japan. We give it to you, and we would like you to think of it as a remembrance."

4

"They say there's been a warning to the Fuji area," said Kunieda, his face pale. "The steam rising from the Ozawa landslide has become more intense, it seems. And, just below the Hoei crater, steam has started to rise. The meteorological station on the crest has been evacuated except for a small emergency group."

"I wonder if we'll be able to see an eruption from here," said the old man, smiling with anticipation. "If Komagadake or some other mountain in Hakone erupted, we'd get a good view, I should think."

"There are three cars at your service, sir. The Prime Minister's strict orders. Please go back to Tokyo as quickly as possible.

If, by chance, something should occur . . ."

"Don't worry. Death and I are on easy terms," said the old man. "I'm resigned. If I have two or three days left, that will be fine. Besides, that matter of ours should be concluded this evening."

"The work has been making progress?" Kunieda asked, his tone edged with irritation. "I had the impression, I'm afraid, that they spent most of the day relaxing and strolling about."

"Yes, and while doing that, they've been thinking," said the old man, giving Kunieda a penetrating glance. "Their whole concern, you see, has been given to this matter. For three days now they've gone without sleep. I'm worried about their health."

They were referring to the group gathered around Fukuhara, the scholar who had come to this mountain villa from Kyoto and remained here ever since. In accordance with Fukuhara's request, two more men, both rather unusual, had come to the villa. One had a smooth, pale face, which made his age hard to determine, and though he wore an ordinary kimono, his manner was that of a Buddhist monk. The other was rather elderly. He had white hair. And then, in order to keep records, deliver material, and establish liaison, three more men had been sent from Plan D headquarters to join them.

The frantically busy Prime Minister had spent a whole night talking with the three of them. Kunieda had been engaged in conversation in the neighboring room, and sometimes, when a maid slid open the door to bring refreshments, he had casually glanced in. Each time the group—Watari among them—had been casually talking of garden shrubbery, tea-ceremony utensils, and the like as they sipped their tea, not a thing on their minds, it seemed, but pleasant conversation. One of the trio, for example, had been relating an amusing anecdote about his experiences abroad while the old man and the Prime Minister laughed uproariously.

A young woman in a rust-colored Yuki pongee kimono appeared at the end of the corridor and came to where the old man was sitting in his wheelchair, gazing out at the garden through the glass doors. She knelt down beside him and whispered something in his ear. The old man nodded slightly. She got to her feet and began to push the wheelchair toward the hall.

"Please come along," said Watari to Kunieda, turning his head.

Making a right-angle turn from the corridor, they proceeded down a passageway leading to a detached wing concealed by a growth of shrubbery. At the end of this, beyond a foyer four and a half tatami mats in size, there was a room ten mats large. Beside it was another room which seemed to be of about eight mats. The sliding door between the two was open a few inches.

Around the edges of the room were piles of books and documents. Periodicals and the like lay scattered about the floor. Some were in European languages, and there were also Chinese books in their distinctive cases. Yearbooks and dictionaries were conspicuous as well as every kind of map—everything strewn about. A middle-aged man, apparently the recording secretary, sat in a corner, his face worn with fatigue. Two men were sitting at one corner of a table. One, a small man wearing a dark blue Oshima kimono, was gazing at the scenery outside, his arms folded. The other, the man who looked like a monk, was wearing a grayish-blue cotton kimono. Sitting with his fingers linked together over his stomach and one leg folded beneath him, he had his eyes closed. On the table before them were three large manila envelopes, each one designated by Chinese characters written in a bold hand.

The man who had been looking out the window unfolded his arms and, with a slight bow, spoke in a low voice: "As for the fundamental principles, they are here for the most part. . . ."

"You gentlemen have completed it?" the old man asked, bowing slightly in return. Assisted by the young woman, he got out of the wheelchair and sat down on the tatami. "What of the Imperial Household—to Switzerland, I imagine?"

"As to that, sir," said the small man, "one of the Imperial Family to America, one to China, and, if possible, one to Africa. . . ."

As he spoke, the small man looked for the first time in Kunieda's direction. Kunieda swallowed hard at the sight of the pain so evident in the man's features. In no more than a week Professor Fukuhara's face had undergone an incredible transformation. Only a short time before, his boyish face had had the glow of youth about it, but now his cheeks were hollow, his eyes were sunken, and his skin grayish, his cheeks covered with a scraggly growth of beard. His face seemed to belong to a man in the last stages of cancer. His eyes alone shone with spirit, but their odd glitter was like that struck from the embers of a dying fire.

"Probably about half will die," said Fukuhara in a low voice, his tone detached. "And for those who survive, there will be much suffering."

"You've made three divisions?" asked the old man, glancing at the envelopes on the table. "In what way?"

"It's not according to geographical areas, sir, but rather as to types," said Fukuhara, clearing his throat. "The first is that portion of the Japanese who might begin a new nation somewhere. The second is for those who would be scattered among various nations as naturalized citizens. The third is for those who could go to no other country."

"The example of the Jewish people is not especially relevant," said the man who seemed to be a monk, his eyes still closed. "The Jews have the experience of a two-thousand-year period of exile. Whereas this island people of ours have had the happy experience of living secure in their own country for a like period. Therefore it would be no easy matter to take on the other role. Would we gain some wisdom from our Diaspora over the course of the years? And throughout such a period, would the Japanese people remain the Japanese people? In that third envelope is enclosed still another envelope. It contains an opinion that is somewhat of a departure," said the monk. "The truth is that not one of the three of us is averse to this opinion. Since, however, the conclusion it presents is not in line with the purpose of the task set for us, we offer it as nothing more than a variant opinion."

"In effect, it proposes that the best thing would be to do nothing whatsoever," said Fukuhara, hiccoughing slightly. "The best thing would be not to lift a finger."

Not lift a finger? Kunieda cried out within himself, feeling his flesh tingle with icy shock. It would be the best thing to let 110 million Japanese die? Was that it? What sort of men were these scholars anyway?

"I see," said old Watari. He bent his trunk slightly, his hands on his lap, as he looked down at the envelopes upon the table. "So that opinion, too, has come forth, has it?"

"That it should has its source, perhaps, in the Japanese people's differing decisively from other peoples." His eyes now half opened, the priest whispered as though talking to no one but himself.

"When you three gentlemen formulated this opinion, could it be that your years affected your thinking?" The old man's eyes peered keenly as he put the question to them.

"True, sir," murmured Fukuhara, once more looking out at the garden.

"Hanae . . . come here," said the old man, gesturing to the young woman, who was sitting in a corner of the room. "Take a good look at this girl, gentlemen. She's twenty-three. She hasn't known any man yet. She's a fresh young girl with her life in front of her. Girls such as she . . . and children, too . . . were they in your thoughts?"

"Yes, sir," answered Fukuhara.

"In any case, that opinion represents a departure," said the monk, his eyes closed again. "Moreover, had we not gone so far, we would have been remiss."

"Our fundamental thought throughout has been that the Japanese people are to make no demands, are to claim nothing as their right from other nations," said Fukuhara, his voice low and hoarse. "For there is simply no way that we can do so. Human society is not ready to recognize the right of the people of any nation to live upon land that lies outside their borders. We must acknowledge as a fundamental truth that this situation will persist for a very long time to come. Thus, the Japanese people, dispossessed of their homeland, will have to ask the nations of the world for corners in which to live. But if we ask this as our right, we'll not get it, so making demands is out of the question."

"Even if our race lives on, then, our descendants, it seems, will have bitter times ahead of them," whispered Watari as he nodded slowly. "From now on, whether it's a matter of going on being Japanese or ceasing to be Japanese, whatever the case —we have to leave Japan out of our consideration. The problems to come will be those dictated by outside elements. Once this Japan of ours is gone forever, once it is taken from the Japanese, then our identity is simply that of human beings, it would seem, but in truth the problem cannot be reduced to terms so simple. For we have our karma—in our culture, our language, our history. And that karma will be resolved when this nation called Japan and its culture and its history—when all alike are swept away with the land itself. But the people of Japan will still be a young people, a people uniquely gifted. And this other karma, a living karma, is one that will go on."

"Begging your pardon . . ." A dry voice came from the corner of the room. The secretary, silent till now, was speaking. "If you would be kind enough, sir, it would be desirable, I believe, to allow these gentlemen some rest. For, having been without sleep or rest, as you see . . ."

"Kunieda, the envelopes," said the old man, signaling the young woman with a wink. "Thank you, gentlemen, for giving so much of yourselves. Please take a good rest."

The three men remained as they were while Kunieda and the girl helped the old man to his feet and into the wheelchair.

"Are you going to leave for Tokyo soon, sir?" Kunieda asked as he pushed the wheelchair. "If possible, these gentlemen might go with you, perhaps. There are cars enough. For, as you know, it seems to be gradually growing more dangerous here."

"Hanae," said the old man, turning his head and speaking in a surprisingly strong voice, "call the doctor right away. See that the three of them in there get examinations."

The old man decided to use one of the three cars for an immediate return to Tokyo with the plans, Kunieda going with him. The preparations made, Kunieda pushed the wheelchair out to the car as snowflakes were beginning to flutter down from a chill sky. Just as he was about to push the chair up the ramp of the specially equipped Mercedes-Benz 600, an echoing roar like that of a cannon seemed to make the gray sky tremble. When Kunieda turned, he saw a cloud of white smoke rising from the slope of Fuji at a point near the crest.

"The Hoei crater has finally erupted, it seems," said the old man tranquilly. "But if it's no more than that, it will be all right for the present, I would think."

At that moment there was the sound of frantically hurrying footsteps, and the girl named Hanae came running up to them, a distraught expression on her face.

"Master . . ." said the girl, stopping beside the wheelchair. "Professor Fukuhara . . . he . . ."

"What is it?"

Turning abruptly back toward the house, Kunieda saw the

monk walking slowly toward them, a Buddhist rosary at his wrist and his palms pressed together.

"All right," said the old man to Kunieda, indicating he was to push the wheelchair into the car. "Hanae—inform the Professor's family immediately. Mr. Tatsuno, I beg you to take care of everything."

The monk bowed slowly, his hands still pressed together. Yet another boom echoed from the direction of Mount Fuji. Ashes fell with a light rustling sound, blending with the snow which was beginning to cover the top of the Mercedes.

5

Onodera had not been in Kansai for a long time. In comparison to the quake-scarred condition of Tokyo, everything here seemed to be far closer to normal. Nevertheless, when Onodera's plane was circling Osaka before landing, there was something about the scene below that struck him as odd. What it was he learned later in a conversation with his brother, after they had accompanied their mother's body to the crematory in the Nada section of Kobe.

"I've been thinking about changing jobs," said his brother as they were driving back. "Here in the Kansai, you see, all kinds of projects have been suspended or else put off. And in my work, too, there's not much at all going on."

"Why is that? The effect of the Tokyo quake?"

"Don't you know the reason? Why, the land in the Kansai is sinking at an alarming rate." His brother's face was grim. "Sinking land is not something new in the Kansai, of course, but now it's at the stage where it's no joke—in economic terms, you see. The fact of the matter is that in some places it's sinking at an average rate of nearly an inch a day."

"Really?" murmured Onodera, at a loss. Though he worked at Plan D headquarters, he had been so taken up with the exploration of the Japan Trench that he hadn't seen any reports about the general state of things.

"Really. This started about a year ago, and it's gradually gotten worse. And it's not just in one or two places. The tide levels throughout Western Japan have gotten higher. They're building emergency sea walls, but if the sinking should keep increasing as it has been, in six more months it will pass four inches a day and there'll be no keeping up with it. That would be three feet every nine days! They say they'll find some way to deal with it before it gets that bad. But at what point are they going to be able to stop it, I wonder?"

Onodera clenched his fists.

"Take us to the airport." Onodera's brother spoke to the driver. "The company has a helicopter. Let me give you a look at the sort of thing that's happening."

"But, dear . . ." Onodera's sister-in-law turned around in her seat beside the driver. "You're in mourning, remember."

"That's all right. The public ceremony's not till tomorrow morning. You go home and get things in order. We'll come right after."

When he gazed down at the Osaka waterfront from the air, Onodera was able to see clearly where the sea had made its inroads. Aside from the places where the dikes had been especially high beforehand or else made higher by emergency measures, the Osaka waterfront section and the strip of filled-in land that fronted Kobe were already half awash. The work on the landfill in Kobe Harbor, meant to extend Kansai International Airport, seemed to have been abandoned. The tide swept over the mud flats, and streams of yellow-brown water flowed far out into the Inland Sea.

"You see? The job isn't an impossible one, but it's going to take a lot of money. And because the Kanto area is still recovering, we can't expect much to be available for a while. Take my company—the stoppage of work on the new airport has left us high and dry."

"You talked about changing jobs. What would you do?" asked Onodera, looking down morosely at the scene below.

"Well, there's no need to worry about taking care of Mother any more, and so what I've been thinking about is work in Canada." His brother's voice had a trace of sadness in it. "There's a development under way in the oil fields of Manitoba. I've been intending to take the family and go, but my wife is not enthusiastic."

"Wonderful!" Onodera blurted out, impulsively covering his brother's hand with his own. "That's a fine idea. When do you intend to go?"

"They'd like me to start as soon as possible. But there are all sorts of things to be attended to first, and that will probably take a month or two. I think that probably next week I'll take a trip there."

"The sooner the better." Onodera squeezed his brother's hand hard. "Don't worry about arrangements and things like that. No matter what your wife says, take the whole family and go."

"You make it sound so simple. I'm changing jobs at forty, remember." His brother laughed, a puzzled expression coming over his face. "Why are you so eager to see me go?"

"Well . . . Japan is . . ." Onodera stopped abruptly. He had to keep quiet, even though this was his own brother. He looked down again, but then he averted his eyes from the scene below.

There were many memories. When he was a mere toddler, he had fallen into a ditch, and his brother had pulled him out. Then there had been a shrine festival in the country, and on the way home he had fallen asleep on his brother's back. That was the time when the thong of his brother's clog had broken and he had had to walk home barefoot. His brother had caught beetles for him, had taken him fishing and swimming. He had taught him to play games and to build model planes and done all sorts of other things for him. His brother had been already in college when he was in elementary school, and Onodera had gazed with awe on the Western books and the difficult novels that his brother had been reading. . . . It was memories such as these that were now coming back to him one after another.

Just a word. A mere word would do it—so wouldn't it be all right? Get away, Brother . . . Japan is finished. The words stuck like a searing lump in his throat. As he gazed out through the windshield of the helicopter, Onodera coughed repeatedly. Suppose he were now to whisper something . . .

His shocked brother would immediately start preparing to leave, heedless of his wife's complaints. And she, most likely, would demand an explanation. His patience at an end, his brother would probably say something to her, a secret between husband and wife. Or when he was about to leave Japan, over a farewell drink, when the talk would naturally take a confidential turn, he might let slip a word to a good friend or someone with whom he worked. Thus the "secret" would become something that was traveling from mouth to mouth and would soon spread beyond all limits. Well, what would be wrong with that? thought Onodera, clenching his fists. This would cause people to flee spontaneously, and thus more might be saved. And yet, thought Onodera, gritting his teeth and clenching his fists so hard that his nails were beginning to draw blood, because I am part of Plan D headquarters, I must keep the secrets that come under the jurisdiction of that headquarters. I have to think that that's the manly thing to do, but at the same time I can't avoid the thought that it's a matter of fleeing to organizational logic in the face of an agonizing human problem. Have I become a faithful bureaucrat? he wondered suddenly. But Onodera rejected that thought at once. The true bureaucrat, secure in his virtue, would never agonize in this way. But when he reflected that among the thousand or so men connected with Plan D there must be other distraught men like him who struggled with their emotions as they debated within themselves whether or not to let the secret out, he felt his mouth going dry. Nakata was obviously right when he said that the time was coming when the secret could no longer be kept. Already, probably, any number of them, rather than bearing the emotional burden, had told their families and were making ready to flee.

Avoiding the routes used by the airlines, the helicopter approached the airport from the northeast, steadily decreasing its altitude. Still avoiding his brother's eyes, Onodera kept looking down. He saw the red, blue, gray roofs of close-packed houses. He saw a procession of grade-school children, wearing yellow caps, their figures wrapped in heavy winter clothes. A group of women, mothers apparently, accompanied them, guiding them across intersections. Since it was a clear, bright afternoon, quilts and washing shone white from open windows. A group of housewives in aprons, kerchiefs wound around their heads, seemed to be doing their shopping. And then, as the helicopter dropped still lower, a young mother pointed up at it, saying something to the infant she was carrying. . . . Such were the scenes that flashed by below him, a panorama flattened by the rush of the helicopter. As he watched, a gathering heaviness clogged his chest. I guess I've never really understood the weight of things like *family* and *life,* he thought. Now the meaning of those words for his brother, with his wife and two children, began to take form in his imagination with a painful intensity. His spirited wife, beginning to grow plump and gritting her teeth as she did her beauty calisthenics . . . the son in his first year of junior high . . . the daughter in the fourth grade, whom his brother, fond of children anyway, so doted upon that she could do no wrong in his eyes. The girl had finished second in a prefecture-wide talent contest, his brother had told him, and he had bought her a grand piano in place of the upright they had had, though his practical wife had opposed it. . . . Such was the joyful weight of *family*, of *home* that pressed heavily upon his brother's shoulders.

And so it was that families like this, more than twenty million of them, led their family lives upon these islands threatened with oblivion.

This kind of flesh-and-blood human life with its specific gravity—these 20 million households—this was what had to be saved. The great effort of moving to a strange land where an uncertain future waited—could such a thing be carried out?

"Well, what are you thinking about? Let's get out," said his brother, tapping him on the shoulder as he unfastened his safety belt. "It's still early, but should we get something to eat? Do you like blowfish?"

After dinner, Onodera and his brother went to a bar. His brother wanted him to stay at his home overnight, but Onodera said that he must return to Tokyo. His hotel was at the airport, and he had a reservation for the earliest flight the next day.

"Please forgive me for being unable to be at Mother's funeral tomorrow," he said to his brother. "I feel terrible about it. I imagine the relatives will have something to say. . . ."

"Don't let it bother you. Leave things to me," said his brother, putting down money for the bill and getting up. "Well then, I don't suppose you'll be coming back this way for a while?"

"No," answered Onodera vaguely, oppressed by the thought of taking up again tomorrow that strange work that seemed to have no limits, "I don't think so. But I'll keep you up to date."

His brother stopped at the door of the bar. He took a long, thin package from his breast pocket and handed it to Onodera: "Well, now is when I should give you this," he said. "It's a remembrance of Mother."

Onodera took it and, instead of putting it in his pocket, stood holding it. Something welled up within him, but the words that came out had to do with something quite different from his thoughts.

"Brother, go to Canada. That's the best thing," he said once again, his voice ringing with fervor. "Believe me, it's the best thing."

"What an odd fellow you are!" said his brother, grinning broadly. He turned on his heel, and as he was starting to walk away, he said over his shoulder: "Instead of minding other people's business, how about your own? Isn't it about time you had a family? Single at thirty—you're going to get shopworn, you know."

They parted in front of the tavern, his brother taking Shinchihon Street toward Midosuji and he walking in the other direction, toward Sakurabashi. In the distance, the latest headlines were moving in flashing lights along the side of some building or other, the characters reading: "Fuji Hoei Crater Erupts."

The freezing chill of the tag end of February gripped the streets, and some snow was falling, but the flourishing night life of Shinchihon Street was as vigorous at eight o'clock that evening as he remembered it from two or three years before. With March, the month all debts had to be paid, approaching, the street was jammed with the cars of banquet-goers and expense-account spenders. And there was one party on foot, the men drunkenly singing war songs. The young hostesses, bare shoulders showing for all their winter wrappings, gave cries of distress from time to time at the naughty antics of one of the drunks. One man staggered along by himself, bundled up in an expensive overcoat. A waitress, her sleeves showing that she was wearing more than one kimono, broke into a trot as though to warm herself. At one corner a young girl was selling flowers, her hair wrapped in a scarf. Street singers stood with accordions and guitars slung from their necks. Sushi and octopus stalls were set up along the street, and it was to one of these that the hostesses were leading their drunken patrons. Steam from the noodles cooking within poured out through the door curtains of a Chinese restaurant. As Onodera plodded on, he suddenly recalled, for some reason or other, that the Omizutori would soon be enacted at Nigatsu Temple in Nara. A shudder ran through him that had nothing to do with the cold. Were these annual ceremonies to end?

He felt his awareness dimming even as his fears and passion grew stronger. All the sake he had drunk earlier had had no effect at the time, but now he found himself overwhelmed. What had he done? Standing in the midst of that crowd before —had he cried out loudly? He suddenly feared that he might have done so. Crying out to passers-by, robbed of all control by his drunkenness . . . Worst of all, grabbing a man from the crowd, shaking him by the shoulders and bellowing: "Hurry up, get away!" Was this what he had done?

Caught between the shock of drunken release and the fear that, by force of that shock, he might have done something foolish, Onodera felt desolate. He hung his head as he walked. He felt himself bump into somebody. He dodged to one side and this time collided headlong with somebody else. When he tried to disengage himself, something that looked like a purse slipped from the hand of the other person, its clasp coming loose, and its contents spilling over the street.

"Ah . . ." said Onodera, shaking his heavy head, his features swollen. "Excuse me . . . please."

When he bent over and tried to pick up the compact, handkerchief, lipstick, and the rest, he tottered forward, almost falling on his face, catching himself then, but this time nearly falling on his back. Finally, as he squatted on the street, he suddenly heard a voice call from above.

"Mr. Onodera . . ."

"Huh?"

Onodera made out a pair of shiny black women's shoes somewhere below his hanging head. Higher up, he saw as he slowly raised his eyes, was a pair of black velvet slacks. And at that moment a hand gently touched his shoulder as he squatted there.

"How I've been looking for you!" said the owner of the hand in a voice suddenly filled with emotion. "I want to talk to you."

Feeling as though his skull were on the verge of splitting, Onodera finally lifted his head and, with great effort, opened his swollen eyelids.

A woman's strong-featured face was smiling at him. Her skin

was dark and her hair was bound in a headband. It was Reiko
Abe.

6

"The lateral pressure from the Japan Sea coast is getting awfully
strong," muttered Nakata, peering at the three-dimensional
light image of the Japan Archipelago suspended within the
block screen and surrounded by a vast variety of colored dots
and lines. "It's more than we bargained for."

"And on the sea floor the elevation of the Yamato Rise, together with the intensity of its earth heat waves, has increased
three times in the past week," said a young man from the
Weather Service in a low voice. "There'll be eruptions, perhaps."

"There's quite a lot of energy stored up in the Noto Peninsula," said Mashita, a university professor from the Earthquake
Research Bureau, as he scanned the block screen with a pola-
rized-light scope. "The portion to the north of the Hakui-Manao
line is moving eastward. There might soon be an earthquake."

"More so than that, how about this energy that's gathered
along the Itoigawa-Shizuoka structural line?" said a man from
the National Geological Institute, his voice somewhat hoarse as
he pointed to the block screen. "According to our calculations,
even though the limit of earth-crust flexibility has already been
passed, the build-up of energy is continuing, going well beyond
the theoretical limit."

"What do you think, Mr. Nakata?" asked Mashita. "It seems
to me that, whatever else, we have to conclude that some phenomenon previously unknown to us is at work beneath the
Japan Archipelago. In effect it's as though a portion of the downward current of the mantle is passing beneath the Archipelago
and is beginning to jut out on the Japan Sea side."

"Yes, so it seems. Tonight we'll run a thoroughgoing simulation and see what we can come up with."

Five men, including Yukinaga, were constantly at work in the
Display Room. The Defense Agency computer, which handled
the complex calculations, was not available to them during the
day, and so yet another sleepless night was in prospect.

The evening was spent in preparation. In the room were
seven cathode-ray-tube devices connected to the computer.

Yukinaga, besides working one of the CRTs, had the task of running the videotape recorder cameras which photographed the block screen from different views. Finally, some time after two in the morning, Nakata stood in front of the huge plastic block and gave the signal to begin.

No more than two minutes had passed, however, before he gave a startled cry: "Stop! Come here and take a look at this."

Yukinaga, after manipulating the buttons on the control board to stop the action, came running up to the screen, joined by the others. They all peered into the plastic block. Yukinaga caught his breath. The three-dimensional pattern of the Japan Archipelago, drawn in pale glowing phosphorescent lines, had broken in two at its center and tipped to one side. The sheet of light that indicated energy distribution, varying from orange to red, surrounded the tipped mass of the Archipelago, pulsating in sinister fashion, now weakly, now strongly.

"Has Japan already sunk?" asked Yukinaga, his voice shaking.

"Completely sunk," muttered Nakata grimly. "Furthermore, before it sinks, it will break in two."

"Isn't that a bit fast?" said Mashita, looking at his watch, his face white. "Couldn't there have been some error in the time scale?"

"No chance of that," said the young man from the Weather Service, glancing back at his CRT. "The scale was the usual: 3.6×10^4 . . . 36,000 seconds. One second being equivalent to about one hundred hours."

"Give me a reading on the time up to this point."

"120.32 seconds," said the young man. "Therefore, 11,232 hours."

"11,200 hours," Yukinaga muttered. "Why, that's . . ."

"A year and three months, I believe," said Nakata, rapping the display block with his fingers. "Let's take a closer look at it, from the very beginning. This time let's drop the time scale to a quarter of what it was. 0.9×10^4—one second equals twenty-five hours."

Everyone hurried back to his post. The phosphorescent image in the block faded from sight, and they were back at the beginning.

The needle on the illuminated clock began to revolve, the ping of each second sending a chill through the silent room.

Then came the tapping of CRT keys and the noise of electronic printers. Finally, much more deliberately than before, the three-dimensional image began to move. As though in slow motion, unfolding leisurely as scattered red lights, orange lights, yellow lights flashed on and off like will-o'-the-wisps. In the midst of these bright points a pulsating sheet of multicolored light took form. Waving as it came, it fastened itself to the long, arc-shaped light image and began to contract upon it. Its ill-omened beauty was like that of a huge, luminescent devilfish attacking the pale, glowing form of the Japan Archipelago.

The first movements of the light image were almost undiscernible. As the intervals between flashes decreased, the points of lights began to form lines. The yellows and oranges began to decrease, and the reds gradually increased, growing ever more intense.

"Stop!" cried Nakata once more.

"How much time up to here?"

"302 seconds, exactly."

"Yukinaga, from here on, besides the VTR, take photos of each quadrant . . . every two seconds. And let's halve the time scale."

"Wouldn't it be better to drop it to a quarter?" somebody asked.

"If you lower it any more, I don't think the detail would be clear enough. All right, start it."

Yukinaga threw the switches, and the second hand of the illuminated clock began to turn again. The tension in the room grew still more acute. The lights blinked slowly, and the waving of the light curtain took on a torpid, dreamlike quality. Only the busy whir of the six camera shutters intruded. The gleam of the red lights grew still stronger, the points growing together. They were like strings of red jewels laid against the coast of the Japan Sea and along both sides of the Izu and the Ogasawara Islands. Along the Pacific coast, following the line of the Japan Trench, a two-layered mass of glowing light took form, the upper green, the lower a vivid scarlet, steadily growing brighter.

"What's that?" asked the geologist in a whisper. "I didn't notice it before."

"The green indicates the deficiency of the mass, an integral calculus with the gravitational irregularity," said Yukinaga.

"Keep watching," Nakata said in a low voice.

"Look! Beneath the Archipelago there."

Two hundred kilometers beneath the surface, the layer of red light under the green seemed to be passing beneath the Archipelago in the form of flowing pink stripes. When these reached the Japan Sea coastline, their brightness grew more intense and they formed specks of light.

"What about those stripes?" asked Mashita in a whisper. "What can they mean? Could energy move that quickly at such a depth—all the way past the Japan Sea coastline?"

"I don't know for certain how it could," said Nakata, shaking his head. "But that's the pattern as indicated by the computer data."

"It's begun," said the Weather Service man, a taut edge to his voice. "The Archipelago is breaking apart."

In the Central Region of the Japan Archipelago, beginning at a point east of Toyama Bay, a brilliant line of red light ran north and south. At the same time, innumberable thin red lines appeared all over the luminescent form of the Archipelago, distorting it. The waving green light mass on the Pacific side spread out to the east and, at the same time, began to sink, while the lateral movement of the stripes below grew frenzied. The pink light mass on the Japan Sea side grew still more immense and began to pulsate like a living thing. The eastern portion of the luminescent image of the Archipelago shifted slowly eastward, and the western portion southward, the whole mass now beginning to tip slightly. As the echoing ping of the seconds and the agitated buzz of the camera shutters continued, the pale image of the Japan Archipelago, still slightly tilted, slid down within the plastic block, a motion like the heaving of a sigh, and finally came to rest.

The pink on the Japan Sea side, the green on the Pacific side both faded. The points of red light forming the red lines began to decrease rapidly, and those that persisted changed from red to orange and then to yellow, flickering as their colors grew dimmer.

"What's the time?"

"Sixty-two seconds from the second start."

"Putting that into days, it amounts to about thirty-two."

"A change of this order taking place within one month?" Mashita gave an irritated sigh.

"How about the movement of the Archipelago?" asked Yukinaga.

"The lateral movement—twenty-seven miles at most. The vertical movement is minus one and a half miles. The eastern portion moves east-southeast on a line that forms an acute angle of almost thirteen degrees with the geodesic line, while the western section slides south at an angle of six degrees. As for Kyushu, the entire island revolves to the left, sliding its south side around to face east."

"The vertical movement is minus one and a half miles," muttered the geologist from the institute. "In that case, the mountain regions will remain."

"Even if they do, it will do precious little good," said Nakata. "Don't forget the landslides and the eruptions. Nor is this the end of things. The sinking will go on."

"That's right," said the young man from the Weather Service, studying the CRT figures. "Even after the radical movement is over, both the sinking and the lateral movement will continue at an average rate of several inches a day."

"And when is this going to happen?" asked Yukinaga hoarsely.

"According to our model, at the 302nd second," said the meteorologist, his voice quavering. "In terms of days, 312.54."

"Less than a year," said the geologist, with an anguished sigh. "Ten months . . . about . . ."

The group stood about the plastic block as though numbed. A mere ten months was all that was left.

The blood seemed to be draining from Yukinaga. He felt as though he were about to vomit. The floor seemed to be dissolving beneath his feet. In a mere ten months *it* would begin. What could possibly be done within so short a period?

Nakata, his eyes raised to the bulletin board, folded his arms and stood rigid as a statue. But then, abruptly making his decision, he picked up the phone.

"Are you calling the secretary general?" asked Yukinaga.

"No, the Prime Minister," said Nakata brusquely as he pressed the call button.

"When will you disclose to us your evacuation program?" asked the leader of one of the independent parties. "You must have it fairly well in hand by now. At the time of the public announcement in two weeks, you'll have to give out some sort of outline at least. Otherwise there'd be an uproar, wouldn't there?"

"Since the obvious course would have been to set up a non-partisan committee to deal with this crisis," said the leader of the major opposition party with a frown, "forgive me if I seem ungracious at hearing the news. The government of the administration party, while keeping this from us, has for some time now been secretly pouring it into the ears of the business world. And what's happened already is that our industrial assets are beginning the flight abroad without anyone knowing about it. The government has the obligation to administer equal justice to all, and what kind of behavior is this partiality shown finance and industry but the grossest sort of inequity? I think that it is but another instance showing the perverse character of the administration party. And with regard to plans for evacuation, what I want to know is this: is the saving of the life of every citizen of Japan the thing that is given priority above all else, or isn't it? Mr. Prime Minister, before a non-partisan group looks into the matter, I would like to hear from you with regard to this point."

"Let this be understood: our overriding intent is to save the lives of the entire Japanese people, making no exceptions whatsoever," answered the Prime Minister. "To accomplish this we are making use of every means at our disposal. However, what about *after* the disaster? How are 110 million people going to live from then on? The government is obliged to face up to this problem also."

"Well and good," said another party head. "But, judging from the conduct of your party, it seems to me that you gentlemen, while giving lip service to the worth of human life, have in fact been most concerned with planning for the continuance of the financial and industrial life of this nation and, more than that even, for the continuance of the nation itself and its structure. Rather than the people, rather than individual men and women, it's the nation and its structure that are more precious to you—the kind of bureaucratic thinking that goes back to prewar days, and it looks as though it's never going to be rooted out. The kind of spirit that in the past has thought nothing of sacrificing fifty thousand or a hundred thousand lives for the sake of the prestige of the nation and the structure behind that prestige doesn't fade so easily. But, at any rate, here's what I wish to know: leaving the future to take care of itself, throwing aside prestige and formalities and hypocritical bureaucratic posturing about equal justice and everything of that ilk, is it your intention or is it not, Mr. Prime Minister, to throw yourself headlong into the task of saving the Japanese people, and to hell with structures?"

"Ogata . . ."

All at once the leader of the third largest of the opposition parties spoke up in his heavy, deep voice, which was like the lowing of a bull. It was a voice of crushing force, forged in the fierce debates and speeches of a long political career.

"You said a short time ago that politics was a backstage affair. But this way of thinking that all political matters can be settled backstage is where your party, with its bureaucratic way of running the government, has most gone astray since the war. And I think that this is the reason why most Japanese think of politics as a crafty, sinister business. Certain backstage activity is necessary in politics. But, at the same time, it is absolutely essential to go onstage, too. Especially in this crisis that brings us to the brink of national disaster. I feel that all is lost unless there emerges a 'nation-saving hero'—a man of stalwart determination, a man who will give light to a fearful people, who will point the way, who will stiffen our resolve, a man with the strength to act forcefully, the strength to snatch the nation from the jaws of ruin. . . . Now, Ogata . . . is there anybody in your party, not excluding yourself, fit to perform this vital *onstage* role? Do you think that you have strength and popular favor enough to turn yourself into the furious devil himself, Ashura, to take hold of the people and slash your way through the danger? Calling on a friendship that goes far back to when we were in school together, I beg your leave to speak frankly. Your political conduct has been a model of bureaucratic prudence, but—pardon me for saying so—I can't see you as having anything like the resolution necessary to see the country through this crisis."

"It's a role, in other words, that you yourself will have to take, then?" said the Prime Minister, a somewhat stiff half-smile forming on his face. "Mr. Atsumi, as yet I have no idea whether or not you will be nominated to head the coalition Cabinet. As for myself, I don't necessarily think that I have the ability that's needed to see this crisis through. However, until such time as your 'nation-saving hero' makes his appearance, I have no choice but to put every ounce of strength into the task of somehow fulfilling the duties now entrusted to me. And then, too . . . in present-day Japan the memories of the War are still vivid, and I have the feeling that there are very many Japanese who have had their fill of 'nation-saving heroes.' They feel in their bones, you see, that heroes and the cult of heroes have had a disastrous effect upon Japan and the lives of the Japanese people."

"Well, at any rate," said the head of the major opposition party, breaking in, "we would like you to give to our representatives just as quickly as you can a thorough explanation of Plan D and of the evacuation program insofar as it's drawn up to date. We can't very well wait two weeks until the Diet session."

"Of course. We have the preparations all in order," said the secretary general of the Cabinet. "Once you've had a conference of your chief secretaries and pick your representatives, we'll be ready at any time to do as you direct."

"You'll have your conference in two days, I believe?" said the Prime Minister. "Two weeks is the time we're aiming for, but the situation is such that the news might leak out at any time, from some source or other. Our foreign ties present a special risk. In that case, we'd have to make an immediate public declaration. So, gentlemen, I'll be depending upon your good will. . . ."

"It looks as though European financial circles have gotten on to something," said the head of the International Monetary Bureau of the Treasury. "This morning large-scale selling of Japanese bonds began. We're supporting them by buying through figurehead groups, but if this flood of selling keeps up, it's going to take a toll of our purchasing assets."

"I think we'd be best advised to let things ride for a bit," said the president of a certain private exchange bank. "If things go

down some and small investors get out, I think that would be
to the good."

"What's the present withdrawal rate?" asked the Minister of
the Treasury.

"Very soon it will be fifty percent."

"Maybe it would be good to hold it temporarily at about
fifty-five percent," muttered the Minister. "After that we'll just
have to let it drop as far as it will go."

"I wondered if anyone has discovered that we're using our
assets to buy," said the president of the Bank of Japan in a low
voice.

"It's hard to say," said the Bureau head. "The idea is to move
deliberately and not stimulate the market, but the rate of increase is steadily climbing."

"In view of the way that European and American financial
interests are manipulating their speculations, this cashing in of
bonds seems to indicate that we're foolishly letting ourselves be
taken advantage of," muttered the president of the exchange
bank. "We shouldn't throw good money after bad. I think that
now is the time to let them take a bit of punishment."

"Fine—in any other circumstances but the present," said the
president of the Bank of Japan. "But even if hard-eyed finan-
ciers call us foolish, we must consider this: it's a matter of the
Japanese people losing their very homeland and thus being
dependent upon the good will of the rest of the world. We
cannot trick either individual investors or even large financial
groups and pin the loss on them. We cannot afford enemies. Nor
are we going to be reduced to the level of beggars. Rather,
holding tight to what is our own, what we must do is see this
thing through in such a way, hard though it be, that no other
nation suffers loss from the sinking of Japan. If we do this, bitter
pill though it be at the time, we will reap untold benefits in the
not too distant future. Our ancestors in the Meiji Era started out
empty-handed and conducted themselves in such a way as to
win the respect of the world."

"But the question is, I'm afraid, to what extent such purity
can stand as currency in world society," said the head of the
International Monetary Bureau.

"It will stand, all right," said the president of the Bank of
Japan forcefully. He had a magnificent head of white hair. "And

more than that, going beyond politics as such, nothing like an international industrial society can ever come into being without such a conviction. In the long run, I believe this has to be so."

"Come to me. . . ." Reiko's whisper sounded in his ear. When he heard it, he remembered that night at Hayama, which already seemed like part of the far-distant past. Now, in place of the bracelet transistor radio whose music had irritated him as they lay together, there was piped-in music that filled this narrow airport-hotel room. For Onodera, Reiko's amber skin seemed to have kept the scent of sand, of sand still warm from the torrid rays of the sun. In the very nadir of drunkenness, desire flamed up, and he grabbed hold of her desperately, roughly caressed her breasts, fixed his mouth upon hers, and did not let her go until, finally, he had wrung passionate, drawn-out cries from her.

"I want to get married," said Reiko, her panting body, awash in sweat, held fast within his arms. "I looked for you all over . . . afterward. I wanted to talk to you."

"Why?" he whispered, his cheek pressed against her breast, white in contrast to the rest of her torso, still tan from last summer's sun. "Why me? You have all sorts of fine boy friends. Me, whom you met only once . . ."

"And the night we met I made love with you on the beach, didn't I?" Reiko smiled. "I was drunk, yes, but still . . . I wonder why. Why this man who had just appeared . . . why did I suddenly feel I wanted you? The group that was there that night —I knew most of them for a long time, but I never let any of them make love to me."

"Well . . . you were drunk," said Onodera, smiling.

Reiko pinched his back lightly with her nails. "I was awfully embarrassed afterward, you see. I thought maybe you'd think I was a sort of nymphomaniac, somebody who slept with anybody at all. But then I realized something. Because I did make love with you, I knew that you couldn't be the kind of man who would think that of me."

But why? Onodera asked her, holding to the question. Why had she picked him?

"I don't know, but . . . That night . . . How was it now?"

She had felt as though she wanted to look at the sea, Reiko whispered. She loved scuba diving, and she had tied a women's record in it. When she sank down, head over heels, all alone, into the gloomy depths spreading out above, below, on every side of her, she loved the isolation she felt at that moment, the chill water gripping her.

"I feel lonely then, I feel so isolated I want to break into tears, but I feel happiness, too. I'm like a fragment of a falling star plunging through empty space, but I'm totally happy. The cold water embraces me. And though I'm all alone, the blue-black water, the wavering seaweed, the fish swimming like clouds of silver . . . I feel as though I'm one with all of these. And that's when this forlorn, isolated happiness that makes me want to cry takes hold of me. . . . But wait! Now I see. I felt just this way, you see . . . the first time you held me in your arms. Why, I don't know, but the feeling was just the same. Even though I didn't know then that you piloted a deep-sea submarine, I sensed the sea inside of you. That's it! It was as though the vast, limitless sea, which had ever held me in its embrace, had seen the tears behind my mask and had taken the form of a young man and taken me in its arms."

Reiko then took his head in both her hands and, lifting it, looked deeply into his eyes. Her expression was like that of a little girl.

"Will you marry me?"

Instead of answering, Onodera gripped her naked body with crushing force, sucked her lips into his mouth, and once more thrust himself forcefully into her still-wet body. It was as though, holding his breath, he were plunging deep down into the warm waters of a tropic sea. Kicking out, reaching out, twisting his body, pushing his breath to the limit, plunging deeper, still deeper. Then in the inky blackness of the ocean floor, with his lungs about to explode, he took hold of the stars that glittered gold, scarlet, blue in the depths. And then those stars burst into brilliant fragments that spread over the sky, scattering to every corner of it. Not uttering a sound, eyes fast shut, panting fiercely atop Reiko's hot, sweaty belly held fast beneath him, Onodera at last came up from the depths and felt the buoyant ease of floating upon the waves. Head down, still breathing heavily, he experienced the rest that Reiko's body had led him to.

He remembered then that it had been over a year since he had last been with a woman. And the woman had been Reiko. Since then, a year and a half . . . day after day, he had sat sealed within that steel ball, operating instruments, moving rapidly from one site to another, fighting wind and waves, carrying on the endless labor together with men whose eyes fatigue and anxiety had fixed in a glittering stare.

"You're tired, aren't you?" Reiko suddenly asked. Her beautiful lips abruptly parted, and her warm tongue licked up a single tear, which had wet his cheek without his having noticed it. As he took her in his arms again, this time gently, cherishing her, he repeated over and over to himself: I must rest. I must rest with this woman. What I thought was mere fatigue was my grief in the face of the fantastic disaster of Japan sinking . . . my fear, my heartbreak.

No more than a few days after the government's decision to make a public announcement within two weeks, a disquieting rumor began to spread through the country. A terrible earthquake and volcanic eruptions far more destructive than the last were going to hit Japan. This time Tokyo would be leveled, and Chiba and the Sagami Bay coast would sink to the bottom of the sea. There was nothing to do but to flee abroad for a time. Though the newspapers had not printed one word of it, the rumor spread rapidly. People whispered about it with anxious faces in offices, in homes, on the street. Every airline was swamped with requests for tickets abroad for whole families. The planes of every international airline that flew into Japan left loaded to full capacity every day, and even though more planes were put into service, reservations piled up three months in advance. Steamship lines, too, began to sell out their passenger reservations.

The government was hit from all sides with questions prompted by the rumors. The faces of newspapermen gradually altered, their eyes became bloodshot, and the press room of every ministry began to echo with angry voices talking over the phone. Though there were still some days left till the opening of the special session, members of the Diet, were holding crowded meetings every day and harassing ministry officials with questions, demanding to know what was going on. Among the public, especially in Tokyo, the flood of wild rumors grew more intense. White-collar workers left the work on their desks untouched, but they came together in little groups in corners of their offices as though they needed contact with one another. What is going to happen, I wonder? Just what are we going to do? Is the government going to do anything for us or not?

Taxi drivers began to greet their customers by saying: "Is it true, do you think—about Tokyo going to sink?" Bookstores sold out everything having to do with earthquakes and geology. Everyone had become convinced that something was impending.

7

On March 11 an American geodesic group made an announcement that sent an electric shock through the world: a massive shift in the crust of the earth was taking place on the continental shelf of East Asia, with the Japan Archipelago at its center. This came three days before the government's intended announcement.

The American statement came at two in the afternoon, Eastern Standard Time. It took the form of an urgent exchange between Dr. Eugene Cox, chairman of the geodesic group, and the director of a satellite research group. The expressions used in the conversation were extremely reserved, but the burden of it was that the information gathered in the previous months by satellites and survey ships pointed toward an immense change, an alteration of the crust of the earth on a scale altogether unprecedented. And it would come, at the latest, within a year. When one of the reporters asked if the area described did not in fact take in the whole of Japan, Dr. Cox's response was unequivocal: the Japan Archipelago would be at the focal point of the change.

Pressed for detailed information, the chairman avoided a direct answer, but said: "Well, it's the kind of thing that makes you think of the Atlantis legend." This was enough to galvanize the reporters. Three hours after the American announcement, the AFP in Paris, citing an "unimpeachable source," sent out the sensational headline: "Day of Japan's Destruction Approaching."

An hour and a quarter before the Diet session was to open,

almost all its members had already taken their places. At precisely one o'clock the presiding officer declared the session open, and the Prime Minister immediately stepped up to the podium, a grave expression on his face. Strobe lights flashed, and the television cameras zoomed in on him. He picked up his speech, coughed faintly, and, in a somewhat subdued voice, began to read it.

"Ladies and gentlemen of the Diet, as the one holding the foremost responsibility in this nation, it is my duty to inform you that Japan is now confronting an unprecedented peril, something that could well be termed national disaster."

Just as the Prime Minister was beginning his talk, Onodera, wearing a topcoat and carrying a suitcase, appeared in the door of the D-1 room at Plan D headquarters. Though it was time for the afternoon's work to be under way, most of the men were crowded into the conference room to listen to the Prime Minister on television. The office next to the Display Room stood nearly empty. In a corner of it Yukinaga and Nakata, listening to the speech on a portable radio, were smoking with weary expressions on their faces.

Seeing Onodera, Yukinaga raised his hand. "You're going today?"

"Yes. A three-thirty flight out of Narita." Onodera smiled faintly, but his expression was melancholy, and he seemed ill at ease. His work was finished. He had faithfully discharged his duties, and yet . . .

"It's good you are. After this speech, tickets and foreign currency alike will be hard to come by."

"He's begun to tell them." Onodera indicated the radio with a nod.

"As some of you may have heard on the news broadcast from abroad this morning," came the Prime Minister's voice, "in the near future a vast change in the crust of the earth will occur, with the Japan Archipelago at its center. Japanese scientists and research organizations set up by the government have informed me of the certainty that this will deal an annihilating blow to our homeland. . . ."

"I suppose that this is the first time the Prime Minister of Japan has ever been on radio and TV all over the world," said Nakata quietly. He laughed faintly.

". . . The various aspects of this change and the time of its occurrence became evident only recently. According to the forecast of our research groups, this change will occur within one year. And it will not only cause immense destruction in every part of the country through earthquakes, but the fact is that Japan in practically its entirety will sink into the ocean. . . ."

A phone rang. Nakata picked it up and hung up after a brief exchange.

"Mount Fuji is showing more and more acute signs of erupting. Smoke is pouring up from two or three spots in the Hoei crater. In Hakone there have been smoke and minor explosions in Kamiyama and Owaku Valley."

"Mount Fuji?" Onodera muttered. An ill-omened shadow seemed to pass over him.

"Evacuation began in that area yesterday. The earth's been rising at the rate of nearly an inch a day in Tonozawa and two a day to the north of Mount Ashitaka."

"Well, goodbye, gentlemen," said Onodera. "I hope we meet again somewhere in the world."

At that moment the glasses and ink bottles on the desks in the room began to rattle. A pencil rolled off and fell to the floor, and there was a light crack as the lead inside snapped.

"It's started," whispered Nakata, turning to the window behind him.

"It looks like it." Yukinaga got up and stood beside him.

The window did not have a direct view of Mount Fuji, but a huge gray mushroom-shaped cloud was rapidly rising and spreading over the clear, pale blue March sky. Shock waves rattled the glass.

"This is going to be big," said Nakata.

"Should we go up to the roof to see?"

The phone rang again. Yukinaga took it this time. His voice grew loud. The connection was apparently a bad one. Then, as though suddenly realizing who the party was, his expression changed and he held the phone out to Onodera.

"It's for you. . . . It's a woman."

Onodera lunged for the phone.

"Hello, hello . . ." Loud static crackled in his ear. Someone was shouting at the other end. "Hello, hello . . ." The distant voice was Reiko's.

"Where are you?" Onodera shouted into the phone, covering one ear with his hand.

"I'm at a place . . . off the Manazuru Road. . . . Traffic is blocked."

"The Manazuru Road?" Onodera's voice grew louder in his excitement. "What are you doing there? We've got to be at Narita by three-thirty."

"Yesterday . . . it came up suddenly . . . to Izu . . ." The static, together with shouting in the background, grew so loud that he could make out little of what Reiko was saying. ". . . by train, but . . . early this morning . . . I started to drive, but . . ."

"Hello, hello . . ." Sweat began to roll down Onodera's body. "I can't hear you!"

"I got as far as here . . . eruption, stones . . . the road was blocked. . . ."

There was a booming noise in the background, and then the sound of hard objects striking, like heavy hail on a roof. He heard the drawn-out screams of women and the cries of children. He heard the crackling sound of wood shredding and of breaking glass.

"Hot ashes are falling. Everything is white outside. Hot stones are flying through the air. . . ." Suddenly he heard Reiko clearly. "Toshio—we were going to go together. You go ahead to Switzerland. Go ahead! I'll meet you, whatever happens."

"Reiko, no . . ." said Onodera, shouting into the phone as he gripped it tightly with his sweaty hand. "Don't talk like a fool."

A thunderous roar sounded in his ear. There were screams, the sound of the earth groaning, of something falling. Reiko's voice had risen to a desperate pitch, but he was able to catch only a single word.

". . . Geneva . . ."

There was a terrible crash, and the connection was cut. Nothing sounded in his ear but a faint hum.

Onodera stood stunned. The blood seemed to be draining out of his body. Covered with sweat, he turned to the window, and as he stared out, his eyes wide and frantic, he felt tears wetting his face.

"What's the matter?" asked Nakata. "Onodera, where are you going?"

Onodera's tall figure, however, had already disappeared through the door.

". . . Such being the circumstances, then, I would call upon the entire nation to remain calm." The Prime Minister's voice was still coming from the radio. Now he was addressing the people of Japan directly. "I ask your cooperation in the maintenance of order. Whatever course events take, this administration, this legislative body will give itself wholly to the task of saving the life of every Japanese in the face of the coming destruction. . . ."

Some minutes after the eruption began, the first sound wave struck, having covered some fifty miles. It was like a thunderclap, shaking the whole sky. Once more the room vibrated with shock. Yukinaga, still in the doorway, instinctively glanced out the window. A pall of smoke already lay over the western horizon.

The great eruption of Mount Fuji, occurring on March 12 at 1:21 P.M. just as the Prime Minister was addressing the nation, began with an explosion on its southeast side, about 1,000 yards from the peak, followed by the bursting open of some twenty craters of varying size, one after another, on the slope below, spewing forth gas, ashes, and fiery projectiles. And at almost the same time several peaks to the southeast erupted. Fiery ashes and rocks bombarded the area, blocking the Tokyo-Nagoya Expressway and cutting both the regular Tokkaido Line and the Super Express.

The first eruption went on for about two hours. And then, after a brief lull, at about 3:45 P.M. there was a tremendous explosion near the peak which carried off the entire crest of the mountain. At the same time a vast crater opened on the northern slope and a flood of lava came pouring out, for the first time in 900 years, rolling down the slope and turning the forests below into a sea of fire. The lava swallowed up a village and a cluster of resort hotels and poured into the Sai and Motosu lakes at the foot of Fuji. This cataclysm, though in fact no more than a prelude, raged for some six hours, and then there was a slackening off which lasted for about four hours. During the entire period a heavy, muddy rain fell, mixed with volcanic ash. Finally, at 1:25 A.M. on March 14 an earthquake struck the area to the southwest, and three minutes later a massive eruption blew the top of Mount Fuji into the air and split the entire mountain on a northwest-southeast line, transforming it at one stroke. Energy stored up for more than 20,000 years, trapped in a volcano that was expected never to erupt again, tore Fuji asunder, and the rain of rocks and ashes, the flood of lava, the shock waves killed more than 20,000 people. Fuji shrank in height by some 2,000 feet, and the entire district sank more than three feet. The lovely, cone-shaped mountain that had been celebrated from the era of the Manyoshu poems as the symbol of Japan was turned into a scarred crater, a hellish caldron several miles in diameter—one, moreover, that was split in such a way that it appeared to be two mountains. The volcanic ash that fell from the sky reached a depth of six feet in the vicinity of Odawara, three feet in Kofu, and in Tokyo itself four to eight inches in some places. A light coat of it covered even the runways of Narita Airport, nearly thirty miles away.

On March 22 a message came from the Plan D field group in central Japan to the Policy Committee informing them that Eastern and Western Japan, divided by the fossa magna, were beginning to slip away from each other at a considerable rate. At present the rate was several millimeters a day, and it was gradually increasing. By mid-April, the report said, the rate would most likely be several inches a day.

8

The Japan Archipelago would sink within a year. The government's announcement shocked the world, but the reaction in Japan itself was strangely calm, though it might be more accurate to say that the news had plunged the Japanese into an enervated, ominous silence. There were those who ran outside screaming, but such cases were extremely rare. As they listened to the Prime Minister's address, a hard, blank expression came over people's faces. When the broadcast had ended, the only show of emotion was, for the most part, a faint sigh. It may have been that the news was so fantastic that, for the moment, everyone was at a loss how to respond to it. At factories and offices, most workers kept on staring at the television screen as though hypnotized as they listened to the commentary and explanation that followed. There were a good number, however, who stole quietly away, and one minute after the Prime Minister had finished speaking, telephones began to ring all over Japan: Did you watch television? . . . Did you hear the speech? . . . Japan sinking—what do you think of that? . . . What are you going to do? . . . Hello, it's me. Did you hear the news? . . . Yeah, I'm coming home. I'll be right home anyway. . . . Call the children home from school. . . .

The strange thing was that there were no discussions in factories and offices. There everybody avoided each other, while some ran to the telephone and others sat thinking, looking off into space uneasily, drumming their fingers upon the tops of desks or tables.

People walked rapidly, spurred by the fear of being hit by the hard chunks of ash falling from the sky. Taxis raced by at reckless speed as though unwilling to stop to pick anyone up. Their drivers were transformed, as they listened to their radios, from men at work to fearful individuals with one thought on their minds: to get home to their families as quickly as possible.

Home! It was as though the people of this great city were crying out with a single voice as they hurried along through the rain of gray-brown ash. To get home—and then what? What could be done? Though this was the thought that loomed up dimly in the heart of everyone, no one confronted it. For now, what had to be done was to get back to one's family. After that there would be time to think about what to do.

The Japan Archipelago continued to shake convulsively. There were earthquakes registering a strength of four in every part of the country, from Hokkaido to Kyushu. Mount Aso, in the south, and Tokachi Peak, in the north, erupted at almost the same time. The tunnel connecting northern Honshu and Hokkaido had already been made unusable by flooding the previous month, and now, at the beginning of April, the rail and traffic tunnels linking Kyushu and Honshu were destroyed in the wake of a magnitude-seven earthquake which rocked Western Japan. It left the bridge over the Shimonoseki Straits so twisted that it was closed to any but light vehicles. More eruptions followed on Kyushu, and its Pacific shoreline began to sink at the appalling speed of nine feet a day. There were further eruptions in western Honshu.

In the face of all this, the people remained calm, docilely

waiting to hear what the government had to say, but since the promulgation of the general plan of evacuation, there had been nothing in the way of detailed instructions. And so the days passed, and those who lived near the international airports would gather to watch the hasty departure of the big jets carrying priority personnel. Though their faces seemed without expression, their eyes, bit by bit, began to manifest growing anxiety and mistrust. Who were these people, they wondered, who were filling the planes now that the government was running everything? The rich? The families of officials? Ward-office hangers-on? How about us? Are we going to be left till last and then abandoned when things get too dangerous? They did not put their discontent into words as yet, but it grew more intense each time they saw a departing jet climbing into the sky.

They still had faith in Japan, however, still had faith in their government. Moreover, they made every effort to strengthen this faith. The government would do something. The government would not abandon them. For politicians and officials were, after all, Japanese just like themselves—a historically rooted sense of identity that everyone shared. The Emperor had had but to speak, and the war had ended. And in the present crisis the nation was waiting in submission for whatever the government had to say, giving it the benefit of every doubt. This was the fundamental spirit of the Japanese, however critical, enraged, or vituperative they could be toward their nation on occasion.

This spirit, however, was being put to the test. The possibility of panic could not be ruled out. People were tending to let their eyes rove anxiously as though looking for a way out. At first whenever two such glances would meet, there would be a quick averting of eyes. But, gradually, people began to seek each other's eyes, as though to share their sense of being trapped. And as everyone looked on with grim, pale faces, small quakes came and went unrelentingly, and volcanic ash kept falling.

9

"A reply has come from China," said Kunieda to Nakata at the headquarters of the Evacuation Committee. "They want it kept confidential, but they'll take two million people right away and seven million eventually. And perhaps they might be willing to take still more after negotiations."

"Why, that's incredible," said Nakata. "No matter how big China is, its per-capita income is too low for that. What about the food supply?"

"Well, what they want are farmers . . . and skilled workers, too."

The United Nations had formed a committee to direct the Japanese relief operation, and gradually it began to take measures, including the formation of a plan for the distribution of refugees in which all the navies of the world would cooperate.

The topic taken up at the first closed session of the committee was the troublesome one of the manner of distributing the refugees. Wilson, the Canadian delegate, proposed considering a distribution based upon each nation's proportion of the world population. A delegate from one of the small nations protested that something like that was far too mechanical. He insisted that a host of other factors be considered, such as the country's economy, political situation, and long-range outlook.

"There would certainly be the ideal," replied Chairman Sabayo, "but it's obvious that there is no time for all that. Japan has been negotiating privately for some time, and there is still no place allotted for three quarters of her population. What we are concerned about now, gentlemen, is immediate succor—temporary refuge, not permanent homes. Once the refugees are safe, then there will be time enough for detailed negotiations."

"It's all very well to talk about temporary shelter," said Dhabi, the Jordanian delegate, "but it could last for a long time and affect a country a great deal. Dirty refugee camps, outbreaks of disease, fights, clashes with the authorities—all sorts of trouble could arise."

At that point Admiral Brubaker of the United States Navy, a special delegate, raised his hand. "If I might be allowed to put in something here . . . After the War I was involved with the repatriation of Japanese in China. And I was much impressed with how well behaved they were in those circumstances. There wasn't the least difficulty."

"But of course," said Denisigyn, the Russian delegate, breaking in. "Groups of Japanese are very submissive and easy to handle—as long as they're not armed."

"And all those I knew who served in the Occupation," said the admiral, going on as though he had not been interrupted, "confirmed my impression."

"But we all know from the Second World War that the Japanese are not always so peaceful," said Malik of Indonesia. "What is going to become of the Japanese armed forces after the evacuation?"

"One suggestion is that they serve in a special UN force. Right now they're charged with keeping order during the evacuation," answered Katsarides, the evacuation director.

"In any case, gentlemen," said Chairman Sobayo, "we have no cause to fear Japan now. Our task, rather, is the saving of her people. I beg you to realize the gravity of the situation and lay aside bitter memories. The tragedy that is about to overwhelm Japan is unprecedented in history. And what is on trial now is not Japan but our own humanity." The idealism expressed was but to be expected from Sobayo, a Tanzanian who from his early youth had been active in the cause of African unity. "Please don't think of this, gentlemen, as happening to one country in the Far East, but as something that's happening to all of us, as something that exerts the strongest possible moral force upon us."

A message was handed to the director, who ran his eyes over it quickly and passed it to Sobayo.

"I have an announcement," said the chairman. "The People's Republic of Mongolia informs us that they will take 500,000 Japanese refugees immediately and more later."

There was restrained applause.

Denisigyn smiled faintly. "They certainly won't lose anything by that, with all that land and so little population, gaining skilled Japanese."

10

While the United Nations special committee was carrying on these intense discussions marked by a show of idealism, behind the scenes political activity was also at a peak. In Washington, Moscow, London, Paris, Peking, hot lines were constantly ringing, and the circuits were filled with voices talking in all sorts of languages, simultaneously translated. Diplomats of the second rank, who could travel without attracting too much notice, were forever on their way to conferences in every part of the world. The subject of all these negotiations did not escape the notice of journalists: how would the disappearance of Japan affect the Far East and, indeed, the world? Of prime importance was the long-range effect upon the military balance. Historically, Japan's role had been one of vast influence in the Far East, both politically and economically. Once that presence was gone, what would happen? This is what the diplomats were so anxiously trying to ascertain as they hurried to develop new options and sought to grasp what was going on in the minds of their opposite numbers.

The Japanese government, the Defense Agency, and Plan D headquarters were besieged with inquiries. In Plan D headquarters, in turmoil because of its crushing work load, research papers disappeared and key personnel were constantly being asked to meet secretly with important foreigners. Foreign newsmen loitered about headquarters, and two staff members disappeared together with important papers.

"It's a matter of life and death for us, but these foreigners don't give a damn about that," Yukinaga cried out in frustration and fatigue when Kataoka brought him the news that these two men had turned up abroad. "How could those two have done such a thing? Their work was vital to us."

"Well, it won't do any good to get angry about it," said Nakata. "And, anyway, there's nothing of much importance that we haven't already told the International Geophysicists. What these people are interested in is the effect upon the surrounding area, and that's something we haven't had time to go into much. If these two want to investigate that for them, let them do it, and good riddance."

In the meantime, as the earthquakes and eruptions continued, as the Pacific coastline sank, and as the lateral movement of the Archipelago became more apparent, the activity of Japanese society slowly began to wind down. People received their food ration every day, and as anxiety mounted to an explosive pitch, they waited for their local government offices to inform them of the location of their assembly points and their order of evacuation.

And all the while a muted power struggle was going on in the international political sphere. The American President announced that elements of the Atlantic Fleet as well as the entire Pacific Fleet would aid in the evacuation of Japan, but there was some indication that, besides humanitarian motives, the Americans were anxious to counter recent Russian moves in the Far East, activity brought about by the imminent demise of Japan. With Japan gone, there would be no strong non-Communist nation in Southeast Asia to back up South Korea. And with Japan, of course, would go the American naval bases at Sasebo and Yokosuka. Also a strain was put upon Japan relations with South Korea by the arrival of refugees, who were fleeing across the straits in whatever craft they could find. South Korea, already concerned about the damage that she would incur in the catastrophe to come, treated these refugees harshly and threatened to sink every boat intercepted. Reverberations from "The Japanese Problem" traveled around the world, reaching as far as South Africa.

In the United Nations, the special committee headed by Chairman Sobayo was in session eight hours a day.

"It looks like it's going to be troublesome," said Secretary Kitowa, of the Zambian delegation, as he and Sobayo sat in a corner of the delegates' lounge. He glanced around the room as he spoke, a frown on his black face. "There's been an unconfirmed report that South Africa has sent a number of units into Nambia."

"Do you think they might have found out about the plan?" asked Sobayo, leaning forward as he pursed his thick lips.

"They could not have done that. We have not even broached it to the Nambian commissioners yet. But they probably see it as a possibility."

Nambia, formerly a German possession called Southwest Africa, had been under the jurisdiction of South Africa until 1966, when the United Nations put an end to the South African mandate and put it directly under the United Nations. The plan that Sobayo and Kitowa were secretly refining was to have the General Assembly pass a directive providing for the settlement of a large number of Japanese refugees in Nambia, providing them with a security force. There were a number of advantages to such a plan. Nambia would benefit immensely from the introduction of the skilled Japanese, and then, too, the introduction of such Asians into Africa might help to lessen the prejudice felt in East Africa toward the native Asians there, the Indians.

"Well, if South Africa has started that sort of thing," said Sobayo, standing up, "we had better bring our proposal to the attention of the commissioners immediately. At any rate, I shall be talking with the Secretary General. . . ."

Just then there was a sudden flurry of activity in the lounge. Everyone was getting up and heading for the entrance, talking excitedly.

"What's going on?" Sobayo asked a passing clerk.

"They say there's a special TV program, sir," said the clerk, turning around. "Ed Hawkins of CBS is broadcasting from Japan by satellite. It's about the sinking of Japan. It's actually started, in Shikoku or some place like that." The clerk hurried out.

"Shall we take a look?" asked Kitowa, starting to follow the crowd.

"Wait," said Sobayo, laying a huge hand on the other's shoulder. "Look there."

With a nod of his head, the chairman indicated a corner of the room where a small gray-haired Oriental was standing quietly, paying no notice to the stream of people hurrying by him, his eyes fixed upon the red sunset that silhouetted the skyline of New York. He had taken off his glasses, and Sobayo and Kitowa could see, even from where they stood, that the hand with which he held them was trembling. The old man's deep-lined face was lit by the sunset glow, and he was lightly dabbing his eyes with a handkerchief. It was Shintaro Nozaki, the Japanese member of the special committee.

VI

Japan Sinks

1

It was on the morning of April 30, at ten minutes after five, that the first cataclysm struck the Osaka-Kyoto area. Never before had an earthquake of this kind been recorded. Never before had a quake struck so vast an area.

Of a total population of 30 million in the four prefectures that made up the district, 3.5 million had already been evacuated by sea and by air during a thirty-day period preceding the quake. The new Osaka Airport had been overwhelmed by the encroaching water, and there was no choice but to fall back upon the old airport at Itami. By dint of frantic round-the-clock labor, the runways, damaged in the previous quake, were made ready to take the huge jet passenger planes just before daybreak on March 1. All the ground crew and other personnel from the now-defunct domestic airlines were put to work here, and soon planes were taking off and landing at the rate of some 500 in a twenty-four-hour period. With the aid of the United States Air Force, close to 500,000 people were flown out of Japan during this period, a figure unprecedented in the history of aviation.

During the period the sinking of the Pacific coast and the rise of the Japan Sea coast became much more pronounced, and the harbor facilities, especially at Kobe and Osaka, suffered immensely. Consequently, in most cases the loading of refugees had to be done with the transport ships anchored either offshore or in rivers, and every sort of small vessel that could be found was pressed into service to ferry the refugees out to the ships, from landing craft to old-style fishing boats. And despite all the obstacles, in this month some 3.2 million people were evacuated. The district evacuation headquarters, however, was determined to spare no effort to raise the rate to 5 million a month. The June rainy season would slow air transportation, and with August and September would come the ever present danger of typhoons.

The day the quake struck, at dawn on April 30, refugees whose turn had come had been massing at the airport and at the harbor all through the previous night. Those not so lucky, their mood desolate, were sleeping fitfully in their homes while light quakes succeeded one another without let-up. Their bags were packed and their personal goods gathered together, in anticipation of their turn coming or of an emergency evacuation.

Buses and trucks arrived at the airport, one after another, and silent refugees, loaded with baggage, streamed into the terminal. Tents had been pitched in front of the terminal, and flight numbers were posted on each. Police and airport personnel kept order in the long boarding lines. The adults were white-faced and silent. Since it was so early, infants were sleeping on their mothers' backs, but little children frolicked about as though they were on an excursion.

And along the flooded coastline of Osaka Bay, at Kobe, Ashiya, Sakai, and other ports, and, along the banks of the Yodogawa and Anjigawa, similar scenes were being enacted. Osaka Bay was filled with ships of every nation, a vast number of them freighters or even ore boats hastily converted to take passengers. Ship after ship got under way with a dull, rumbling whistle, the water boiling up at its stern, and turned its bow toward Kii Strait and the open sea. The screeching, piercing whistles of the tugs that guided them echoed beneath a leaden sky.

At 5:10 A.M., a Sabena Boeing 707, making its approach from the southeast, landed on Runway B at Itami. The refugees waiting in the terminal fixed their eyes upon the jet as it taxied by them, the roar of its engines' reverse thrust filling the air. At that moment those by the windows saw a white flash light the overcast sky.

Down by the harbors the people aboard ship saw the flash more clearly. Like a brilliant curtain of white, it rushed from east to west along the southern horizon, silhouetting the surrounding mountains as far off as Kii, Awaji Island, and Shikoku.

Three times it raced from east to west and back again, touches of purple and green flickering here and there against the whiteness. A surge of dread went through the crowds.

The captain of the *Okuma Maru*, a 26,000-ton freighter loading passengers from one of the still-usable piers in Ashiya Harbor, had just come up onto the bridge, rubbing his sleepy eyes and yawning, when he heard a deckhand yell something. He turned to look at the southern sky, and the next instant he was jamming his finger against the emergency alarm button.

"Start engines!" he roared to the watch officer. "Prepare to cast off—emergency procedure."

His mouth agape, the watch officer relayed the command to the engine room.

"The passengers—how many of them are still not on board?" yelled the captain, grabbing hold of the purser, who had come running up to the bridge at the sound of the ship's siren.

"About two hundred. They're coming on now."

"Hurry it up. Put more men on it. The gangplank goes up in five minutes. We've got to get out of here as quick as we can. Get the radioman. Have him call the transport office and tell them we're getting under way at once. Blow the whistle and let the other ships know. We've got to get out to the open sea."

"What's happening?" asked the startled purser.

"You damn fool! Chances are we're going to get hit with a tidal wave."

The boarding passengers had stopped in their tracks at the sound of the alarm, but crewmen with megaphones now rushed over the pier, hurrying them on board. It was then that the first shock struck. A terrified cry went up from the crowd standing on the half-drowned pier, and the violent up-and-down motion of the quake caused two or three people to lose their footing and fall into the water.

"Prepare to get under way," said the captain to the watch officer. "We'll go with the diesels. There's no time for the turbines."

The *Okuma Maru*'s whistle, like the sinister moan of some monstrous beast, echoed against the dark sky. The captain took hold of the portable speaker and called down to the pier: "Get those people out of the water. There's still time. Another quake is coming. But take care in coming on. Don't get excited."

Then he turned to the deck crew: "Loosen the hawsers! Relay it to the stern. Prepare to cast off."

On a runway at Osaka Airport the captain of a Pan Am 747 jumbo jet, loaded to capacity with 490 passengers, had just opened his four engines to full thrust and had started his quivering 350-ton plane on its takeoff run when the first shock struck.

Cups flew from a table in the control tower, and so violent was the up-and-down motion that some lights went out.

"An earthquake!" someone yelled. "Stop Flight 107. Don't let it try to take off."

It was evident even from the tower, however, that the plane had already reached a speed of well over 100 miles an hour. The air controllers watched through the rattling windows of the tower as the huge body of the plane began to shake with a rising and falling motion, its wheels bounding slightly. The chief controller's face turned ashen as he gripped the microphone.

"Aren't you going to stop him? What are you doing? Hurry!" shouted another controller in a frenzy. He tried to snatch the microphone away, but the chief controller pushed him roughly aside. The chief controller had been in the tower at Haneda Airport in Tokyo when a passenger plane landed at the very moment the great quake began. He knew how quakes behaved, and thus made his decision. The epicenter of this one had to be very close, and even if the runway was long enough for the Pan Am jet to come to a stop, the second shock wave would hit with disastrous effect before it was able to do so.

Flight 107 attained a speed of 115 miles per hour, then 140, its great mass bouncing up and down. Its wheels seem to leave the ground and then touch down again as it bounded along.

God help them!

Modern skeptic though he was, the chief controller's heart cried out at that moment. He thought of the captain and co-pilot bent over the controls in the cabin, their eyes fixed on the end of the runway toward which their huge plane was hurtling at full throttle. As the distance remaining melted away, the captain would have to make his decision, and the point of no return was rushing to meet him.

Take off! the chief controller shouted within himself. In a brief moment his whole body had become wet with sweat. Don't stop! Give it all you've got! Get into the air. Don't get caught!

"He did it!" somebody yelled.

The chief controller brushed the sweat from his eyes as he watched the giant plane's front wheels lift off, followed by its sixteen main wheels, with a bare fraction of the huge runway remaining.

"To all planes on the ground—this is the tower," said the chief controller into the microphone. "Emergency! Cut your engines. An earthquake is coming."

At that instant there was a sound like a thunderclap, and he was thrown from his chair.

"Take over for me," he said in a hoarse voice to a colleague who came to his assistance. "Put the planes waiting to land in hold patterns. And get out of here. There's a rough one coming."

The first shock wave passed. No sooner had it done so, however, than up from the depths of the earth there came an uncanny groaning sound. The control tower, struck with a dreadful force, spun around as though upon a giant turntable. The assistant controller shouted desperately into the microphone to the planes circling above, but his voice was lost amid screams and crashes and the awful rumble of the earthquake.

At this same moment the American satellite *Manned Orbiting Laboratory #3,* having passed through the already bright Northern Pacific sky, was moving through the predawn darkness that still covered Japan at an altitude of seventy miles. The commander was monitoring the vast array of cameras and other instruments trained on the scene below. Two other crewmen were sleeping, and the fourth was peering out the observation window, watching through binoculars the smoke still pouring up from shattered Mount Fuji and the flickering points of fire that marked the newly active volcanoes strung through the central mountain ranges. With dawn just breaking, he found his vision obscured, and he switched on the night vision screen.

"Hey, look!" he shouted, grabbing the commander's shoulder. "There's something going on in Western Japan."

The area covered by the screen was Ise Bay and the Kii Peninsula, south of Osaka. The commander turned to look over the man's shoulder, and then he immediately switched to a wider coverage and started the video transmission.

"What's the matter?" said a third man in a sleepy voice as he got out of his bunk.

"I don't know. Get Pat up. We'll need him. Look! The color of the water's changing."

On the almost black surface of the sea, just off the Japanese coast, blue-green splotches took form and then spread at incredible speed, moving east and west. And at the same time they began to move out into the Pacific, coalescing to form an advancing blue-green line behind which new splotches, light blue in color, began to appear. "Keep those cameras going. Jimmy, look out the other window."

The fourth crewman, too, sprang into action. He threw switches on the control panel and fixed his eyes to the quivering needles, some of which began to spin erratically.

"Damn! This is really something," he said, frantically making adjustments. "Both gravity and terrestrial magnetism are all screwed up. Bill, are we on the frequency of any ships in the area?"

"Yes. The *LaFayette* should be right below us. Should I tell them not to get too close to the coast?"

"My God!" cried the crewman with the binoculars. "Look what's happening. Japan is breaking up!"

Before the horrified eyes of the four Americans, the outline of Shikoku and the southern part of the Kii Peninsula below suddenly seemed to blur slightly, as though trembling. The now blue surface of the sea became covered with small pale splotches, which spread out to the east and west, forming a single line. A shock sent a ripple over the surface of the ocean, and this, gathering up the splotches as it went, began to spread outward with awesome deliberation, a dark, sweeping curve.

"A tidal wave," cried the crewman with the binoculars. The dark line of the wave spread across the blue surface of the ocean beneath them. It would strike the islands of Eastern Asia and even the coast of Chile.

"Hey, the southern coast of Japan is changing," said the crewman at the movie camera.

"Pat! Get Houston," shouted the commander, staring at the screen. "Tell them that Japan is going under."

The southern portion of Shikoku and the Kii Peninsula along the structural fault line of the Yoshino and Kiino rivers had begun to move southeast into the Pacific, rocked by quake after quake. The rest of the Western Archipelago was moving too, but at a slower pace. The sea swept into the breach, and the Yoshino and the Kiino grew broader and broader. When the detached land mass reached the end of the continental shelf, it began to sink at the incredible rate of several yards an hour along a line some hundreds of miles long. Several hours after the first quake had struck, most of the towns along the southern coasts of Shikoku and the Kii Peninsula had disappeared, the ocean coming as far as the foot of Nachi Falls on the Kii.

The slippage between north and south along the central structural line gradually spread eastward. When the quake had struck Western Japan at dawn, the whole Central Region too, had experienced a medium-grade quake. Afterward the earth had continued to rumble in sinister fashion. Now at 10:47 a quake of like severity struck Central Japan, and a new fault developed on a line running from the mouth of Ise Bay to the Fuji River at the base of Mount Fuji. A tidal wave nearly thirty feet high swept into Sagami Bay, devastating the coastal cities. Destroying as they went, the ocean waters surged over the area depressed by the great eruption, moving along the line of the Fuji River as far as Fujinomiya.

A vast quantity of ocean water poured into the still-active Ashitaka volcano, southwest of the shattered slopes of Fuji. Mount Ashitaka shook throughout the day with minor eruptions, and then, at two in the afternoon, a thunderous explosion destroyed every vestige of it. The hostile elements clashed again, and firestorm and flood ravaged Central Honshu.

2

The television-equipped helicopter carrying Kataoka on a Plan D inspection mission crossed from the Kii Peninsula to Shikoku, following the fault line. The heavy rain brought on by the shock of the quake had slackened after an hour and a half, and Shikoku's mountains had begun to show through the clouds. The helicopter pilot flew as low as he dared through the treacherous air currents, and as Kataoka looked down, he saw, through the breaks in the clouds, traces of the havoc below. He caught glimpses of ravaged earth and the dull, leaden glint of flooded fields. Furthermore, he could see any number of crevices cutting diagonally through the mountains from northwest to south-east. The green mountainsides were rent, exposing the raw texture of the earth beneath, red, brown, and black scars. In places the dark crevices seemed to gape open to incredible depths. It was as though giant hands had wrung the earth below like a mop. Kataoka could see landslides still taking place and steam boiling up from the crevices.

A colleague sitting beside him tapped his shoulder and pointed down. A passenger boat lay on its side in the rice paddies below. From such a height it was of course impossible to make out any people, but when Kataoka looked down at the red bottom of the stranded vessel, he thought of the crowds massed on the docks and shorelines that morning, fearful of what was ahead but relieved that their turn to leave had come, and a black depression took hold of him. His own family had been wiped out in an instant by the tidal wave that had followed the great Tokyo quake, and now he imagined he could hear the cries of his young brother and sister rising from the drowned fields below. He covered his ears with his hands.

"What's the matter?"

"Take over for me, will you?" said Kataoka, getting up from the television monitor. "I have to vomit."

At Plan D headquarters Yukinaga and Nakata were staring somberly at the television screen, watching the transmission from another helicopter, this one flying above stricken Osaka.

The three low-lying districts adjacent to the harbor were almost completely submerged. The water that covered them was an inky black, probably because the silt at the bottom of the bay had been churned up by the tidal wave. The dark water flowed through the city and, twisting and eddying as it went, surged farther inland. The factories and petroleum tanks clustered at the mouths of the rivers that flowed through Osaka had taken the brunt of the quake and the tidal waves. Some had been obliterated and others lay in ruins. And as Yukinaga and Nakata watched, those left standing were collapsing one after another into the murky water that flowed around them. A floating dock, the ship that had been under repair still within it, lay upon what seemed to be Benten Pier like a ship run aground. Only a portion of the roof of the huge pier facility was still above water. A capsized ocean liner was jammed into a shattered street, its red bottom pointing upward. The black oil which lay like a blanket over the bay and was flowing into the city as well had begun to flame up here and there. Even in the wards somewhat removed from the waterfront, the water had reached the third and fourth stories of buildings.

The elevated expressways lay twisted and shattered. The supports of the section running through the Nakanoshima district in the center of the city had been torn away, and it lay beneath the murky water. In this area only the tops of trees and buildings were to be seen and a flat-bottomed riverboat, its prow stuck fast in the side of a building.

The black water that had worked so stunning a transformation of Osaka was now lapping at the high ground in the eastern section of the central city, where Osaka Castle and the government buildings stood, twisting its way toward the northeastern suburbs along the banks of the Yodogawa. And to the south, the turgid, backed-up waters of the Yamatogawa merged with those that had swept over the dikes to the north, and began to move relentlessly toward Ikoma Heights, to the east of the city.

According to legend, when the Emperor Nintoku had founded his capital, the waters of the bay had covered most of what was to be modern Osaka. And now after earthquake and tidal wave, at the foot of Takatsu Shrine, where ships had moored in ancient times, what looked like a roofed oyster boat lay tilted, its prow aground on the shrine steps.

The roofs of the apartment buildings were crowded with refugees, who looked up with grim, anxious expressions, waving and shouting at the helicopter flying overhead. The murky water that swept around the buildings was filled with corpses, bobbing in the midst of debris of every sort. Such was the force of the current that in some places automobiles were swept together into a mass blocking a street, and here the black water turned white as it raced over these obstacles.

"It looks like we'll have to fall back on Senriyama for a marshaling point," muttered Nakata as he watched the screen. "Get in contact with D-3," he said to the radio operator. "Find out what they think. The Expo 70 grounds are big enough for both the big helicopters and the STOL planes. And find out what damage they've suffered."

The operator struggled to get through to the Ground Defense Force at Itami, where the D-3 group was located. When Itami finally came in, the reception was bad and it was difficult to get the message. It seemed that all road traffic had been blocked as a result of damage done by the quake, and the large ponds in the area had overflowed, causing extensive flooding. As a result the refugees, some of them nearly out of their minds with desperation, were besieging the Ground Defense headquarters. A helicopter sent from the naval station at Maizuru had been destroyed by the crowd, and a young officer had lost his head and fired.

"Fired? Into the crowd?" shouted Nakata, jumping up and lunging toward the radio operator.

"No. Into the air, I think," answered the distraught operator, trying frantically to maintain contact. "What happened was that the crowd turned on the soldiers then. Two were badly hurt. . . . No . . . one man was killed."

"What's the matter with the military down there?" shouted Nakata, angrily pounding his fist on the table. "Tell the commander that the officers have got to set an example. They've got to keep their heads!"

"Don't get excited," said Yukinaga. "They know what they're doing."

All at once the various pinging sounds that filled the communication room were drowned out by the emergency buzzer. There had been a time when this sound would have galvanized everyone, but now they heard it with weary resignation.

On the fluorescent map on the wall, two, then three red lights flashed on in the North Central Region.

"From Matsumoto . . . Mount Norikura erupted. Yake and Fudo are on the verge," a technician reported. "That was at seven thirty, and right after, a report from Nagano . . . in the direction of Mount Takazuma . . . eruptions along the western slope . . . at eight three."

"Takazuma?" Yukinaga whispered, taken aback.

"That's sooner than we thought," said Nakata, clucking his tongue and glancing up at the board. "We thought it would start there sooner or later. . . . Well, at any rate, it's on both sides of the Itoigawa fossa magna now. Lateral movement is more than two yards. Everybody along the coast there should have been moved out by now."

"I hope so, but . . ." muttered Yukinaga in a hollow voice as he gazed vacantly at the flashing red lights on the board.

The buzzer rang again. Two red lights flashed on the extreme northeast.

"From Morioka . . . Iwate and Koma starting to erupt," came the technician's voice, echoing mechanically through the room.

Yukinaga stood in front of the board as though he did not hear. The glowing map of the Japan Archipelago seemed to blur before his unfocused eyes and take on the form of a dragon. The spine of the dragon, the central mountain ranges, was speckled with orange dots glowing like an ugly pox. The familiar outline of the Archipelago was being altered drastically by the encroaching blue spreading over its coasts. And crossing it and recrossing were countless vertical, horizontal, and slanted lines, each scarlet stroke representing a structural break. The most recent had flashed on the board that morning, the slash running from the Kii Peninsula across into Shikoku. Scattered from one end of the main island of Honshu to the other, the red dots, which stood for eruptions, glowed like clots of blood. Off the coast of the Kanto Region, though the Izu Islands had been all but overwhelmed by the sea, more red dots marked the volcanic fires still bursting up from the ocean floor.

The dragon was stricken.

A fatal illness was eating at him, destroying his very marrow. Racked with fever, his vast bulk covered with bleeding wounds, he thrashed about, vainly struggling against the fate that was tearing at him. The encroaching blue sliding over him was like the shadow of death.

Yukinaga was lost in reflections of his own. His vacant gaze was now fixed on the North Central Region, where clusters of red lights were flashing insistently.

3

When Mount Takazuma erupted that morning, Onodera was flying over the North Central Region in a small Defense Force helicopter on an inspection mission. Since the entire population of the region had supposedly been evacuated, he and the pilot were startled to see a group waving up at them from in front of a mountain shelter house. They landed, and Onodera got out of the helicopter to discover three parties of mountain climbers, fourteen people in all, students and young office workers. They had come into the region despite the evacuation orders and had been trapped by the cumulative disasters and bad weather. Two of them had already died from injuries and exposure. A girl was ill with pneumonia, and a young man was badly injured.

Onodera was enraged: "What the hell did you people have in mind when you did this? Did you have any idea at all of what was going on?"

"Yes, we did," said a youth with high cheekbones in a weary voice. "Our parents and everybody else tried to talk us out of it. But we love mountain climbing. It's what we live for. If these beautiful Japan Alps are going to disappear from the face of the earth, we wanted to bid a last farewell to them. What's so bad about that? We came knowing that we might die here, and, if so, well and good."

"I see," said Onodera, turning around and starting back to the helicopter. "Well, if that's the way you feel, it'll make things a lot simpler for us."

Onodera's mood was a bleak one. What's happened to me? he thought as he returned to the helicopter. The memory of Reiko came to him, a memory that had to be repressed violently lest it tear at him. The day that he had run blindly out of Plan D headquarters, volcanic ash had been falling on Tokyo and the trains had stopped running. He had had but a single thought: to get somehow from Tokyo to the Izu Peninsula, to the spot where Reiko had called from. He had run to the Defense Force helicopter base at nearby Ichigaya and demanded to be flown there. After an officer had refused him, Onodera had grown violent and had to be thrown off the base. Later, however, he had been able to get a ride on an armored troop-carrier. At Odawara, at the head of the Izu Peninsula, however, ash and falling rock had blocked the vehicle's way. When Onodera had leaped down to the ground, his feet had sunk more than three feet into the gray wasteland. He had screamed out in frustration. After his return to Tokyo he had gone to Evacuation Headquarters and, disregarding the pleas of Nakata and Yukinaga, had demanded to be used in the most dangerous rescue missions. And so he had gone on these past weeks, sleeping and eating less than even his hard-driven companions, growing ever more haggard and desolate, and making a name for himself by the reckless heroism of his conduct. What am I doing to myself? he wondered groggily. I'm like a man already dead.

"Sergeant Tomita?" he shouted to the pilot above the roar of the rotor. "How many can we carry?"

"Two. Ordinarily it would be six, but there's the equipment, and there's no time to dismantle it."

"Make it four. One of them's sick. Two others are injured."

"Can't be done," said the pilot, gesturing behind him. "No matter what you do, there's not enough space for four."

"I'll stay here. So you can put one beside you and squeeze two more back there with the equipment somehow. You can do it, can't you? And as for these other idiots, do you think you can get a helicopter to come from the squadron at Matsumoto?"

"No, I don't think there's any chance— But wait. A UH-1B is at Matsumoto Airport. It developed engine trouble the other day and had to stop for repairs. If it can fly, maybe I can have them send it. It would take all of you . . . but the problem of fuel . . ."

"Okay," said Onodera, looking at his watch. "See what you can do, anyway. We don't have much time." Onodera turned away and walked back toward the youths, four or five of whom were standing a short distance away with worried looks on their faces. One of them, a young man with long hair and glasses, spoke to Onodera: "You weren't really serious, sir, were you? Before, I mean. You wouldn't just fly off and leave us, would you?"

"We can take three. Get the sick girl and the two injured on board. Hurry up."

"There's one more girl. She's not in good shape. Can she go, too?" asked a strongly built youth.

"No. Only three. Even with me staying behind. So let's get moving!"

Onodera went into the dimly lit cabin with the young men, and as the sick and injured climbers were being carried out, he noticed a young girl standing as though in a daze, with the side of her face pressed against the cabin wall.

"Better leave her alone, sir," said one of the youths, frowning. "She was almost out of her head before. She's suffering from shock."

Disregarding this advice, Onodera walked up to the girl and

put a hand on her thin shoulder and shook her. Her cheeks and clothes were stained with tears, and from the gaudily stylish cut and color of her mountain-climbing attire, it was obvious at a glance that she was not an outdoor girl. She was frowning and her body shook from time to time as though with sobs.

"Let me alone!" She shook off his hand, her voice like a scream, and shrank away from him. "I can't walk any farther. . . . Mama! Please help me!"

Onodera took hold of the sobbing girl and gave her two light slaps across the face.

"Pull yourself together. Another helicopter will come to pick us up soon. Now help us load up these people."

The girl stared up in shocked surprise, her eyes swollen from crying. Onodera thought that in the dim light of the cabin he saw a sudden awareness come over her face, but with no time for such considerations, he turned and ran out of the cabin.

"When you get them back, Sergeant, don't tell anybody what really happened."

"I understand. They're refugees who were trapped by landslides. And as soon as I find out the situation on the helicopter, I'll contact you."

Onodera slapped the pilot on the shoulder, slammed the door shut, and turned to see a slight figure in bright-colored mountain-climbing garb walking unsteadily toward him.

"Mr. Onoda!"

Onodera was stunned. Then something stirred faintly in his memory.

"You're Mr. Onoda, aren't you, sir?"

"Onodera," he said, staring at the girl.

"Why . . . imagine you here, sir!"

It was Mako. It was the little hostess he had met on the Ginza what now seemed long years ago. She threw herself into his arms and sobbed like a little girl as he stood buffeted by the wind and by the blast from the rotor.

"I'm frightened, Mr. Onoda! I'm tired. I can't walk. I'm cold. Please let me get on the helicopter."

"No," he said, gently moving her away from the helicopter. "That's for the sick and injured. Don't worry. A big helicopter will come soon and take all of us."

He gestured to the pilot, and the helicopter lifted off with a roar and a still stronger blast from its rotor.

"Does anybody know this girl?" he asked after the helicopter had gone.

"Nobody here, sir," answered one of them. "I was with her group. Another one, my friend, went in the helicopter, and the fourth one died. He was her boyfriend, and my friend and I never met them before this."

"All right," said Onodera, taking hold of Mako's arm and supporting her, "let's get into the cabin."

"What do we do now, sir?" one of the youths asked.

"We wait," he answered, looking at his watch. It was 7:35.

"How long, do you think?"

"I don't know. A big quake and tidal wave hit the Kansai Region this morning. Hundred of thousands of people were killed. We have perhaps a fifty-fifty chance that they'll be able to send a second helicopter for us."

"And if they don't?"

They had reached the cabin door. Onodera stopped before going in and looked back at the windswept ridge. "Well, three have been saved anyway, and we will have had a chance to get to know each other." Ignoring their varied reactions, Onodera helped Mako to lie down on a cot and then turned his attention to the wireless set he had taken from the helicopter.

"Let's take a look at your map. If worse comes to worst, we'll have to try making it out on foot."

Just then the radio began to sputter. The voice was Sergeant Tomita's, but it was hard to make out. Onodera pressed the receiver to his ear and spoke into the microphone as he balanced the set on his knees.

"This is Shirauma. It's Onodera. Sergeant Tomita, do you hear me?" Onodera repeated the question again and again. Finally his expression brightened. "Cheer up, gentlemen," he said after he had put down the microphone. "A helicopter's leaving Matsumoto in about a half-hour."

Though they had little strength left, the youths gave a hoarse cheer.

Onodera raised a warning hand. "It's not coming direct but by way of Nagano. So we have a good hour and a half to wait yet."

Before Onodera had finished speaking, however, the earth

began to groan and the cabin began to creak as it rocked back and forth. A dull booming sound echoed through the mountains. Onodera bent quickly to pick up the radio, which he had put back down on the floor, but as he was lifting it up, a second shock hit the cabin, and he collided with one of young men, whose arm knocked the set from his hands. Before it struck the floor, however, a transmission came through marred by terrible static: "Attention . . . emergency warning . . . Norikura is on the verge of eruption."

There were explosions that sounded like fireworks and then a cannonlike booming that seemed to reverberate through one's whole body.

"An eruption!" shouted someone in a shrill voice.

"It's started. We can't get away."

"Take it easy," said Onodera. "Norikura's way to the south."

"No, it's here. There's another Norikura, and it's right above us."

Onodera glanced at his watch. It was 7:45. Outside there was a rumble as though the very axis of the earth had been shaken. One youth ran outside.

"It's water," he cried as the thunderous rumble grew louder. "Water's coming down the slope."

"It's from Shirauma Lake," said a tall young man quietly, his face white.

"We'll get swept away!" somebody shouted. "We'd better run."

"Wait," commanded Onodera. He shouted to the boy outside: "Where is it going?"

"It's all right," the boy answered. "It's turning toward Ume Pond."

Onodera went to the door and looked out. The muddy water mixed with snow rushed down the slope close to the cabin with the force of a cascade, sending up a spray of snow and water. From time to time it would strike a rocky outcropping, and a plume of muddy water would spurt skyward. The mountains around echoed and re-echoed its deep rumble, and the valleys below, from which the mist was starting to rise, seemed to tremble. Part of the flow, arching like a waterfall, was falling into a crevice that had opened just below. Gradually its rumble subsided, but the sinister explosions and the roar that came from beyond the ridge line did not grow any less. Suddenly Onodera threw away his half-lit cigarette and sniffed the air. He could smell sulfur.

"Let's go. We'll go north of Akakura and down to Otani. It's our only chance, and we should be able to make it."

He rushed out of the cabin and drew an arrow in the snow with his foot. Beside this he wrote: "To Otani." The wind would probably blow it away before the helicopter came, but with a wind like that no helicopter was likely to come anyway. He looked up to see Mako's bright jacket in the midst of the wind-blown group that had come out of the cabin. He went over and took her by the arm.

"I can't walk," she said, sobbing. "I'm freezing . . . let me die. The helicopter won't come, will it?"

"Come on now. Pull yourself together and walk. If you fall down, I'll pick you up."

Fighting the wind-driven snow, they made their way across an open meadow and then began their descent of the east slope by means of a ravine. The sulfur smell grew more intense.

Heavy mist was rising from the Itoigawa Ravine in front of them, hiding the Togakushi Range on the other side. A chill suddenly ran through Onodera.

"Sir, look at that!" came a shrill voice behind him. "There's fire behind the mist over there."

Red flames tinged the dirty gray mist that was covering the sky, and as the ever present rumble of the earth grew louder yet, a second layer of flame appeared below the first, and a curtain of inky black smoke began to blot out the little brightness left to the sky. What was falling around them was no longer small rocks falling down the sides of the ravine but a steady rain of still-warm volcanic fragments.

Onodera stopped in his tracks and stood gazing at the red hell seething behind the mist. The sulfur smell had been in front of them, not behind them. It had been coming from Mount Togakushi.

"Sir, what are we going to do?" a youth beside him screamed as the hot ash poured down on them.

On April 30 at 8:03 A.M. Mount Takazuma in the Togakushi Range erupted with an explosion that blew off its crest. And an instant later there began that series of eruptions that tore open twelve distinct craters along the western slopes of the Togaku-shi Range.

Epilogue

The Death of the Dragon

At the eastern edge of the Eurasian land mass, which covers half of the Northern Hemisphere, a dragon lay dying. As he twisted his huge body and thrashed his tail, smoke and fire poured from every part of him. He shook convulsively, racked by spasms. His once powerful back, covered with towering spines surrounded by green forests, had been hacked asunder, and from his wounds hot blood poured out spasmodically. And from the depths of the sea, whose Black Current had gently caressed his belly from ancient times, there now rose the chill jaws of death. As savage as a school of crazed sharks, it shook the dragon's body as it tore away piece after piece of flesh from his belly, gulping them down one after another into that vast stomach that covered most of the earth.

Kyushu, Shikoku, the southern half of the Kii Peninsula were already torn away and nearly swallowed up. The Boso Peninsula, which had formed one side of Tokyo Bay, had also been severed from the body, and its tip was already plunged some fifty feet below the sea. In northeastern Honshu the coastline had slid some sixty feet into the Pacific. The waters were rushing in on Hokkaido, too, and sections of it had fallen away. As for the islands to the southwest of Japan, the transformation had become evident more than a year and a half earlier, and by now many islands had vanished entirely.

An unseen giant stood behind the dragon, pressing upon him. It was this same giant who, 400 million years before, had helped to form the young dragon, thrusting him away from the continent that had conceived him. But now the giant's benevolent strength had turned into something vicious. It had shattered the dragon's backbone, twisted his body, thrust him down into the sea.

In the short space of two or three years Japan had been pushed nearly thirty miles to the southeast. The pressure on Central Honshu was especially intense. Such was the heat coming up from the earth that the rainy season began in May, and as the soft rain fell upon Japan, coastlines melted away and plains became shallow seas. Sea then linked up with sea, and ocean-going ships were able to make their way to what had once been inland cities and towns.

The agonized dragon fought back against the violent forces that were pushing him away from the continent and down into the sea. At the beginning of June four fifths of his body were still above water as he tried to shake off the cold hand of death that had reached up from the depths. And as the dragon writhed and bellowed, smoke and fire pouring from each gaping wound, there perished vast numbers of the tiny creatures that had lived upon him. And the rest were fleeing over the encroaching sea, leaving behind the body that had for countless centuries given them sustenance. The dragon still lived, but his death was quite near. And the eyes of the whole world were fixed upon his death agony.

Planes laden with cameras, flying through smoke and fire, ranged far and wide over the sinking Archipelago. Every major television network throughout the world had its men on the scene.

Ordinary men and women mourned what was happening as a great tragedy for humanity, but for them it was also a spectacle of immense fascination. What was sinking into the ocean was not some shadowy Atlantis of legend, but a modern industrial nation of immense wealth and power, a nation, furthermore, rich in history and culture. A great island nation which some massive force deep within the planet was breaking apart, tearing with eruptions, shattering into fragments, and, finally, drawing down into the depths of the sea. For scientists, of course, the cause for fascination ran far deeper. Never before had they had the opportunity to witness such a thing, and never would they again. What did this phenomenon mean? Had the earth reached a new stage of existence?

The emotions of the rest of the world were complex, therefore—sympathy, curiosity, a zealous desire to help, a feeling of relief that this was not happening to one's own country, concern about what effect the flood of refugees might have. . . .

The only ones who could face the tragedy in simple, straight-forward fashion and throw themselves headlong into the struggle were the Japanese themselves. And soon the rescue units were performing in such spectacular fashion that the world began to speak of the "Japanese Miracle." They worked without sleep or rest, and as the end drew near, their casualties mounted at an incredible rate. Among the foreign rescue units, the largest contingent and the group that worked most closely and most effectively with the Japanese was the United States Marines, who lost more than 200 men.

In a television interview the Marine commander, Brigadier General Grant, expressed himself in highly emotional terms: "The Japanese relief organizations—government officials, soldiers, civilians alike—have been performing with incredible courage. I've seen situations where even veteran Marines who have been through all kinds of combat would have held back, but these people rushed fearlessly ahead. It's their fellow countrymen they're saving, of course, but they have so little regard for danger, no matter how desperate the situation, that sometimes when we talk it over among ourselves, we wonder if perhaps this tragedy hasn't made them half crazy."

This was all that was actually broadcast, but General Grant in fact went on to say: "I think that as a people they have a Kamikaze instinct. Or else you might say that they're all soldiers at heart. Why, even the supposedly weaker younger generation has fitted right in. . . ."

As the end drew nearer and nearer, the Japanese Miracle went on, a desperate challenge flung in the face of death. Despite earthquake, eruption, and flood, 65 million people had somehow been evacuated, at the incredible rate of some 16 million per month. As the devastation and sinking began to reach a more acute stage, however, with a large-scale breakdown of communication and transportation facilities, the pace of evacuation began to slacken. It became difficult to marshal large concentrations of refugees, and soon there was no choice but to pick up small groups isolated throughout the country.

By the beginning of July there was only one international airport left in operation, at Chitose, in Hokkaido, and it was only a question of time before that, too, was gone. There were some smaller airports remaining in the north of Japan as well as some military airports, which were used as much as their capacity allowed. For the rest, the transport planes were reduced to landing and taking off on whatever broad, open meadowland still remained beyond the reach of the sea.

Now instead of airliners and ships, the burden of the rescue came to rest entirely upon helicopters, STOL aircraft, and other kinds of military planes that could operate under difficult conditions. The huge Soviet transport planes proved especially valuable, as they were able to carry heavy loads and negotiate the worst possible terrain.

By mid-July more than 70 million had been evacuated, at the cost of the most desperate labor. The toll of victims, including those who had died in the Tokyo earthquake, had passed 12 million. Among these, many had died after they thought they had been saved, perishing in air crashes or sea disasters. The rescue units themselves had suffered more than 5,000 casualties. And 30 million Japanese were still left upon the ravaged, sinking Archipelago—frightened groups scattered throughout the country, in isolated inland sections or on high ground near the seacoast. The rescue units threw themselves into the task of saving each and every one of them with an almost insane zeal. They hardly noticed whether it was day or night, spending themselves without rest or sleep, carrying through their desperate missions even at the cost of life itself.

As July gave way to August and rescue became more difficult, the cataclysm claimed more and more victims and the casualties of the rescue units themselves shot up sharply. Many dropped from exhaustion as they toiled unremittingly beneath a sinister sky covered with a pall of smoke, the stink of sulfur in their nostrils and the taste of ashes in their mouths, while the never quiet earth rumbled beneath them. All this took its toll of their morale. As they grew wearier with each passing day, a growing despair took hold of them. How could they hope to win their battle against the violent, overwhelming force of nature? Their fate was sealed, and nothing they could do would alter it. Together with the scattered remains of their countrymen, they would perish beneath the smothering ashes or be swallowed up by the voracious, dark sea.

In the middle of August the first typhoon of the season took form in the South Pacific and began to move toward Japan. In the midst of her other torments, she was now to be afflicted with that of a raging storm. The fleet of rescue vessels sought the relative safety of the open sea, and many among them sailed for home. The efforts of June and July had brought more than 4.5 million people out of the country, bringing the total to some 70 million. During these same two months, however, the toll of dead and presumed dead had increased by more than three million. Among these were many who, either overwhelmed with despair or crazed with shock, committed suicide. And of the 20 million remaining, a considerable number yielded their turns to others and went off by themselves. The vast majority of these were men in their seventies and older. They would leave notes for their families and disappear from the marshaling points in the middle of the night. The future could be entrusted to youth. They had lived long enough, and what happiness could there be in living on away from their beautiful homeland, gone forever?

Oldest of them all was probably the man who now lay in a room of his imposing mansion in Fuchu, just outside of Tokyo. The town was covered with a thick layer of reddish-brown ash. Built of reinforced concrete, the house had withstood the successive quakes relatively undamaged, but nothing could keep out the fine stream of ash that worked its way in through every crack, covering not only the sleeping kimono the old man was wearing but even his face, which was like a skull etched with wrinkles. The dust lay on it like the cosmetics that are applied after death.

"So . . ." said the old man, mumbling, "it's all settled. His Majesty and the Imperial Family are safe in Switzerland. . . . And the government?"

"The Paris arrangement seems to be working out, sir," answered the huge young man with close-cropped hair who sat, back straight, on the tatami mat beside where the old man lay. "And the headquarters of the Evacuation Committee is now in Honolulu."

"Yukinaga and Nakata?"

"On board the *Haruna,* sir, together with the rest of the Plan D staff."

"Very well. Are you leaving by helicopter?"

"No, sir. There is too much danger of the ashes choking the engine. A large-sized jeep is coming to get us. Then we shall be transferred to an amphibian."

"All right, Yoshimura . . . you'd better be off. What's Hanae doing?"

"I believe that she's all ready to go, sir."

"Bring her here at once."

The huge young man named Yoshimura got to his feet and hurried out of the room, the tatami mats squeaking beneath him. As soon as he was gone, a young girl appeared in the doorway, as though she had been hiding in the corridor.

"Hanae!" said the old man, raising his eyes. "You're going to ride in a jeep dressed like that?"

The girl was wearing an Akashi kimono of deep, glowing purple, fastened by a silk obi of an old-fashioned morning-glory pattern. She stood gazing at the old man, her eyes passionate, and then she suddenly began to walk toward him, her tabi-shod feet moving with exquisite grace. She knelt beside him, her head and shoulders drooping.

"I'm . . . I'm not going," she said, covering her face with her hands. Her voice shook with emotion. "I want to stay just like this . . . at your side."

"No," said the old man calmly. "You're young. You're not meant to die with an old man like me."

"No! No! I can't leave you."

"Hanae, what a way to carry on!" said the old man wearily. "I never expected to hear such nonsense from a girl of your breeding. You must go. You must live. That's what's important."

The girl threw herself down, the sleeves of her kimono spilling over the floor. Her slender shoulders trembled from her sobbing.

The old man glanced up to see Yoshimura looking hesitantly in through the doorway. He raised his voice: "Bring her some clothes. Something she can wear in the jeep." He coughed faintly. "What a bother you are, girl."

A dreadful roar rose up from the earth, rocking the room. Yoshimura staggered as the sliding door tore loose and collapsed. A cloud of powdered ash filled the room. The air echoed with the loud noise of something falling, and the steel reinforcing rods rang ominously. From outside came the rumble of sliding earth.

"Hurry up," said the old man. "The roads are going to be blocked."

Yoshimura turned and ran down the corridor.

"Hanae . . ."

The girl raised her tearful face.

"Would you let me see . . . ?"

She drew in her breath with a quick movement of her white throat. Then the girl stood up and loosened her obi. There was a faint rustle of fabric as the kimono slipped from her shoulders. With this single graceful gesture, her naked body stood revealed in the desolate room. Its firm and rounded flesh shone in the gloom like a secret cache of snow.

The old man looked at her but for a moment before closing his eyes.

"A daughter of Japan," he whispered to himself. "Hanae . . . have children. . . ."

"What, sir?"

"You must have children. You could have good, strong babies. Find a good man. . . . He doesn't have to be Japanese. Have many children."

Yoshimura reappeared in the doorway with the girl's clothes. The old man glanced up at him. "Take her with you."

The huge young man draped a coat over Hanae's shoulders and then knelt beside the old man's bed.

"Farewell . . . Master," he said, bending forward and pressing his palms to the ash-covered tatami.

"Hurry up," said the old man, shutting his eyes once more. "There's no time to waste."

The sounds of footsteps and quiet sobbing receded. Then there was the sound of an engine at the front of the house, and soon that, too, grew more distant and faded away. There was no dearth of other noises, however; the air was filled with them. The continuous rumble of the eruptions that were shattering the mountains of the Kanto Region, the convulsive shuddering of the earth that rocked, the creaking house . . . Then there was another sound, a rustling in the air that gradually grew stronger until, finally, a strong gust of wind blew in from the ravaged veranda, stirring up the ashes and bringing still more in its wake, which formed new piles.

The old man opened his eyes slightly. The figure of a man had appeared on the veranda.

"Would that be Professor Tadokoro?" the old man asked in a hoarse voice.

"It looks like the typhoon is almost on us." Tadokoro came in and sat beside where the old man lay. "Miss Hanae is safe by now, I imagine."

"So you didn't go, after all? Why not?" The old man closed his eyes, and his expression became somewhat contorted as another fit of coughing took hold of him.

Tadokoro's eyes had sunk deep into his head. His cheeks were hollow. He seemed to have aged at least ten years. Even his broad, heavy shoulders had grown thin and were sagging. The crest of hair that surrounded his bald head had turned pure white.

"If there had been a jeep left that ran, I think that I might have taken a ride up into the mountains," he said quietly.

"I don't think you would have gotten very far," said the old man, opening his eyes from time to time. "How much time do you think is left?"

"About two months, I'd say," said Tadokoro, rubbing his eyes as though ashes had gotten into them. After he took his hands away, several tears rolled down his cheeks. "But as far as staying alive goes . . . then I think that it's a matter of only two or three weeks."

"Professor Tadokoro," said the old man in a louder voice, as though something had just occurred to him, "how old are you?"

"I'm sixty-five," Tadokoro answered, smiling slightly, the tears still wet on his cheeks. "I'd be retiring this year. There'd be the ceremonial speech to give, and all that. . . ."

"Sixty-five? You're a young fellow. Why do you want to die?"

"Oh, I don't know. I'm sad . . . that's why," Tadokoro answered in a low voice, his head drooping. "After all, I've lived to a good age."

"Because you're sad? Hmmm . . ."

"At first, you know . . . I thought that I'd say nothing." All at once, as though stirred by some strong emotion, Tadokoro spoke out in a loud voice. "When I saw that it was going to happen . . . well, for a long, long time the scientific world had been giving me a wide berth anyway. Remember when we met for the first time at the hotel and you asked me what was the thing most important in a scientist? I told you it was intuition. And the only proof lay with my intuition. It was obvious that no one was ready to see it my way, no matter how I protested. I felt a chill of dread when I put everything together . . . and then the thought came to me: Wouldn't it be better to keep it to yourself anyway?"

The old man said nothing. Tadokoro heard him cough faintly.

"I know it sounds strange, but the truth is that this is what I really wanted to do. I wanted to speak out to my fellow Japanese. I wanted to say: Listen to me. This country we love, this island country, is going to break apart and sink into the ocean. Since we love it so, let us die with it. . . . And even now I think that might well have been the better thing. Why? Because those who have escaped overseas are going to experience hardships worse than any the Japanese race has ever before encountered."

Another strong gust of wind blew into the room. Tadokoro felt a stream of ashes brushing his cheek. Was it his imagination, or did the wind carry the scent of the sea? Had it come that close?

"Professor Tadokoro . . . I think I understand now. You're in love with Japan herself, aren't you?"

"That's right, I am," answered Tadokoro, as though he was happy to hear it put into words.

"It's as though the woman you loved were dying."

"Exactly." Tadokoro covered his face and began to sob. "And when I found out that she had to die, I wanted to die with her."

"A love suicide, eh?" A wheezing sound came from the old man's throat. It was not a cough. Tadokoro must have said something that had struck him as funny. "Ah, the Japanese . . . a strange race indeed."

Tadokoro raised his face, still streaked with tears, and gazed up at the somber sky. "It's not as though we were a race that came from somewhere else to these four islands. We were formed here, and we've become one with this land—with these mountains, these rivers, these cities and villages, these monuments left by our ancestors. Once these have all been destroyed, what meaning could there be in being Japanese?"

Suddenly there was the boom of an explosion, and a moment later the sky seemed to shake with an ear-splitting roar. Somewhere nearby, it seemed, the earth had been rent yet again.

"I pride myself in not being an especially provincial or narrow-minded person." Tadokoro was speaking again. "I've seen most of the world. I've been almost everywhere. I've seen other peoples. I know their customs and their environments. The truth is that I *am* in love with Japan. And now, when her end is near, I can't bear to leave her."

Once more emotion overcame Tadokoro, and he could not speak.

The old man's coughing fits had become more severe. Nonetheless, he began to speak in his hoarse, quavery voice: "The Japanese are a young race," he said and then paused for breath. "They're like infants who have had a happy time of it . . . these two thousand years . . . clinging to their mother's bosom . . . these four islands, with their warm, gentle climate. If they ventured out into the world and suffered mishap, they could always run back to their mother. Now that mother, whom they loved so much, is dying."

Tadokoro listened with the intensity of a disciple hearing his master's words.

"From now on, the Japanese must experience suffering. As long as these four island were here, there was a home to return to, a place to raise children, children who would live exactly as they . . . but there are not many races who have been so fortunate as to have so secure a home of their own for so long a period. Through thousands of years of history there have been countless races that have experienced the bitterness of exile. This, then, will be a test for the Japanese. Their bridges have been burned behind them. They have no choice but to go forward. Whether they wish it or not, the chance to achieve adulthood is being forced upon them. Let them be swallowed up by the world . . . so much the better! They can emerge as a mature people, with their language and customs intact, ready to take their place in the world of the future. . . . But if they bewail their fate and cling to past glories, then there is no hope for greatness. This is what's now at stake. . . . Professor Tadokoro

. . . it's well for you to mourn for the passing of the woman you love, but spare a blessing for the future of your fleeing younger brothers and sisters. They have no idea of what I've been trying to tell you. Nor will they ever realize that it was you who saved them. But I recognize it . . . I realize it. Well and good, Professor Tadokoro?"

"Well and good, sir," said Tadokoro, nodding. "I understand what you said."

"Well, well . . ." whispered the old man, taking a breath. "You understand me, do you? I'm gratified. Come to think of it . . . Tadokoro . . . you're the last stiff-necked Japanese I'll have to deal with. The truth is I didn't want you to die thinking as you did . . . taking the whole Japanese race with you. When I was listening to you just now, I suddenly felt as though for the first time in my life I fully understand the Japanese character. For, you see, there have always been aspects I did not quite grasp. . . ."

"How do you mean, sir?" Tadokoro asked, even though he did not expect a significant answer. The old man's words had suddenly become much more labored. He sighed briefly and then said nothing for a few moments. When he spoke again, his voice was a bare whisper.

"Perhaps . . . because I am only half Japanese." He paused to take a breath. "My father . . . he was a Chinese monk. . . ."

Startled, Tadokoro looked down intently at the old man, waiting for him to go on. But no more words would come.

"Mr. Watari . . ."

Tadokoro studied the old man's face for some time. Then he took up the purple Akashi kimono which lay on the mat and placed it gently over the old man's face. The wind was growing stronger. He got to his feet and stepped down into the garden, where he picked up two small rocks. He returned to the old man's bedside and placed one upon either sleeve of the fluttering kimono. Then he sat down once again, his back straight, his arms folded.

A thunderous roar of awful force drowned out the noise of the approaching typhoon. The earth began to quake with a terrible frenzy, and from somewhere in the house came the sound of steel reinforcing rods being torn asunder.

The end came in September. Despite the typhoons, the rescue units had pursued their task with a still more frantic zeal, but toward the latter part of September four groups were wiped out in eruptions, and the LST carrying the last few hundred refugees was lost in a typhoon.

Shikoku had moved more than a seventy-five miles to the south and was completely submerged. Kyushu had broken in half, and the southern part of it was overwhelmed. The two great peaks in the central part of the island, Aso and Unzen, barely showed above the surface, though they continued to erupt. In the Northeast Region of Honshu the mountainous area had already slipped beneath the sea. In Hokkaido, reports said, only Mount Daisetsu remained. The final drama was played out in the Central and Kanto regions of Honshu, with no witnesses. The slipping of the earth had generated so much heat that when the waters rolled in, there were explosions of such cataclysmic force that the mountains were blown apart and shattered to fragments. While the Pacific coast slid away into the deep, the Japan Sea coast rose up for a brief moment, like one side of a capsizing vessel. But then the same blind force took hold of it and plunged it, too, down into the sea.

"Are you still working?" said Yukinaga in surprise as he came into the wardroom of the *Haruna* to find Nakata with an unlit cigarette dangling from his lips. The strain of the past year had drastically altered the appearance of both men. "Everyone says there are no more plans to be made."

"Do you have a match?" asked Nakata. "So . . . Japan has gone under, eh?"

"There was a television relay. A half-hour ago there was a final explosion in the Central Region," said Yukinaga, holding up his cigarette lighter. "There's still something left, but the sliding and sinking are continuing. It'll all go under, it looks like."

" 'Oh, have we sunk the *Teien* yet?' " said Nakata his voice harsh as he quoted the dying sailor's words in the old Navy song. He blew out some smoke. "How many were saved in all?"

"I don't know. We don't have the figures tabulated even up to the end of August," answered Yukinaga, yawning wearily. "The Secretary General of the UN is going to make an appeal to the world on television, and the Prime Minister is going to make a speech, too. Do you want to hear them?"

"To hell with it." He crushed his cigarette into an ashtray and got to his feet, apparently in good spirits. "It's over, it's over— no more plans to make. Should we go on deck?"

Nakata led the way, walking with long strides and whistling cheerfully. Yukinaga came along behind, a disturbed look on his face. The sun was hot out on the deck. The dark blue water was free of the ashes and pumice stone that had covered it through-out their time on board. The *Haruna* was speeding along at twenty-eight knots, and a brisk wind was blowing.

"It's hot," said Nakata, squinting in the dazzling sunlight. "The sun is high in the sky. Is it morning?"

"We're not on Japan time any more. We moved fourteen hours ahead. The *Haruna*'s going to Hawaii."

"I see. So I suppose we can't see the smoke over Japan any more. . . ."

Nakata shadowed his eyes as he looked back at the western horizon. Cumulus clouds were towering there. Their trailing edges seemed to be gray, but since he was uncertain as to the position of the *Haruna,* there was no way of knowing if these clouds were in fact rising over Japan.

" 'Oh, have we sunk the *Teien* yet?' " Nakata's tone was jocular.

"Wouldn't it be a good idea to get some rest?" asked Yukinaga, frowning at his colleague's levity. "You seem a bit odd, you know."

"So this is it?" Nakata leaned upon the rail. His teeth were bared. "The end of the Japan Archipelago . . . it's goodbye, Japan. . . . Give me a cigarette, will you?"

"The end? Yes, it's the end, all right." Yukinaga held out a pack of cigarettes.

Nakata took one, put it in his mouth, and then, instead of lighting it, he stared down at the water rushing by below.

"You know," said Yukinaga absently, "last night I dreamed about Onodera. I can't help but think he's still alive."

There was no response from Nakata. After a few moments Yukinaga turned to look at him. Nakata's huge body was slumped over the rail. The cigarette had fallen from his lips.

"Nakata!" said the startled Yukinaga, reaching out to put a hand on the other's shoulder.

Before he could catch him, however, Nakata fell heavily to

the deck and rolled over upon his back. His arms flung out to either side of him, he began to snore loudly, as the sunshine poured down into his wide-open mouth.

It's hot! Onodera felt himself wanting to yell out. He wanted something cold to drink. A cold beer . . . that would do it. He opened his eyes. The round face of a little girl appeared in the semi-darkness. Her eyes were big, and there was a worried look on her face.

"Does it hurt?" she said.

"No . . . it's just hot." He could only move his mouth, since his face seemed to be swathed in bandages. "I'll bet we're in the tropics by now. . . ."

"Yes . . . that's it," said the little girl, her eyes sad.

"Have you heard from Nakata and Yukinaga?"

"Not yet."

"No? Well, we'll be hearing from them soon."

The girl's face disappeared, and a moment later Onodera felt something cold pressed to his head.

"Ah . . . that feels good."

The girl's face came back. Her eyes were filled with tears. With the coolness, memories seemed to be coming back to Onodera. A volcano . . . an eruption . . . a helicopter . . . Reiko —was it Reiko? There was an earthquake in the midst of the snow . . . more eruptions . . . a wave of glowing lava rolling down toward him . . . Yes, he remembered now.

"Japan . . . did it sink?" he asked the girl.

"I . . . I don't know. . . ."

"It's sunk . . . it has to have sunk. . . ."

"I think it did."

He shut his eyes. Tears gathered behind the lids and rolled down his cheeks.

"You must go to sleep," said the girl, wiping away his tears.

"I'll go to sleep. . . . Who are you?"

"You don't remember?" asked the girl, smiling sadly. "I'm your wife."

Wife? Onodera tried to think, but his head was burning up. How strange. There must be some mistake. Hadn't his wife died beneath a rain of volcanic ash? But what difference did it make anyway?

"Can't you sleep?"

"Maybe I could if you told me a story," said Onodera like a child coaxing his mother.

"A story?" said the girl, taken aback.

"Yes . . . any at all. I don't care."

"I do know one story," said the girl hesitantly. "My grandmother told it to me. She was born on Hachijo Island, and she came to Tokyo when she got married. When she died, they took her remains back there. I visited her grave every year when I was a little girl." She stopped. "I don't think you'd like this story. . . ."

"No, no . . . go on," said Onodera.

"It's the story of Tanaba. It's a terrible story. And it's sad, too. Long, long ago there was an earthquake, and a tidal wave swept over Hachijo Island, killing everybody except this woman called Tanaba, who clung to an oar. She was pregnant, and so after the wave was gone, she gave birth to a son there on the island. It was long ago, so no boats ever came there. The son grew up into a strong, handsome man, and one day Tanaba told him what had happened. She said to him: 'All of them are dead. Only the two of us are left. If there is to be an island race after this, then it must come from us. Lie down with me, then, and let me conceive your sister. Afterward, lie with her and have children by her.' Her son did as she told him, and, according to the story, this is where the people of Hachijo Island came from."

As he listened, Onodera focused upon a clear image in his fevered head: Tanaba . . . Hachijo Island. . . . Then another: the cold darkness of the ocean floor beneath Ogasawara.

"It's a dark and frightful story. . . . Tanaba's grave, even today . . . up to just a while ago, I mean . . . was there on Hachijo Island. Just some stones beside the road. There was nothing written there. I used to look at that little grave and feel sad and a little frightened, thinking about what it stood for." The girl drew in her breath and bowed her head. "I forgot that story for a long time, but then, after this happened, it came back to me all at once. Tanaba was a terrible woman. It's a dark and terrible story, but somehow that story has been my support all during this. I'm a girl who has island blood, and I would do just what she did."

Onodera began to breathe a slight noise as though he had

fallen asleep. But when the girl moved quietly away from his berth, he spoke.

"It's shaking."

"Yes," said the girl in surprise, turning back to him. "Do you feel pain?"

"Ah, I know what it is. We're probably running into the Black Current south of Cape Nojima. Hawaii's still a long way off," said Onodera groggily.

"Yes," said the girl. "Try to sleep."

He became quiet for a moment. But then he spoke out, his tone urgent and insistent: "Has Japan sunk?"

"I . . ."

"Look out the porthole there. Can't you see?"

The girl looked hesitantly out the window.

"Can you see Japan?"

"No."

"It must have sunk. . . . You can't see any smoke either?"

"I can't see anything at all."

After a while Onodera began to snore. His breathing was painful.

Mako raised her right arm instinctively, and with the bandage-wrapped stump of her wrist she wiped away her tears. Outside the window there was not a single star to light the black Siberian night. The train sped westward, plunging ever deeper into the chill darkness of an early winter.